JUSTICE IN JUNE

ALSO BY BARBARA LEVENSON
Fatal February

Justice in June

A Novel

Barbara Levenson

Oceanview Publishing
IPSWICH, MASSACHUSETTS

ISBN: 978-1-933515-71-7

Published in the United States of America by Oceanview Publishing, Ipswich, Massachusetts
www.oceanviewpub.com

10 9 8 7 6 5 4 3 2 1

PRINTED IN THE UNITED STATES OF AMERICA

To Brad and Tony
for their constant encouragement and belief that
Mary Magruder Katz had a future in books and movies

ACKNOWLEDGMENTS

While the characters and their adventures are totally fictional, many of the Miami locations are actual places. Two locations mentioned in the book that are outside of Miami deserve special attention.

Wolf Haven as described by Catherine is an actual nonprofit shelter for wolves who have been abandoned as pets or who have been injured in the wild. Wolf Haven is located in Tenino, Washington, south of Olympia. The wolves are housed in open areas in habitats made to look and feel like the dens where wolves live in natural surroundings. My husband and I have visited this very interesting facility. Because of our interest in German Shepherds, who are descendants of wolves, we were fascinated to be able to view these beautiful animals. Wolf Haven relies on contributions and grants for their work, not only as a shelter, but also for its breeding program of the red wolf.

The Pontificia Universidad Católica Argentina is a well-respected private university located in Buenos Aires, with branches throughout the country. To learn more about this facility, visit its Web site or that of the Argentine government.

One person named in the book is an actual person. Max Mayfield was the voice that has guided the citizens of South Florida through hurricane warnings and actual hurricanes. He is the retired director of the Hurricane Center located in Miami-Dade County, Florida. Mr. Mayfield's calm, reassuring directions on radio and television were relied on by the citizenry for many years as we prepared for and lived through the storms that are part of life in the area.

Justice in June

CHAPTER ONE

The Miami Herald, June 1, 2005
INFORMANT SHOT IN COLD BLOOD ON CITY STREET

A Miami-Dade Police informant was shot this morning while being escorted to the office of the state attorney in the Civic Center.

Rolando Malaga, a Colombian national, had been working as an informant in the Jack Carillo drug-trafficking case. His identity and whereabouts were kept secret by the police and prosecution following the arrest of Carillo. Malaga was on his way to a deposition when he was fatally shot

Judge Elizabeth Maxwell granted Carillo's motion to depose the informant prior to trial. At the conclusion of a two-day hearing, Judge Maxwell ruled that the informant was the most material witness in the case. She ordered that the deposition be held in a secure location known only to the attorneys and the court reporter. The deposition was to be kept under seal until the time of trial, along with the informant's name.

When Malaga and several police officers approached the building on N.W. Twelfth Street, shots were fired from an unidentified vehicle. The informant died immediately. At least one shot grazed one of the officers.

"There was a lot of confusion," Officer Michael Noonan

said. "No one got a good look at the car or the shooter. They approached us from behind."

Police are asking for the public's help as they continue to search the area.

"This investigation will continue until we find the shooter who endangered the lives of innocent bystanders on the street. Anyone who witnessed the shooting or has any information that will assist us in the investigation is asked to call Miami-Dade Police, the Office of the State Attorney, or Crime Stoppers," police spokesperson Adam Foster stated.

Jack Carillo, a Miami Beach resident, and son of a prominent physician, was indicted on numerous drug and money laundering charges. He posted a one million dollar bond and is awaiting trial, which was set to begin June 30.

The Miami Herald, June 2, 2005
ARGENTINE FOUND MURDERED IN DOWNTOWN HOTEL
Links to terrorists suspected

A maid at the Floridian Inn on Brickell Avenue discovered the body of a male who had been shot. The room was registered to Roberto Gomez of Buenos Aires, Argentina.

No identification was found in the room, so police are uncertain if the registered name is actually that of the murder victim. A large amount of money was recovered from a safe in the room along with correspondence from the group called "The Army of Allah," a known terrorist cell operating out of several countries in South America and the Middle East.

The CIA and FBI have both expressed interest in assisting local police in the investigation.

CHAPTER TWO

It was a Monday morning in early June. The rain that pelted South Florida for the entire weekend had not abated. June is the rainiest month in Miami. Most of the storms occur during the morning and evening rush hours. The morning rain comes off the ocean in intermittent showers. The evening deluges form over the Everglades brought on by the heat and humidity that build throughout the day. It doesn't matter if the storms come from the east or the west. The end result is clogged roads and traffic nightmares. That's how Monday began.

My name is Mary Magruder Katz. I'm a criminal defense attorney in Miami. I live in a 1950's house in Coral Gables with my mostly German Shepherd dog, Sam. (Short for Uncle Sam since I found him on the Fourth of July.)

I have a sexy boyfriend, Carlos Martin. He develops all kinds of buildings and homes, and sometimes I act as his lawyer and not just his girlfriend.

Life is good since I got rid of my old fiancé, Franklin Fieldstone, and left his snooty law firm. Now I have my own law office in Coconut Grove, and, if I do say so myself, I'm doing pretty well. Lots of new clients have come my way after I won the Lillian Yarmouth murder case last February.

If you're wondering about my name, Magruder was my mother's maiden name. Her family of Southern Baptists settled in Miami when she was a teenager. She met my dad, Abe Katz, on the beach one weekend. His family owned the famous Katz's Kosher Market on Miami Beach. Hence my Magruder Katz name. My background isn't at all unusual in Miami, where the melting pot often takes place in the wedding chapel.

Carlos is a mixed migration story too. His mother's family came from Cuba before Castro. His grandfather was a revered professor at the University of Miami. His father came from Argentina to attend the university. Carlos has some German blood somewhere on his dad's side, but no one is sure whether his relatives ran to Argentina to escape the Nazi's or whether they were the Nazi's. Either way, it doesn't matter. We all share the urban dream that is Miami, and the urban nightmare that it sometimes becomes.

Like two front-page murders in two days.

I was sitting in my law office that Monday morning when two telephone calls changed my life. I wasn't really working. Just staring out the window at the rain.

Carlos and I spent the weekend at his parents' beach house on Marco Island. It rained the whole weekend. There isn't much to do on the island when it rains. Somehow, Carlos and I found much to occupy us, which is why I was sleepy, but content, as I stared out the window.

Files were piled on the desk, but I hadn't touched them. *Thank God I'm not due in court today*, I thought.

I came directly to the office from the island, so Sam was with me. Sam did not enjoy the weekend; no stick chasing on the beach. He was a little stir crazy. I was contemplating getting into my rain jacket and taking him for a walk when the intercom buzzed and Catherine's excited voice came on. Catherine Aynsworth is my A-1 paralegal and guardian angel.

"Mary, it's Judge Maxwell's chambers. They said she needs to speak to you right away."

I grabbed my calendar. I couldn't remember any cases pending in Maxwell's division. Had I forgotten a court date? Not possible. The last time I saw Judge Maxwell was at the hearing where I won the case Franklin Fieldstone filed against me after our breakup.

I grabbed the phone. "Mary Katz here. How can I help you?" I said in a congenial voice.

"Mary, it's Liz Maxwell. This isn't about any official case. I need to come and see you. I have a problem I'd like to discuss."

"Of course, Your Honor. I'll fit my schedule to yours, and I'll come over to your chambers."

"No, Mary, it'd be better if I came to your office. Can I come after five o'clock? I'd rather not run into anyone else there. This is very confidential."

CHAPTER THREE

The second earthshaking call came right before the lunch hour. It seemed innocuous. Catherine had taken an early lunch, and I was holding down the fort. I was contemplating half a leftover peanut butter sandwich lurking in the fridge, or the rest of the chocolate chip cookies that had been left on my desk by one of my nephews. I opted for the cookies.

The phone rang and I grabbed it. "Mary Katz here."

"Mary, why are you answering the phone?" It was Carlos.

"You must miss me a lot. Didn't I just leave you at your house three hours ago?" I asked.

"I do miss you *mucho, mi amor*, but that's not why I'm calling. Remember when I told you about my cousin?"

"Which cousin? You seem to have dozens."

"My cousin, Luis Corona, from Argentina."

"What has he done?" People only mention their relatives to criminal defense attorneys when the relatives are facing criminal charges.

"I don't know, but it couldn't be too bad. He's a really nice kid. His father called my father and I said I'd call you. He's at the Dade County Jail. Can you go see him?"

"Okay, Carlos, I'll go this afternoon, but I've got an important client conference late this afternoon, so I have to be back by five. I wish you'd give me a heads-up about what his problem is."

"I don't know, but you should know, he really isn't my cousin exactly. He's the son of a friend of my father's brother, my uncle, but we think of him as a cousin."

As soon as Catherine returned, I left for the jail. I was lucky. I only had to circle the block three times before finding a parking place. I walked the two blocks from the car to the jail in the continuing rain. I was accosted only once by a recently released inmate begging for bus fare, which I readily handed him. It's always good to have a couple of dollars handy in my suit pocket. The alternative to a "no" answer may be a purse snatch.

The lobby of the jail was filled with bail bondsmen filling out paperwork, family visitors waiting for visiting hours, and a few other attorneys. I filled out the appropriate forms and inched up to the front desk. The sergeant behind the desk was an old friend. I smiled and handed in my purse and cell phone. The sergeant looked at my paper work. I held out my hand for my visitor's badge.

"Luis Corona?" he asked. "Sorry, Mary, you can't visit Luis Corona. He's in a special cell. No one's allowed up there. He's being picked up for transfer by the feds anytime now."

"Well, I'm his lawyer, and he has a right to see his lawyer."

"Not if he's accused of trying to blow up an airplane on his way into the U.S. I got my orders from the Homeland Security boys. He's probably on his way to Guantanamo."

"There must be some mistake," I said. "Look, I'll just stay five minutes. You won't get in trouble. Just sit here and think how much fun you're going to have at the Marlins game Sunday." I fished in my briefcase and handed him my two tickets to the baseball game. Well, actually, Carlos's two tickets.

Soon I was in the elevator on my way to visit Luis. I was buzzed into the isolation section. A young guy sat on the cot with his head in his hands.

"Hi, Luis, I'm Carlos Martin's friend. I'm a lawyer. Carlos said you needed help."

It only took a second to realize that Luis spoke little English. He turned my card over in his hand, looked at me blankly, and began to sob. Between the sobs and the rapid Spanish, I couldn't understand him at all.

I managed to tell him in my hesitant Spanish that I was a lawyer and could I help him.

After that, the only thing I made out was that he didn't do it, and if he did, he didn't mean to. He was only helping his family.

"What about the airplane?" I shouted at him.

Just then, three burly Secret Service agents appeared at the cell. I think they were Secret Service because they were wearing those earpieces and talking into little microphones attached to their jacket lapels.

"Get out of here, Miss," one of them said, as he not so politely moved me out of the cell. "No one was supposed to be seeing this prisoner. We need to remove the prisoner now."

I watched them attach leg irons and handcuffs to Luis, who was now totally hysterical. I tried to tell him that I'd find out where he was being taken. Then I split before the agents decided to chain me up too.

I picked up my purse and phone and sprinted out of the jail. As I emerged, I was blinded by bright flashing lights. I knew it wasn't the sun, because the rain was still falling. Rows of TV and newspaper reporters swarmed toward me.

"Are you the terrorist's lawyer? Is he involved in the killing of the Argentine?"

"Will you be going to Guantanamo with him?" They threw questions at me while video cameras whirred.

One of the TV reporters yelled that the agents were coming out of the back entrance. The whole pack ran to the south entrance. I ran north to my car and hightailed it out of there. I kept to the back streets and when I was sure I wasn't being followed, I raced back to my office.

On my way, I called Carlos on both of his cell phones but only got his voice mail. I reamed him out on both voice mails. "Couldn't you have told me your cousin was an accused terrorist? Couldn't you have given me some preparation that the media from around the world would be outside the jail? Don't you understand that my other clients might fire me? Even other criminals don't like terrorists," I screamed. Finally, I hung up. It's hard to have a good argument with voice mail

CHAPTER FOUR

Catherine was on the phone when I raced into my office. The second line was ringing. I glanced at her computer screen and saw e-mails popping out like kernels of popcorn in a microwave.

The first e-mail I opened said, "You lawyers are all alike. You take money from anyone. Don't you care about the safety of our country?" The second one was worse. "I hope they hang your terrorist client and you with him." The third one was unprintable.

I reached over and turned off the computer. "Catherine, don't answer anymore calls. Don't even put the answer machine on."

Catherine hung up and looked at me with a dazed expression. "What in God's name happened? The phone has been ringing for the last half hour with the worst people I've ever talked to, which is saying something. My dad was an army sergeant, and I was married to a race car driver."

"Carlos's so-called cousin is being held as a terrorist. He allegedly tried to blow up an airplane, and the media accosted me when I left the jail. I guess they mentioned my name."

"Not only your name. Your picture is all over CNN and Fox News." She pointed to the little TV I had put in the corner of the waiting room. There I was in living color, and rain bedraggled clothes.

Catherine thrust some phone messages into my hand. "Your mother called. I think she was crying. She said something about how she had failed to give you an adequate religious faith."

"Oh, shit. It always comes back to a guilt trip with her. I thought only Jewish mothers took their kids on guilt trips. I think my dad's mother rubbed off on her," I said as I rummaged through the messages.

"Oh, she also mentioned that I should get you to do something about your hair." Catherine suppressed a giggle.

"I'm not in the mood for jokes," I said. "What's this message from Carlos? It just says, 'He will bring you dinner.' What does that mean?"

"Just what it says. He said he would be bringing you dinner at your house. I told him that you had a late appointment and probably wouldn't be home before seven or later, but he said it didn't matter. He'd wait. He said he'd feed Sam and walk him, but I reminded him that you had Sam here all day."

"Oh, God, I forgot. Poor Sam. Where is he?"

"In your office sleeping under your desk. I walked him about two hours ago."

"Well, he'll just have to stay put. I've got to pull myself together before Judge Maxwell gets here. My suit is rain soaked and so are my shoes, and for once, my mother is right about my hair." I plopped down in the chair next to Catherine's desk and covered my face.

"Come on, Mary. We can get you fixed up. You've still got your suitcase in the car from the weekend. What's in there?"

"Hey, I forgot. I've got slacks and a blouse that I was wearing in the office on Friday and some sandals. And my hair dryer. And Sam's bowl and his food bag. Catherine, you're a genius."

"No, just a great legal assistant. Let's get everything out of your car. I'll feed Sam. You get changed and put on some makeup. And for heavens sake, do something about your hair."

I thought about how lucky I was to have Catherine come to work for me. She's a single mother with two great boys. She lives in the neighborhood and rides her bike to work. She only asked for three things when she applied for the job: decent pay, time off to see her boys play soccer once in a while, and that there be no dress code for her. She prefers to come to work in jeans. I'm okay with all of it as long as she keeps the office ticking, which she always does.

By five o'clock the office was cleaned up and so was I. Sam was back asleep under my desk. A freshly brewed pot of coffee was on the table in front of the sofa along with the left over cookies that we had rehabbed in the microwave. I could hardly wait to hear why Liz Maxwell was coming to my office.

I glanced around my little office. I moved here after I broke my five-year engagement to Franklin Fieldstone, who also had been my boss at the very highbrow Fieldstone law firm. If I hadn't met Carlos and hadn't been immediately turned on to him, I guess I'd still be sweating out billable hours, and putting off the oft-planned wedding to Frank. Instead, I had a hot Latin boyfriend, and this great law office all my own.

My old office overlooked Biscayne Bay and the sailboats docked in the harbor. This office overlooked the parking lot, but I felt at home here. I had managed to buy two slightly used desks at a furniture rental store, a sofa and table at the Goodwill Thrift Shop, along with two chairs for the waiting room. My parents bought me the microwave and the coffeepot after they got over the shock of Frank's exit from my life. Things were not so bad. Now, if only I could trust Carlos to tell me the whole truth most of the time — well, you can't have everything. What's more important, truth or good sex?

Catherine appeared in the door. "Judge Maxwell is here. If you don't need anything else, I'm out of here."

CHAPTER FIVE

I ushered Judge Maxwell into the office. "Let's sit over here." I indicated the sofa. "How about some coffee?"

"That would be great," she said.

I poured two cups of coffee as I looked at Liz Maxwell. She's a cool, reserved woman. She always looks put together and never raises her voice in court. I was shocked as I surveyed her. Her eyes were red and puffy. Her makeup was smeared. Her usually well-coifed hair was pulled back in a ponytail. She looked much younger than she appeared on the bench. She also looked very vulnerable.

"How can I help you?" I asked in the soothing voice I reserved for the parents of juveniles who have just been arrested.

Just then Sam crawled out from under my desk. In one swoop, he located the cookies and gulped them down in a single mouthful. I opened my mouth, but nothing came out. Then I saw that Judge Maxwell was laughing. She patted her lap and Sam put his front paws up. Liz scratched his ears. Her face relaxed.

"I love dogs," she said. "Listen, I won't beat around the bush. I want to hire you. I believe I'm in need of a good criminal defense attorney. I'm under investigation by the state attorney. From here on out, drop the judge and 'Your Honor' stuff. Please, call me Liz. I saw you on TV this afternoon. I

hope you aren't too busy. I could see that you have an important federal case. Can you make time for me?"

I felt slightly dizzy from all the events of the day so far,
and now I had a judge asking me if I had enough time for her.
I may be exhausted, but I'm sure never bored.

"Of course, I have time to help you. Just start at the beginning and tell me everything you know about this investigation. Do you mind if I take notes?" I asked as I pulled out
my yellow legal pad.

CHAPTER SIX

Liz's Story

Judge Elizabeth Maxwell was glad to be back in criminal court after a six-month sojourn in the civil division. Defendants are on their best behavior in criminal court, but litigants in civil court exhibit their worst behavior since their beef is over money.

She was happy in criminal court, but glad to be through for the week on this Friday afternoon in June. Her bailiff, Gladys, grabbed the judge's files, and hurried to keep up with the judge who was sprinting down the hall, her robe flying about as she shrugged it off.

The courthouse was emptying even though it was only three o'clock. The hall echoed with their footsteps. Gladys unlocked the door to their chambers and Liz stopped for a second at her judicial assistant's desk. Patricia, her judicial assistant, handed Liz a few phone messages.

"These can wait 'til Monday, can't they, Patricia? I'm really in a hurry."

Patricia nodded and took them back.

Gladys picked up a sheaf of papers from her desk. "Wait, Judge, you need to sign these before you leave."

"What are these? I thought I already signed all the orders." Liz tried not to show her annoyance. Patricia and

Gladys were a great support staff. The three enjoyed an easy camaraderie. They took a lot of kidding about their all-female division, but having their support canceled a lot of the stress of the job.

"These are just boilerplate stuff. The continuances for Monday. I put all the signature pages on top so you can sign them quickly. You must have a fun weekend planned," Gladys said.

"I'm driving down to the Keys for the weekend. I'll have my cell phone on, if anybody needs me. I want to get on the road before the traffic gets too bad," Liz said as she signed the orders.

"The Keys this weekend?" Patricia frowned at Liz. "It's the rainy season and the weather guy says it's gonna rain most of the weekend."

Liz smiled at Patricia, whose maternal instinct was directed at Liz most of the time. "Well, you have to go when you get invited to stay with friends. We can still fish and have a few beers," Liz said.

She went into her private chambers, shut the door, and locked it. She hung up her robe, and retrieved her overnight bag she had brought with her that morning. She was out of her dark suit and into jeans, a pink shirt, and sandals. She put on fresh makeup and sped out the back door into the private judges' elevator that took her to the garage.

As soon as she turned on her car, she grabbed her cell phone, hit the speed dial and said, "I'm on my way." She roared away from the Justice Building and headed south through Miami-Dade County.

Liz hadn't totally lied about her weekend plans. She was headed for Key Largo, but she didn't expect to do much fishing. She didn't care if it rained all weekend.

She joined the crawling traffic down the turnpike through

Homestead, past the tomato fields and strawberry stands now closed until next winter's produce season. She turned onto U.S. 1, also known as Useless One. The narrow highway was the only entrance and exit to the Florida Keys. One accident could mean hours of delay. She breathed easier when she saw traffic was moving, and there was no red line of brake lights ahead.

The rain began as a drizzle against the windshield. Soon it turned into a steady pelting. The anticipation of the weekend filled her with nervous energy. The drive seemed extra long.

An hour later she stopped in the village and bought two bottles of wine and a few breakfast and sandwich provisions. She turned off a side road and smelled the fishy, salty smell of the Atlantic. She passed two motels and finally came to a driveway in front of a tall house built on pillars. Stilts is what they called them in the Keys. She pulled into the ground-floor parking area and saw that the red BMW was already parked there.

Liz struggled to pull the grocery bags and her suitcase from the car as the door of the house opened above her.

"Let me help you," a male voice called. Joe Fineberg ran down the steps and grabbed Liz and her packages in a hug. Then he took everything out of her arms and kissed her hard.

"You should park your car in back," Liz said. "It's easy to spot out here."

"Quit worrying. It's my house. Why shouldn't I park here?"

They entered the house. Joe had opened the blinds. The ocean view was mesmerizing, even in the rain. The mist over the water added to the feeling of secrecy.

"Joe, I know we can't keep coming down here like this," Liz said. "Where is Janey this weekend?"

"Visiting her mother again in Atlanta. She spends more time with her than she does with me, anyway," Joe said. "You know my law practice takes so much of my time. That's just the way a criminal trial practice is. I think Janey has been paying me back by going off on her own. I don't know why she married me in the first place. Please, Liz this isn't your problem. I want to be here with you. Don't spoil our weekend."

Liz put her arms around Joe. She loved being here with him, but she knew everything about this affair was a disaster waiting to happen.

Joe stroked her hair and kissed her. He unbuttoned her jeans and they moved together into the bedroom. He began to undress her. She was so eager to be with him that she quickly pulled her shirt and jeans off and dropped them on the floor. She pulled at his tee shirt. In a second, they were involved in passionate and enthusiastic sex.

CHAPTER SEVEN

Liz looked at her watch. She must have fallen asleep. She glanced at Joe. He was sound asleep. She got up, and pulled on Joe's shirt. It smelled of his aftershave. She went into the kitchen and opened the wine. The rain was coming down in sheets now, obscuring the view.

She looked down at her hands. They had begun to look old. She was forty-five. She was lonely. Except for a brief marriage right after law school, she had been alone. Her career took up all of her time. Her goal was to be a judge. She handled every high-profile case she could get her hands on while in practice. She developed feminist connections through NOW and courted gay and lesbian causes. Ten years ago she put all her energy into the election campaign and beat an incumbent to achieve her seat on the bench. The years on the bench were exciting at first. Then the loneliness began to creep over her like a thick, suffocating blanket.

She was ripe for an affair when Joe came along. He tried a case in her court. He was a skilled criminal attorney. His good looks appealed to women jurors, and to Liz. The jury acquitted his client, a midlevel drug dealer who was not without his own charm.

A week later, Liz was seated at a Dade County Bar dinner when Joe took the seat next to her. They had a great time talking about the Justice Building characters. He walked her to her car, and they went to have a nightcap in the Grove near her condo. He suggested that he drive her home. Drinking and driving are not a good combination for a judge. She invited him in and she was hooked; flattered that he was a few years younger than she. He made her feel beautiful and sexy. She also felt scared. She could be throwing away her whole career.

As she began to put together a simple dinner, she felt another emotion that was becoming all too familiar. She was angry; at herself for being available every time Joe snapped his fingers, and at Joe, for not being able to take her out to dinner for fear of being recognized. He never made any mention of leaving his wife. She knew this was a dead-end relationship. Soon she would be lonely again.

CHAPTER EIGHT

Liz overslept on Monday morning. She awoke to the same gray drizzle that permeated the weekend. She felt exhausted from the drive home in Sunday traffic and from the emotional traffic that accompanied being with Joe.

She arrived in her chambers with just five minutes to organize her calendar and take the bench. Gladys met her as she opened her door. Her bailiff looked frantic. "Thank goodness you're here. Judge Marconi has been calling for you. He wants you in his chambers now," Gladys said in a whisper.

Several attorneys glanced up, but went on with their gossip. Patricia always had a pot of coffee ready, and attorneys dropped in on a regular basis.

"What now? Can't it wait 'til I get through the arraignments?" Liz couldn't hide her annoyance.

"No. He said to come over the minute you got here and not to start your calendar."

Liz put her briefcase away and pulled on her blazer. She walked back to the elevator and went to the top floor where Chief Administrative Judge Paul Marconi's chambers took most of the floor. He had awarded himself two judicial assistants, a secretary, and a bailiff although he had removed himself from the regular case assignments, handling only a few high-profile cases.

"Is he available?" she asked the secretary in the outer office. "He's expecting me."

"Oh, yes, he is and he's been waiting for you," she answered as she motioned Liz through the office to the mahogany-paneled door marked "private."

Liz knocked and entered before Judge Marconi answered. He was on the phone and motioned her to a chair across from him.

"Yes, she's here now and I'll take care of this. No need for you to come over," he said as he hung up.

Marconi stood up and reached across the desk extending his hand. He was a short, heavy man who generally appeared ill at ease. This was especially evident this morning. The hand he extended was wet with a cold sweat. It felt like a shrimp in need of refrigeration.

"Good morning, Paul," Liz said as she shook his outstretched hand. "What's up?"

"This is very painful for me, Liz. There's no easy way to approach this. I have to remove you from criminal court."

"Why, Paul? You promised me if I played ball and went to civil court, you'd let me come back here. I've only been back six months. You asked me to be a team player, and I have been."

"This is very difficult for me. I was informed on Friday that you're under investigation by the State Attorney's Office. It would be impossible for you to sit in judgment of the state's cases in this situation." Paul cleared his throat and looked over her head as he spoke.

"Investigation? For what? And why didn't you tell me on Friday?"

"The state attorney and I thought it best to wait until this morning." Paul cleared his throat again. Liz thought he looked like a rabbit about to be hit by a car. He almost smelled of fear.

"So I was to get no advance notice in order to defend myself. Thanks, Paul. What happened to your speech before we elected you chief judge? You know, the one where you told us how you would always stand behind your judges. I guess you meant way behind us. I deserve to know what this is about."

"I really can't tell you much. It has to do with some drug cases that you've handled. It seems that you've dismissed some cases prematurely. Your sentencing in some drug cases is said to be much lighter than in other types of cases. The prosecutor in the case that Joe Fineberg won in your courtroom complained that you cut the defense some breaks. I guess it's triggered some concerns."

"If they were concerned they could have spoken to me about this. Are these concerns or is this an investigation?"

"It's an investigation. That case where the informant was murdered was in your division also. He was murdered after you ordered his deposition. My hands are tied. My choices are to suspend you altogether, pending the outcome of all this or to remove you from the criminal division and send you to a division in family court. It's up to you."

Liz felt ill. Her ears were ringing and she felt sweat under her blouse. She couldn't believe that this was happening to her, after all her years of hard work. She realized that she was still standing in front of Paul clutching the chair in front of her.

"I'll report to family court tomorrow. Today I will be busy hiring a lawyer. And I will not be meeting with you or the state attorney in the future without my lawyer present, so pass that on to the state."

She slammed the heavy wooden door on her way out.

Gladys and Patricia were watching the door as she returned to her chambers. She was shocked to see retired Judge Stanley Franks in his robe looking through her docket.

"Hello, Stanley. I guess you're here to fill in for me," Liz said as she brushed past him. "Girls, start packing. It seems we're moving to family court."

"But why?" Patricia asked.

"I'll discuss it with you later. Don't worry," Liz said as she looked at their anxious faces. "And please, get Mary Magruder Katz on the phone for me right away."

CHAPTER NINE

I had been taking notes furiously as Liz talked nonstop. She seemed unable to draw a breath. I had seen this reaction in many clients. The ability to unburden oneself to someone with no preconceived bias is cathartic. I looked up from my notes when I realized that Liz had stopped talking and was staring at me. The silence lengthened in contrast to the torrent of words that had gushed out of her.

"What is it, Liz?" I asked, still not comfortable calling her by her first name.

"Is everything I've told you totally confidential?"

"Of course. You know as well as I that attorney-client privilege means exactly that. I will never divulge what a client tells me, unless the client directs me to do so, or gives me permission to do so."

"It's just that I haven't told anybody about the affair with Joe Fineberg. He's married. You probably know that, and you probably know him. I would never have mentioned it, if Judge Marconi hadn't brought up his name. I can't risk having the entire legal community gossiping about Joe and me." Liz's face turned a deep red.

I've never been known for my poker face, but I prayed I looked cool. Liz Maxwell, who some people called the ice judge, had just opened up her inner life to me. My guess was that Joe was part of her global warming.

"Sure, I know Joe," I said. "He's a good guy. We tried a case together a couple of years ago. We represented two brothers. You might remember the case. The Moldovan Brothers. The paper played it up as the family business that became dysfunctional."

"Well, when Joe tried the case in my court, we weren't seeing each other. That only began after he got an acquittal. Now Marconi says I cut him a bunch of breaks." Liz began to cry.

I grabbed the handy box of tissues on the table and put some in her lap. "Do you think you cut him any breaks? He is a cute guy."

"Of course not. He's a good lawyer. He probably wins a lot of cases, but if it gets out that we're having an affair, it'll be extra nails in my coffin. Besides, he's got a wife. I don't want to be a home wrecker." Liz was fighting to control the sobs that were escaping.

"Don't worry about Janey. No one knows why they're still together. She's a complete JAP, you know, Jewish American Princess. She spends his money, but I've never seen them out together at one event."

"What can I do? I'm putting my career in your hands," Liz said.

"Let me start to work on this," I said. "I need to start making some phone calls, so we can find out just how far this has gone. But I need your help. Can you put together a list of all the defendants you've sentenced in the last six months, what crime they were sentenced for, and what your sentence was? I also need a list of your office staff, how long they've been with you, and what you know about them."

"I'll get my staff working on it as soon as we finish our move to family court," Liz said.

"No. Do it all yourself. The fewer people who know about

this the better," I said. "I also need a complete transcript of the trial that Joe tried, and I need it fast. Who's your court reporter?"

"It's Glenda Goodwin. But it'll take time to get that. The defendant was acquitted so there's no appeal, so no transcript has been ordered."

"Believe me, there's a transcript, or Marconi wouldn't have brought it up. He and the state are probably pouring over it now. I'll call Glenda. She'll get me a copy. As long as she gets paid by the page, she doesn't care who gets the transcript." I paused and looked at Liz. "There will be some costs associated with this case."

"I know that, Mary. I'll pay you whatever your standard fee is. Don't worry, and don't cut me any breaks because I'm a judge. Someone would investigate that too. Judges live in fish bowls."

"By the way, Liz, this is confidential from me to you. Most of us think Marconi is a worm," I said.

For the first time, Liz smiled.

CHAPTER TEN

I walked Liz to the door and glanced at the clock. It was 7:20. I hadn't realized how long the interview with Liz took.

I returned to my desk and reviewed my notes. Catherine had placed a reminder tag on a big file in the center of the desk. "Ramon Molina's hearing Weds. A.M., Federal Courthouse, Judge Baum." Thank God for Catherine. I had forgotten. I opened the file and began to prepare for the hearing.

Ramon Molina was an important client. He was accused of money laundering, bank fraud, and violations of interstate commerce. He also was vice president of Granada National Trust Bank, located on Brickell Avenue in the heart of Miami's financial district. The feds were jumping with joy over this prosecution of a well-known banker. They were eager to file as many charges as possible against him. I was fearful that they would invent some special new laws that he had violated, like maybe wearing dirty underwear or picking his nose in public.

Ramon was not used to taking orders. Since his arrest, he had been ordered to go to sleep at nine p.m. and arise at five-thirty a.m.; to wear an orange jumpsuit and to work in the laundry. In short, he was being held at the federal detention facility under a no-bond status, due to the fact that he was born in South America and had only been an upright citizen of the U.S. for twenty years.

He was not a happy camper, but his wife hired me and was now in control of the purse strings. She paid all of my bills promptly, and didn't seem all that upset to have Ramon out of the house in a place where he couldn't cause trouble.

I threw what was left of my mind into preparing for Ramon's hearing. The next time I looked at the clock, it was after nine. Sam had begun to pace. It was time to get out of here and head home. Then I remembered the message from Carlos about dinner. He might still be waiting for me at my house. I was in no mood to argue with him. All I wanted was a glass of wine and a dumb TV program to push every thought out of my head.

I put Sam on his leash, gathered up my overnight bag and briefcase, and locked the door. The parking lot was completely dark. The security light was out. I would have to complain about it tomorrow. The building caretaker was careless about a lot of stuff.

As soon as we walked toward my car, Sam stiffened. The hair on his back stood up and a low growl formed in his throat. Mine was the only car left on the lot. It was parked near the hedge that separated the parking area from the next door building. That building was dark too. I wished I had a flashlight. I approached the car. Dammit, I should have gotten my keys out before I left the office. My hands were full, so I laid the bags down and fumbled in my pockets for my keys.

Sam pulled hard on his leash. Then I was on the ground. Sam turned behind me and jumped on someone. His sharp barks pierced the darkness. I felt a sudden dizziness and an awful pain. I touched the back of my head. There was something wet. I got up slowly, got my key out, and opened the car door. In the light from the car, I saw the blood on my hand. Sam jumped in the car and I fell across the front seat. Then I blacked out.

CHAPTER ELEVEN

The next thing I remember was a light shining in my eyes and male voices shouting. I tried to sit up, but Sam was lying across my chest.

"Mary, what happened? Over here, Carlos. She's in the car."

I recognized Carlos's cousin, Marco, the head of Pit Bulls Security. He was checking my pulse. Then I saw the worried face of Carlos looking down at me. He propped up my head and saw the blood beneath it.

"Marco, call the police and fire rescue," he yelled.

"No, Carlos, please, I just want to go home," I said.

"You need medical attention, Mary. Let me drive you to the emergency room. I can have my family's doctor meet us there. You may need stitches or something," Carlos said. He kissed me several times and I felt dizzy again.

I nodded agreement. Carlos moved into the driver's seat. Marco followed us out of the parking lot, and we headed to Mercy Hospital with Sam in the back seat licking Carlos's head.

"How did you and Marco get here?" I mumbled.

"You mean how did we find you?" Carlos asked. "I got worried when you didn't come home. I called the office and your cell. Then I called Catherine's house. She said she left you at the office, so I called Marco and we came directly to the office. I knew you wouldn't just not show up for dinner without even calling me, even if you are mad at me. And I knew you wouldn't be hitting the bars with Sam still waiting to get home. Thank God I got here right away." Carlos put an arm around me as we pulled into the emergency room parking lot at the hospital.

Marco must have phoned ahead because an orderly was waiting outside with a wheelchair. An elegantly dressed white-haired doctor appeared as we entered the emergency area. Carlos shook his hand as our little army proceeded to a curtained-off examining room. I was startled to see Angelina Martin, Carlos's mother, waiting inside.

"Mary, this is Doctor Andreas. He's treated our whole family for years. He called me after he got the call from Marco. Of course, I came right over," Angelina said.

I looked at Carlos with as threatening an expression as I could muster. "All this fuss really isn't necessary. I'm feeling better," I said as I tried to sit up with little result.

"Mi amor, this is necessary. You've been attacked and injured. This is what Hispanic families do. If someone goes to the hospital, the family goes too. You understand?" Carlos said.

It was then that I realized that this was Angie's way of accepting that Carlos and I are a couple. Even in my muddled state, I realized that this was some kind of a breakthrough.

"Angie, thank you for coming, and thank you too, Doctor Andreas."

"Darling, I knew you wouldn't want to scare your parents. Of course, I came right over. J.C. would be here, too, but he's away on a business trip." Angie patted my hand.

Carlos's parents had been cordial to me each time we met, but it was clear that they were hesitant about his having a girlfriend who wasn't Hispanic. Seeing Angie waiting for us at the hospital must mean that she liked me a little. Or maybe she was hoping my injury was fatal.

"Okay, enough of the talk. Everyone clear out while I examine the young lady," Doctor Andreas said.

A nurse cleaned the wound, and a little later the doctor announced his diagnosis to the waiting group. They hung on his words, delivered in stentorian tones. "No stitches are necessary. She must have been hit with a heavy object with a sharp edge, but the cut is small. The more important problem is that a blow to that part of the skull often leads to concussion."

The doctor suggested that I stay awake for a while, and in bed resting for the next day. Carlos, Marco, and Angie took turns shaking hands with the doctor. Then the curtains parted again. Two Miami cops walked in.

"Is this the woman who was attacked?" the one in uniform asked.

Marco nodded. "Mary, I'm sorry. I know you want to get out of here, but it's hospital procedure. They have to report any acts of violence."

"Okay, let's get this over with. Get out your notepad. The doctor just said I had to stay awake for a few hours anyway," I said.

"I'm Detective Avery, robbery division," the one in a sport coat and tie said. "Marco filled us in on your name and occupation and how they found you. It was reported as a robbery attempt, but Marco said he found your bag and briefcase intact right outside your car."

I explained what I could remember about leaving the office and Sam's intervention. Then I remembered, "Where is Sam?"

"One of Marco's investigators came over and got him. He's in my backyard by now waiting to see you," Carlos said. You're going to be staying at my house for the next few days."

"No, I'm okay now. I need to go home."

"Mary, please, you took care of me a few months ago when I broke my arm. Let me do the same for you."

Angie interrupted. "Or you can come home with me, if you'd rather."

I gave up the fight, and let them wheel me out to my blood-stained car. The cops left their cards and said they'd talk to me again when I was more coherent.

Carlos drove to his house in Pinecrest, and for once, he didn't speed. "I should have told those cops that's as coherent as you ever are, and it's a good thing the bad guy hit you in your hard head or you might really have been hurt."

I had to laugh and Carlos smiled his heartbreaker smile.

CHAPTER TWELVE

The next morning I awoke to the sun slanting through the wooden shutters in Carlos's enormous bed in his enormous house. We call these new monsters "starter castles." The clock radio music player with its twenty buttons and switches rested on the night table. It read nine fifteen. I tried to jump out of bed, but fell back against the pillows. My head felt like men in spiked shoes were walking around in there.

I sat up slowly this time and made it into the bathroom. I threw cold water on my face. A glance in the mirror scared me. I couldn't go to work looking like this.

"So, Sleeping Beauty, you are awake already." Carlos stood in the doorway. He had a large mug of steaming coffee, the morning papers, and Sam at his side. "Now get back in bed like a good girl."

"I'm already late getting to work." I felt disoriented and put up no fight as Carlos led me back to bed. He put the mug of coffee in my hands and sat down next to me.

"I've already called Catherine. She's canceling your schedule. She said to remind you Molina's hearing is not until tomorrow and she can take care of everything today. You need a day of rest."

"I think you're right, but I need to go home. I haven't been there since Friday."

"No, you're staying right here. We don't know who gave

you that wallop last night, but it wasn't a garden-variety robbery. All your stuff was right next to your car, untouched. Marco's guys are going by your place. They'll check it out. And Franco already picked up your car to clean it up. He'll bring it back this afternoon. I'll drive you home later this evening and you can pick up what you need for court tomorrow. But you're staying put right here."

Franco is Marco's brother. He owns some kind of car repair garage and seems to stay in business by servicing the cars and trucks of Carlos and his family, including a cast of dozens of cousins or adopted cousins. He automatically turns up whenever a car needs work. Sometimes he turns up to work on a car even when it doesn't need work. He always finds something wrong with them.

"I didn't want to leave for work until I saw that you were awake," Carlos said. "There's plenty of food in the fridge so, please, eat something. Before I leave, I think we better discuss something. I don't want to upset you, but that was some kind of angry rant I got on both my cell phones yesterday. Why are you so ticked off about Luis?"

"I'm upset because you didn't tell me that Luis was being detained as an enemy combatant. You know I'm trying to build my law practice. You should have seen the hate e-mails and phone calls that poured into the office. People don't much like terrorists. Even other criminals don't like them."

"First of all, I had no idea why Luis was arrested. His parents are old friends of my father's family in Argentina. His family was worried sick because Luis never reached his hotel in Miami. They didn't hear from him for two days. I don't even know how they found out he was in jail. Someone in his family called my dad. When I got a call, I called you. I figured you know how to handle such a situation and, as a plus, you'd have a new, paying client. He's such a nice kid. I thought maybe he got picked up on a D.U.I. or something."

"Well, you should have found out more." I felt my anger from yesterday returning, but Carlos interrupted me.

"Listen, Mary, if you are the defender of people accused of crimes, and you really believe in what you do, it shouldn't matter to you what a person is accused of. How many times have you scolded me, and told me just because someone is charged with a crime doesn't mean they did it. Innocent 'til proven guilty. Aren't those your words? Oh, and also, even if someone is guilty, they still deserve the best defense you can give them. Isn't that what you've told me over and over?"

"Yes, that's true," I said.

"Well, either you believe what you say or you don't. Think about that while you're resting today. I'll try to call you later, but I'm going to be in meetings most of the day. I'm trying to negotiate for that land in Palm Beach for the shopping arcade. And the cops who came to the hospital last night may call you here today. They need to get a complete statement from you. Now that you tell me about the hate e-mails and calls, maybe that's what led to your being attacked. I hope not."

I sat up and pulled Carlos down next to me. "I'm sorry if I've made you late for your meeting, and — well, I guess I'm just sorry about everything."

Carlos looked at me for a minute. Then he kissed me and held me for a few seconds. He left the room quickly, and I heard his Escalade drive out of the garage.

I must have slept again. This time when I awoke, the pounding in my head had stopped. I felt totally grungy. I took a long shower in the bathroom with the three pulsating showerheads. I put on some of Carlos's cologne, which made me feel hot. I found an old shirt of his. With the sleeves rolled up, it covered me like a bathrobe.

I actually felt hungry, so I descended to the kitchen where Sam was sprawled out on the cool tile floor. I opened the refrigerator and found more food than I keep in mine in a month. I grabbed eggs, cheese, and peppers and fixed an omelet. I nuked some bacon in the microwave, one slice for me and one for Sam. We took our food out to the pool. The screened enclosure around it keeps the sun away. I watched the wild parrots swoop in and out of the bottle brush trees. Their green bodies and the red flowers of the trees looked like a Christmas display. The rain had finally stopped. Everything looked fresh and green.

I was beginning to relax when the doorbell rang. You can't miss it even from a block away. It sounds like church bells calling the faithful. Sam bounded in and galloped to the front door. He loves company. I do not, especially when dressed in nothing but an oversized shirt. I peeked through the stained glass in the mahogany double doors and saw Detective Avery. He was dressed in the same sport coat and tie as last night. He was carrying a tape recorder and a camera.

I opened the door a crack, trying to stand behind it. Detective Avery stepped through it with little or no effort. I guess cops are used to reluctant door openers.

"Good morning, Mary. Do you remember me? I'm Detective Jim Avery, Miami Police." He flashed his badge. Sam put his paw on Avery's leg and the detective instinctively rubbed his ears and chest. "I'm sorry to barge in, but I need to complete this report. You didn't seem to be able to tell us much last night."

"I can't tell you much today either, because I don't really know much."

"Okay. Can I sit down? I'd like to tape whatever you can tell me. Is that all right?"

"Sure, come with me. I was just having a late breakfast on the patio. May I get you something?"

"No, I'll just get your statement and be out of your way." He followed me out to the patio, and turned on the recorder as we settled on opposite sides of the glass-topped table.

"I was leaving my office after working late. I had Sam on his leash and bags in my hand. It was very dark out there. The safety light was out. I was trying to get my key out. The next thing I knew Sam pulled me and ran behind me. I think he jumped on someone. He was barking and growling. Then I was on the ground with a terrible pain in my head."

"Can you remember anything about the person? Was it a man or a woman? Did they say anything? Did you get a look at their clothes?"

"I never really saw the person. Just as I tried to turn, I got hit. It was super dark too."

"The safety light was shot out. We found the glass and a bullet casing. That's why it was so dark. You're lucky your dog was with you or you might be dead. I know you were in the news yesterday, representing the guy who is accused of trying to blow up a plane over the Keys. Has anyone threatened you about that case?"

"Anyone? Try everyone. Before I could get back to my office, horrible e-mails and phone calls were bombarding us."

"Can we get access to the e-mails and the phone messages?"

"Sure, you can have whatever my assistant kept. She's at the office now. I'll call her and tell her you'll be stopping by."

"I'll go right over there. Has anyone else threatened you? Any of your clients?"

"No, no one. I still think maybe it was just a robbery that went bad when Sam attacked."

"You may be right, but we need to look at everything. Now, I need to take some photos of your injury."

"Are you kidding? Photos the way I look? No way."

"It's just the back of your head. The State will kill me if I don't get pictures, and we arrest someone."

"Well, too bad. You and I both know you'll never find anyone. There are dozens of these robberies every day around Miami."

CHAPTER THIRTEEN

By the time the cop left, I was feeling antsy. I called Catherine, who assured me that everything was quiet. She said that Judge Maxwell had phoned to leave her new number at the family courthouse and to say she was working on the lists that I had asked for.

With everything that had happened, I had put Liz's case out of my mind. I went into the home office that Carlos set up down the hall from the kitchen. The computer beckoned. I began searching the back issues of the *Miami Herald*, looking for any information about the murdered informant that Judge Marconi mentioned as part of the investigation of Liz.

I found the headline only a few weeks back. INFORM-ANT SHOT IN COLD BLOOD ON CITY STREET. A sidebar article contained snippets of the case, *State vs. Carillo*. Jack Carillo, twice arrested, but never *convicted*, stood accused of attempting to import cocaine. A sting operation was set up by the Miami-Dade Police. They used an undercover informant who persuaded Carillo that he could bring him copious amounts of cocaine. The informant was from Colombia, and was not known by Jack Carillo before the meetings set in motion by the cops. As soon as the arrest was made, the informant was secreted by the state and the police. Carillo's attorney was quoted, complaining about the need to depose the informant. The next paragraph jumped out at me.

There was the whole description of Liz ordering the deposition to be taken with her special instructions; location to be secret, only the state, defense, and court reporter to be present, the deposition to be kept sealed until the trial. Nothing in the article sounded an alarm that Liz was doing anything but her job as the judge in the case. On the other hand, nothing in the article exonerated Liz from blame for the informant's murder.

I stopped reading and gripped the desk. I remembered going to a party with Carlos right after we started dating. The host was Jack Carillo. He and Carlos were high-school buddies at the Miami Academy, a private school for the rich and connected. The party was at Jack's home on Star Island, an enclave of mansions with views of the skylines of Miami Beach and Miami, and surrounded by Biscayne Bay. The place looked like a setting for *Lives of the Rich and Famous*. The grounds were magnificent. We spent most of the evening on the terrace overlooking the water. The next thing that I recalled gave me goose bumps. Joe Fineberg was a guest at that party too. I printed a copy of the article and shut down the computer. My head had begun to throb again. This time I wasn't sure whether it was from last night's debacle or the fact that I had no idea how I was going to rid Liz of the state's accusations, an even worse debacle.

CHAPTER FOURTEEN

Franco delivered my car at three o'clock. I grabbed Sam and my dirty clothes and headed home. I left messages for Carlos on his cells and at his office explaining that I felt just fine and needed to see my own four walls.

Marco must have been by the house, because I found my overnight bag and briefcase on the back porch. All seemed to be in order in the house, which is to say that it was the way I left it last Friday morning. No one had touched the dishes in the sink, or picked up the newspapers left strewn on the living room floor. Nothing was missing from either bag. My wallet was intact, credit card and driver's license still there.

I decided not to worry about anything else. I turned off the phone and crawled into bed.

The next time I was conscious again, the clock said eight. Ramon's hearing was at nine. The answer machine was blinking wildly. Catherine had called at seven thirty reminding me to be at the federal courthouse by nine. Carlos left three messages reaming me out half in Spanish and half in English. That meant he was really angry that I left and came home. The end of his message dripped gloom. "I failed to get the land for the shopping arcade. The bastards wanted more money than anyone in his right mind would pay."

I threw Sam in the backyard with his food bowl, dressed, and was in the car by eight thirty. After shortcutting through a maze of side streets, I hit the federal plaza area by nine twenty. I pulled my car into the closest lot that still had space. Twenty dollars whether you parked for fifteen minutes or five hours, but it was only one block from the courthouse.

I sprinted the block and arrived at the concrete barriers that ringed the area surrounding the federal courts. Since 9/11, no cars were allowed around the perimeter. This created not only an auto traffic nightmare, but a pedestrian one as well. Crossing the street and finding the openings in the barriers was like a rat traversing a maze. Every few weeks the pedestrian paths changed. Finally, I reached the entrance and saw the long line waiting to go through security.

Federal marshals barked instructions to the line approaching the metal detectors. "Have your ID ready. Place all bags on the screening table. No cell phones allowed inside."

"Here's my ID." I waved it at the guard who stood with his arms across his chest. He looked like the concrete barriers dressed in a uniform. I started through the metal detector. Buzzers screamed and a light went on.

"Step to the side, Miss," the beefy marshal said.

"I'm sorry, sir. I think my bracelet must have set it off," I said.

"No, it's too small," he said as he started running hand wands up and down my back. He tried to put the wand under my skirt, but I jumped back, so he zeroed in on my pockets. Loud squeaks and squawks filled the air. Impatient attorneys behind me were muttering obscenities.

"Hey, aren't you the lawyer representing that dirtbag terrorist guy? I saw you on TV the other night," the marshal said. "Better come with me. We'll finish this search in a private area."

"This is ridiculous. I'm late for court. My pockets are what squeaked. Go ahead and stick those big paws in my pockets and see what caused it. I'm not going anywhere with you."

A female marshal hurried over. "I'll take over," she said.

She ran the wand over my skirt and jacket with the same results. She put her hand in my right pocket and pulled out my cell phone. She extracted two quarters and two dog biscuits from my left pocket.

"You know you can't bring cell phones in here anymore." She reached for an envelope. "Fill out your name and phone number and put the phone in here. You can pick it up on your way out."

"Thanks. You can keep the dog biscuits," I said. I rushed to the elevators where a huge crowd was waiting, so I opted for the stairs. When I reached the sixth floor, panting and sweating, I saw that it was almost ten o'clock.

The courtroom was filled with attorneys and litigants, but the atmosphere was hushed. The pew-like benches and the quiet reminded me of my mother's church. The atmosphere in federal court differed markedly from the state court. More marshals in uniforms, eyeing the crowd, stood in the back of the room and along the sides.

I consulted the calendar posted in the back of the room. My case was toward the end. I saw Tracy Steinfield at the lectern addressing the court. I looked down the list of attorneys printed next to each case name. What a relief. There were four more cases before Ramon's would be called.

I was looking forward to Ramon's trial. If I did a good job, I could expect more clients from the financial world. The feds were sure to go after other bankers. Not to brag, but I am great with juries. I had some good stuff lined up. I had already prepared Mrs. Molina for her role as sympathetic spouse. We had selected her wardrobe, a simple navy dress and pearls, and her hairdo, a graceful chignon. Several high-powered witnesses were prepared to testify about Ramon's charitable work in the community, in Miami and Granada. We had pictures of the rebuilding of the island after the hurricane, all underwritten by the Molinas.

An hour later, Ramon's case was called. Assistant U.S. Attorney Lenore Forbes stepped behind one lectern, and I stepped up to the other. Ramon was not with the other prisoners who had been brought out.

"Good morning, Judge Baum. I am Mary Katz, representing Ramon Molina. I don't see my client in the courtroom. He's in custody. I made sure that the order was processed to bring him here for this hearing."

"Yes, Ms. Katz, I see the order in the file," Judge Baum said. He sighed and frowned. "Where is he, marshals? We can't wait all day."

One of the uniformed guys approached the bench. "Your Honor, he's in the back. There was a mix-up about his clothes for the hearing. His wife brought them to the wrong check-in area yesterday, but we have them now and he's getting dressed."

"I don't care if he's in his underwear or his birthday suit. Get him out here. We've got more cases after this. I have a meeting at noon, and I'm out of here in forty minutes no matter who's wearing what." Judge Baum slapped his desk for emphasis. I jumped. This hearing was not off to a great start.

Two marshals hurried out of the courtroom through the locked side door into the prisoner area. I apologized to the judge for the lag time, and assured him the hearing would be brief. I was keeping the time filled so he wouldn't call up another case while I sat nursing my headache that had returned with a vengeance.

The side door opened and Ramon entered flanked by the

two marshals. He was wearing grey flannel slacks, a white shirt open at the neck, and a blue blazer; very Ralph Lauren by way of Brooks Brothers. The reason for the open collar without a tie was not a fashion statement. Inmates are not allowed to wear ties. The theory is that they may hang themselves or harm others. Ramon was not the suicide type, but as to harming others, I wouldn't take any bets.

I moved over next to Ramon as he was being led to the lectern. I extended my hand, but he looked straight ahead and ignored my attempted handshake. He looked angry.

"Judge, now that my client is present, I have a few motions we can address in preparation for our November trial date," I began. Before I could finish my sentence, Ramon began to speak.

"Your Honor, I need to address the court," he said.

I tried to quiet him by gently grasping his elbow and shaking my head.

"Mr. Molina, please address the court through your attorney. Let her know what it is you wish to say, so she can advise you," Judge Baum said.

"It's not possible for me to discuss anything further with Ms. Katz. I no longer wish to have her represent me," Ramon said in a loud voice

The other attorneys in the courtroom turned to stare at us. I felt the inquisitive eyes boring into my back and sides. They were onto the morning's newest hot gossip. I half expected someone to leap forward and offer Ramon their card. I stared at Ramon, mouth gaping open, just the way I looked on CNN two days ago.

"Ms. Katz, were you aware of your client's intention to terminate your representation?" Judge Baum was now clearly annoyed.

"Absolutely not, Your Honor. If I might have a few

minutes to talk with Mr. Molina, perhaps I can clarify the situation."

"I would prefer not to do that," Ramon said.

"Counsel, approach" Judge Baum motioned us forward. Lenore and I hustled to the side of the bench.

"What gives, ladies?" Has Molina lost his mind?" the judge asked.

"Well, if you ask me, this is just a stall tactic. He doesn't want to go to trial," Lenore whispered as the court reporter strained to catch each word.

"Are you sure you didn't know about this Ms. Katz?" the judge asked.

"Of course I didn't. Do you think I would allow a client to fire me in front of a whole courtroom if I knew about it in advance?" My voice was rising above the approved sidebar whisper.

"You need to find out what this is about. Step back, please," the judge said.

"I can't, Judge. He's refusing to speak to me," I said.

"Okay, Ms. Katz. Both of you step back. Looks like I'll have to inquire of him myself."

We resumed our positions at the lecterns. Judge Baum looked over the top of his reading glasses and eyeballed Ramon.

"Mr. Molina, since you won't share your concerns with your attorney, I am forced to make inquiry into this decision to reject your current attorney."

"You mean why am I firing her?" Ramon asked

A few attorneys in the audience were stifling giggles.

"Have you been dissatisfied with her work on your behalf, sir?"

"No, she's been doing okay," he said.

"Well, what's the problem?" Judge Baum's face was turning florid.

"Last night it came to my attention that my lawyer is also representing a terrorist. My wife and I discussed this by telephone, and we both feel that we don't want to have a lawyer who represents somebody who would hurt citizens of this great nation. We love this country, even though we weren't born here." Ramon was warming to his topic.

"Mr. Molina, please don't make a speech. All I wanted to know was the reason." Judge Baum cut him off, much to my relief.

"Are you saying, sir, that some people accused of a crime are entitled to be represented by competent counsel, but others aren't? If, indeed, you love this country, you should understand the presumption of innocence by which you have also been protected." Judge Baum leaned forward as he spoke.

"Judge Baum, it seems best that I withdraw from Mr. Molina's case, as he wishes. I will make his file available to whatever new counsel that he hires. Trial preparation is nearly complete, so there shouldn't be any lengthy continuance in the case. May I be excused, Your Honor?"

"Yes, Ms. Katz. Under the circumstances, I will allow you to withdraw from this case, but I am not happy about what has transpired here this morning. Ten minute recess." Judge Baum left the bench, shaking his head.

My face was burning with embarrassment as I grabbed my file and made a rapid exit from the courtroom.

Lenore followed me hurrying to catch up with me. "Sorry, Mary. I had no idea that Molina would make such a statement. I'm sorry I accused you of helping him stall."

"Thanks, Lenore. I said, as I rushed to the ladies' room, always a good place to hide out from questions from colleagues.

CHAPTER FIFTEEN

I went down the stairs to the main lobby, avoiding the crowded elevators.

I retrieved my cell phone, and walked out of the icy air conditioning into the hazy June heat and humidity. I walked toward the parking lot, but took a detour into the park that bordered the bay. It was quiet except for the usual downtown characters, some homeless, some elderly and bored. A few pigeons trotted around the benches looking for crumbs.

I took off my suit jacket and plopped onto one of the benches facing the water. I had never been fired by a client before, and it hurt. When I told Carlos that some of my clients would be upset about my appearing to represent an accused terrorist, I hadn't fully anticipated that I would lose an important client like Ramon.

Carlos told me to think about what I really believed, and Judge Baum reiterated the basic code of justice in this country. Innocent until proven guilty is not just rhetoric. The whole meaning came home to me. I knew what needed to be done.

I speed dialed the office. "Catherine, it's me."

"How do you feel? How did the hearing go?"

"You don't have to worry about Ramon anymore. He fired us."

"What? The ungrateful bastard. After I spent an hour on the phone tracking down his clothes for court. That dumb airhead wife of his couldn't even get it straight where to leave them." Catherine was an army brat, and her language reflected her background.

"Forget about him. I want you to start making some calls to find out where the feds took Luis Corona. Check the federal jails in the area. We need to find him. Any messages?"

"Well, your mother called. She said if she didn't hear from you, she'd come down here and sit in your office. She still has her southern accent, doesn't she?"

"Okay, I'll call her from the car. She picked the wrong day to give me an ultimatum."

Mother and Dad moved to a retirement community complete with a golf course, guard gate, and look-alike red roofed villas on tiny patches of land in Boynton Beach. My brothers and I were shocked when our father sold the Katz Kosher Markets and the wholesale supply business two years ago to a national chain. The Katz name was maintained, but the friendly feeling is gone. Then they turned around and sold our family home on Miami Beach. It was the only house I had ever lived in growing up. A developer bought the place and promptly tore it down. In its place are two town houses three stories high that crowd the half-acre lot. So when Mother threatens to hold a sit-in in my office, it means she would have to drive for ninety minutes to get there. This is her way of insuring my overwhelming guilt.

I eased the car out of the parking lot and into the line of traffic. As soon as I got to the highway, I called my mother.

"Hi, what's up?" I asked. She had picked up on the first ring.

"I'll tell you what's up. I had to learn from Angelina

Martin that my daughter was accosted, injured, and taken to the emergency room. She said this occurred two days ago. Mary, why are you shutting me out of your life?"

"I'm not shutting you out. I'm just trying not to worry you over nothing. I'm just fine. But more importantly, why were you talking to Angelina? Did she call you to tell you about this?"

"No, fortunately for me, I happened to call her this morning."

"What in the world for?"

"Well, I thought it was high time that we met the Martins, so I invited them to go to dinner this Saturday night, with you and Carlos, of course. It's all set. We're meeting at the Ocean Inn in Fort Lauderdale. That's sort of halfway between where they live and where we live."

I was speechless. Just the kind of additional stress I needed right now.

"Mary, are you there?"

"Yes, I'm here. I'm just amazed that you would do something like this without consulting me. What's the point of this dinner?"

"How can I consult you when you're never available. Always too busy to call. The point is that you and Carlos are practically inseparable. It's only reasonable that our two families should meet."

"I'm over thirty years old, Mother. Don't you think I should be the one to tell you when a relationship is serious? When it's time to meet the family?"

"I know how old you are. That's just the point. Your time is running out to know the joy of having children. Although, I must say, lately you haven't been much of a joy. What about this blow to your head in your parking lot? Are you really okay?"

"I can't discuss this any further right now. I'm trying to drive through traffic, and I've got a dozen problems at work. I'll talk to you later." I closed my cell phone and slammed my hand against the steering wheel.

CHAPTER SIXTEEN

"No one has any information about Luis Corona. I've called every holding facility, state and federal, from Monroe County all the way through Palm Beach," Catherine said as soon as I walked in the office door. "They all say he's not on their roster. What else can we do to find him?"

"He could be anywhere. The feds truck defendants all over the country, or worse, he could be on his way to Guantanamo. Once they lock him away there, we'll never get access to him."

"I thought you weren't interested in representing him," Catherine said.

"I wasn't at first, but Ramon has already fired us, and I guess I felt ashamed of leaving Luis in this mess. He really doesn't look like a terrorist, not that I know what one is supposed to look like. He just looked like a scared kid."

"On another note, a packet of papers was delivered by messenger from Judge Maxwell." Catherine laid the packet on my desk. "Any other calls you want me to make about Luis? Do you think you'll be on TV again? Maybe the media will come to the office and we can all be on CNN. My kids would love that."

"I'm not doing this for the publicity, but I'll keep your kids in mind if the horde descends on us. Try to get Lucy Stern's husband on the phone. Steve Stern at the U.S. Attorney's Office. Maybe he can help me find Luis."

"I remember Lucy. She's your old friend who brought you flowers for the new office," Catherine said. "Is she a lawyer too?"

"No, she's actually a friend all the way back to elementary school. She married Steve before she finished college. She's mainly a mom. Leave word for Steve to call me."

I opened the packet that Liz sent over. The first set of papers outlined the defendants she had sentenced over the last six months. It appeared that she exceeded the sentencing guidelines in several cases. There was an armed robbery of a seventy-year-old woman in a bank parking lot. The woman suffered a debilitating heart attack. Liz used the "three strikes law" to give the defendant a life sentence. His priors included another robbery and a burglary. A twenty-year-old was convicted of stalking several girls on a school playground. She gave him twelve years, although the state had asked for only six. That one was sure to come back after an appeal. There were a few other violent crimes in which the defendants had received high sentences.

The drug cases were a different story. Several low-level sellers had received the bottom of the sentencing guidelines. One woman who was a confirmed addict with a long record of petit thefts was sent to a treatment program where she could also house her baby. None of these matters seemed enough to trigger an investigation. There was no mention of any drug cases being dismissed by Liz.

Next I turned to the descriptions of the employees who worked for Liz.

Patricia Patterson was her judicial assistant, the euphemistic name the court system gives to judicial secretaries.

She had worked for Liz for her entire tenure on the bench. Before that, she was employed by Judge Streeter, who retired. Patricia was an African American, fifty-seven years old, married to a Miami-Dade police major who headed the internal investigation unit. Her children were grown. All were college graduates and were career military officers.

Millie Clancy was Liz's courtroom clerk. She was responsible for the court files and for keeping all docket sheets. I paused a moment. Here was someone who could alter case files. I read on. Millie was sixty-one years old, a widow near retirement. She had been in the clerk's office for twenty-nine years. Her husband had owned a small grocery store. He was shot in his store when two warring drug dealers held a shootout. Her one daughter was married and lived in Atlanta.

Gladys Perez-Martinez had been with Liz for six of her ten years on the bench. Her prior employment was with a private security firm. Liz described her as a highly competent bailiff. She kept good order in the courtroom and kept the attorneys in line. She was always impeccably professional, her white shirt starched, tie straight, shoes shined, long hair pulled back in a bun. Liz also described a different Gladys. An after-hours party was held for Patricia's birthday. Gladys came dressed in a miniskirt, high leather boots, and her hair loose in long curls. No one recognized her for several minutes.

Gladys was thirty-five years old. She was married two years ago to a Colombian who had his own import-export business. She and her husband, Billy Martinez, purchased a house in a fashionable subdivision in Doral. Gladys performed a variety of duties, including courtroom organization, conforming and dispersing orders, and opening mail.

I finished reading and dialed the state attorney. It was time to find out just how far this investigation was going.

Jason Jimenez-Jones had been elected state attorney two

years earlier based on his campaign pledge to go after crooked officials. This was a pledge made by numerous Miami office holders, some of whom eventually landed in jail themselves.

I was impressed enough with Jason to work for his election. I liked the fact that he was a typical "mixed breed" Miamian, like so many of us. I also thought he was sincere about making Miami a better place. Now I was in an awkward position. He was doing what he promised and I wanted him to stop.

I got through the first layer of phone answerers and reached Olga, Jason's first assistant.

"Olga, this is Mary Magruder Katz. I believe we met during Jason's election campaign."

"Yes, I remember. You're the defense attorney with the Fieldstone firm, correct?"

"Well, I was at the time. I have my own law firm now. I need to set an appointment to speak with Jason."

"If this is about employment, I can put you through to the chair of our hiring committee," Olga said.

"No, I'm very happy where I am, thank you. I need to discuss a matter regarding one of my clients."

"Jason doesn't meet with attorneys about individual defendants. You need to take up such matters with the assistant handling the case."

"Look, Olga, this is a highly confidential matter. I'm quite sure Jason is the only one I need to speak with." I was becoming more irritated by the minute.

"Well, tell me the name of your client and the case number and I'll see if Jason will see you, but he doesn't have any openings until a week from Thursday."

"I think you better jog Jason's memory. I dropped my entire schedule to assist Jason's campaign two years ago. He will be facing election again soon. The Criminal Defense Bar

Association will be interested in hearing that Jason's open-door policy has been closed and locked. Now go tell Jason I'm on the line and that I need to see him immediately about a current investigation. I'll wait while you consult him."

Olga hesitated. "I'm not sure if he's in his office."

"Well, the best way to find that out is to buzz his intercom. I'll wait."

A few minutes passed. I reread Liz's papers and my notes from our meeting while I waited.

Olga returned to the line. "Ms. Katz, Jason said to come over tomorrow morning at ten thirty, and he said to tell you he was sorry you were kept waiting."

I hung up and gave myself a hug. Never take "no" for the final answer.

As soon as I hung up, Catherine buzzed me. "Steve Stern is on the line. He wants to know if you can meet him and Lucy for lunch tomorrow. He's meeting Lucy at noon at that new bistro on Brickell Avenue, The Green Toad. What an unappetizing name. What should I tell him?"

"Tell him that'll be perfect."

The day was winding down. My head still hurt. Now all I had to do was find Carlos and hope he wasn't still angry with me, because I had to tell him about my mother's devious dinner on Saturday.

CHAPTER SEVENTEEN

Carlos answered his second cell phone. I could hear construction noise so I knew he was still at a job site.

"Carlos, I'm so sorry I ran out on you yesterday. I just had to see my own house. And I'm really sorry your land deal didn't go through in Palm Beach. Let me make dinner tonight. Whatever time you say."

"You'll make dinner? Is this your way of poisoning me in order to end our relationship?"

"Hey, I'm not that bad a cook. Okay, how about I pick up dinner that someone else cooked. I can stop on my way home."

"I'll be there by seven. We'll talk then." Carlos hung up abruptly.

By six thirty, I had showered and changed into shorts and my sexiest tee shirt. The table was set. The wine was poured and *arroz con pollo* was keeping warm on the stove, courtesy of the Spanish chicken place in South Miami.

I knew when Carlos was turning into my driveway. Sam began to pace by the front door. As soon as I opened the door, I tried to hug Carlos, but Sam bullied his way between us and put his paws on Carlos's chest. When I finally got my turn, I could smell Carlos's shampoo. His hair was still wet. He must have showered instead of arriving in his construction clothes. He returned my hug, but it was less than enthusiastic.

He picked up his glass of wine and stared at it. "You don't have any Scotch, do you?"

"As a matter of fact, I do. Want it with water or soda?"

"Neither. Just over one ice cube."

I handed him his drink and started to serve up the dinner plates.

"Could you keep it warm a bit longer?" Carlos asked. He drained the Scotch in the glass and poured himself another shot.

"Carlos, what's wrong? If it's about yesterday, I'm really sorry. I was thoughtless. If it's about Luis Corona, I'm sorry about the fuss I made. I'm trying to locate him so I can help him."

"Listen, I'm not mad, just tired and disappointed. I thought I knew you, but, as you have pointed out often enough, we don't know each other that well. I can put up with your wacky side and even your stubborn side, but I didn't think you were selfish and uncaring about my feelings. I'm not Sam that you can have around just when you want him. I'm not prepared to be your puppy dog."

"Are you breaking up with me?" I asked. Because if you are, you picked a shitty time to do it. My mother called your mother and arranged a dinner party for the six of us for Saturday night. I knew absolutely nothing about this, until she sprung it on me on the phone today."

For the first time since he arrived, Carlos smiled. His smile just makes me tingle.

"So your mother has decided that we are official. Well, I guess we better not break up this week. Maybe we wait until next week." He began to laugh.

"What's funny about this?"

"I'm not breaking up with you. I love you. I just want you

to stop acting like a spoiled child. Go put that chicken on the table. I've had a terrible week. Besides your antics, I've lost out on my next project. I'm behind on the condo project, and the investors are on my neck along with the people who put deposits on the units. They want to move in in two months and we aren't half done."

"Well, let's have some dinner, and maybe we'll both feel better," I said.

When we were almost done with dinner, I brought Luis up, again.

"Please, tell me everything you know about Luis. I have nothing to go on. I don't know why he was coming to Miami, or anything about his background."

"It's good that you're going to represent him. I really don't know what he was doing in Miami, but I can find out from his parents. In fact, you can talk to them yourself. His parents own some high-end boutiques in Argentina. Our families have known each other for years, and they've been very good to my brother, Jose, and my sister, Celia, since they've been living down there. Jose and his wife and kids run the cattle ranches that were my grandfather's. But they keep an apartment in B.A., too. And the Coronas take Maritza under their wing when she's in the city by herself."

"B.A.? Maritza?"

"Yeah, Buenos Aires. Maritza is my sister-in-law. She'd kill Jose if she didn't get into the city pretty often. You know living in the cattle region is like living in Texas. And my sister has a little apartment in the city too. God knows what she's into. Mama is so upset with Celia for staying away so long. Cuban kids don't move far from their parents, but Mama forgets that we are only half Cuban."

"So you're the good half. You stayed here."

"Yeah, well, I'm the oldest. I also like making a healthy living. That's easier here. Governments come and go in Argentina, and sometimes they take people's money with them."

"I'll call Luis's parents tomorrow. Right now, how about dessert?"

"Only if we're having it in the bedroom," Carlos said.

CHAPTER EIGHTEEN

I was in the office early the next morning. It was the first morning that I didn't awaken with a throbbing head. I placed a call to the Coronas at their home number. They would be able to talk more freely than at their office.

A maid or some servant answered immediately. "*Hola, buenos dias, casa de los Coronas,*" she said.

"*Señor o Señora Corona, por favor. Yo soy abogada de Luis.*" When I told her I was Luis's lawyer, she hurried from the phone.

"*Uno momento, por favor. Señor, Señora, rápidamente. El telefono. Es muy importante.*" I heard the excitement in her voice.

"This is Señor Corona," a deep voice said.

"Señor, my name is Mary Magruder Katz. I'm an attorney in Miami, and a friend of Carlos Martin, the son of Angelina and J.C. I wanted to talk to you about Luis."

"Just a minute. Let me get my *esposa* on the other phone."

In a minute another voice joined us. Mr. Corona explained to her in rapid Spanish who I was.

"Have you seen Luis? How is he? Where is he?" Mrs. Corona sounded like she was crying.

"I saw Luis briefly at the Dade County Jail. However, federal agents came to move him before I could interview him. He appeared healthy, and showed no signs of any injuries."

"This is good, but where is he now?" Mr. Corona said.

"We aren't sure, but I am working on it. I have a meeting set today with someone from the federal prosecutor's office. I wanted to introduce myself to you and find out what I can that may help me to assist Luis. Have you been able to speak with him?"

"Not really — only once for a minute. They let him call and he told us he had been arrested on the airplane. He didn't even know why," Mr. Corona said.

"I need to ask you some questions. Do you know why Luis was coming to Miami?"

"Of course, we sent him there," Mrs. Corona was definitely crying.

"Maria, please, let me give some information to Ms. Katz. You just listen," Mr. Corona said.

"Okay, Miguel." I heard Maria Corona blowing her nose.

"Ms. Katz, we own several boutiques here in Buenos Aires. We feature Argentine designers. We have been trying to expand into the States. We got an opportunity to purchase an excellent location in Coral Gables. Paulina Lowy was closing her shop. Luis was entrusted with the money to make the purchase. It was our hope to give him the confidence to purchase the shop and to stay in Miami to run it."

"Was he carrying funds with him to make the purchase? How much money was involved," I asked.

"He had a hundred fifty thousand dollars in cash with him to make the initial payment. The rest was to come in payments from the proceeds of the shop on a monthly basis."

"Why did he bring cash? Was it American dollars?"

"Oh, yes, that's what Paulina wanted. You know many people outside the United States prefer to deal in currency, especially American dollars. Some South Americans don't really trust bank checks, or even banks at all."

The call that you got from Luis, when was that? Give me a timetable. When did he leave Argentina?"

"He left on Friday. It's a long flight so we didn't expect to hear from him until late Saturday, but there was no word, so we called the hotel on Sunday morning where he had his reservation. They said he never checked in. We checked the airline thinking something had happened to the flight, but they said it landed on time. We got his phone call at five a.m. on Monday morning. He said they arrested him on the plane. No one told him why. He mumbled something about smoking. Then he said he was being booked into the Dade County Jail. Then they made him hang up. That's when I called the Martins for help," Mr. Corona said.

"Smoking, you said? What hotel was he going to stay at?"

"Yes, smoking. I don't know what that meant. For a minute after he hung up, I thought maybe it was a code word, but we couldn't relate it to anything. Oh, the name of the hotel is the Floridian Inn on Brickell Avenue.

"Please don't be offended, but has Luis ever been in trouble before? Arrested for anything? How old is Luis? He looks very young. Is he over eighteen?"

"Luis is a good boy," Maria broke in.

"Maria, *por favor*," said Mr. Corona. "Luis is twenty-two. He is, how do you say, a free spirit. A high-spirited boy. He's never actually been arrested, but he and his friends have been known to drink a bit much. We have a club scene here in B.A. like your South Beach. A few years ago, he got tossed out of a club for trespassing after being asked to leave, but he's been improving, trying to be more adult. That's why we thought if we showed him our trust, it would be good for him to have some business to attend to."

"Okay, I understand. I'll be working on locating him and finding out what he's been formally charged with. Before you hear this from someone else, I should tell you that the media has written that he may be charged as a terrorist. Please, don't be alarmed. Rumors get blown out of proportion, especially after 9/11. If you like, you can call or e-mail me on a daily basis, and I'll keep you informed of everything I know. I'll put my assistant, Catherine, on the line now so she can tell you how to reach me, and she'll get all of your information."

"Ms. Katz, please, do everything you can, and please know that I will pay whatever fees and expenses are necessary," Mr. Corona said.

"Please, call me Mary, and I appreciate your generosity."

"And you must call us Miguel and Maria. I'll call you tomorrow." I heard Maria crying softly in the background.

Things were beginning to add up. The Floridian Inn was where a murdered man was found last week, and he was registered as a citizen of Argentina. The cops found a large sum of money. Along comes Luis from Argentina, also carrying a large amount of cash. He's also booked into the Floridian Inn. But smoking? What is that about? This was like trying to assemble a huge jigsaw puzzle with half the pieces missing.

CHAPTER NINETEEN

I pulled off of the freeway and into the lot in front of the office of the state attorney, part of the Justice Complex. Besides the courthouse, this complex consists of the multistory office housing most of the two hundred plus assistant state attorneys and their support staffs, a smaller building for the public defenders, and some low-rise office buildings that handle the overflow. Defendants call it the Injustice Complex, and I'll admit some of the attorneys do too.

I entered the reception area, which was teeming with impatient citizens. Six receptionists sat behind glass windows attempting to triage the continuous lines of people. Those arriving for depositions were sent to an adjoining waiting room filled to capacity. Members of the public who had come to complain or file complaints were sent to the third floor where desks filled with paralegals would interview them.

Police officers arriving for pretrial conferences were dispatched to various paralegals and assistant state attorneys.

Those of us with actual appointments were allowed beyond the receptionists to the inner sanctum. After being issued my visitor's badge, I was admitted to the suite of offices housing the state attorney. More receptionists were seated behind a counter. I checked in and was told to wait a minute. Olga appeared almost at once and took me directly into Jason's private office.

Jason was munching on a doughnut as he rose to greet me. A telephone on his desk had ten buttons, all of which were lighted.

"Sorry," Jason said as he stuffed the rest of the doughnut in his mouth. "I didn't have time for breakfast, again, and this is the first chance I've had to grab some food. My wife is threatening me with divorce or a new will if I don't start eating regular meals."

Jason looked very thin. I noticed that his hair had begun to recede.

"Are you still sure you're glad you won the election? Somehow, this doesn't look like fun," I said. I grabbed the chair across from him. "I'm really sorry to bother you with a new problem. It looks like you've got plenty already."

"Let me hear what's up, Mary." He leaned back in his chair and smiled at me.

"I've been retained by Judge Elizabeth Maxwell. I think you're off on a wrong track with one of your investigations. Judge Maxwell was informed that your office is investigating her concerning her handling of some drug cases. As I'm sure you know, she has an excellent reputation. The stigma of this investigation is career threatening. From what she was told by the chief judge, there is a very flimsy foundation that triggered this investigation. I'm sure I needn't tell you that your office could open itself to a civil suit for libel or slander."

Jason straightened up in his chair. The smile disappeared and was replaced by an angry look. Sort of like a sudden summer storm. "We don't investigate based on flimsy evidence. You know damn well we can't be sued for doing our jobs as prosecutors. Are you threatening me? I think this meeting is over."

"Wait, Jason. You know I'm just being an advocate for my client. Help me out here. If you think Judge Maxwell warrants this investigation, let me know why. You'll have to anyway through discovery. As her attorney, I'll be entitled to witness lists and documents. Calm down and let's work together here."

Jason relaxed a little and settled back into his chair. "I thought you knew me better than to think I'd go on a witch hunt. I couldn't ignore the fact that more than one of my prosecutors believes something funny is going on in Maxwell's division. Since she came back to the criminal bench six months ago, several cases involving drug dealing have been dismissed without any reason at a very early stage of the litigation. Some of these cases were dismissed after the filing of perfunctory motions by the defense. No hearings were held, and the orders were form orders with no reasons stated for the dismissals. In some cases, form orders were signed right after the arraignments. No other judge has such a practice. Frankly, this is against the rules of criminal procedure and against all the local rules in this jurisdiction."

"Well, the criminal caseloads are heavy. Maybe there were reasons that just weren't in the orders. Maybe they were articulated in open court."

"No, don't you think I would have checked all the transcripts? Then there was the murder of the informant in an important state case. Judge Maxwell directed the state to produce the guy. She could have tipped off someone about the time and place he would be produced. Things began to add up."

I was feeling a little shaky. It looked like the State was not just on a fishing expedition, and Liz was a big catch.

"What added up?" I asked. I assumed as haughty an attitude as I could muster.

"Judge Maxwell is unmarried and lives on the income of a judge. We couldn't find any other income such as an inheritance, and she didn't declare any other income on her financial disclosure forms. You know the judges have to fill out those forms every year, and swear to the truthfulness of the answers. She has quite a few bills. Maybe she needs money. I don't know if you're aware of this, but there are rumors that your client is pretty friendly with a local defense attorney," Jason said.

"All I'm asking at this point is that you keep me informed if you plan to file an indictment, and that you let me know if you have questions for my client. Some of the points you've raised may be easily explained. If there is no indictment, I'm sure you'll keep this away from the media. And one more thing. I'm investigating these allegations myself as a service to my client. I promise that I'll share my findings with you, because I am certain that they will exonerate the judge." I extended my hand to Jason as I turned to leave his office.

"Mary, I sincerely hope Judge Maxwell is not dirty. I'm not out to screw the judiciary. My assistants have to practice in this courthouse, but if she is dirty, I have a sworn duty to get her off the bench. I hope you understand this," Jason said.

I retraced my steps to the parking lot. As I drove toward downtown and my lunch with Lucy and Steve, I was filled with a feeling of fear. I realized how big Liz's case was. If I screwed up and lost, I might have the animosity of the entire bench in Miami-Dade County. I would also have lost one of the best women judges on our bench. This case was a must win.

CHAPTER TWENTY

As I turned off the freeway onto Brickell Avenue, my new BlackBerry phone rang. It was a present from my brothers, William and Jonathan. They are both lawyers, practicing in wills and estate planning and real estate; what we criminal attorneys call the death lawyers and the dirt lawyers, and what I personally call boring. They had insisted that I couldn't possibly keep up with my practice without the latest in telephone, calendar schedules, and music without this device. I still loved my camera-cell phone and hadn't given it up. I wasn't sure who even knew what the number of the new phone was unless it was one of my brothers. Additionally, I wasn't sure how to answer it.

I fumbled around with the buttons still trying to drive. The relentless ring continued to the tune of "When the Saints Go Marching In." Jonathan is a jazz freak. I noted that I would have to change that as soon as I learned how to answer the thing.

Finally, I hit the right button. "Hello, Jonathan?"

"No, bitch. It's your worst fucking nightmare. Keep your ass out of what doesn't concern you or you'll regret it, bitch." The male voice hung up. I pulled into the garage at the restaurant. I was sweating as I tried to find the caller ID. The screen showed cell caller 213-323-9050. The 213 area code was not in Florida. I wiped my face and clammy hands and made my way into the crowded Green Toad Restaurant.

I spotted Lucy and Steve in the line for a table. The place was jammed with lawyers, bankers, and other office workers. The Toad was this month's lunch hot spot. If you wanted to keep up with the gossip, it was essential to see who was lunching with whom.

"You are just in time. They just called our table," Steve said. He steered Lucy and me forward.

Lucy hugged me as we walked. "Mary, are you okay? You're so pale."

We gathered ourselves into the booth. I collapsed onto the bench across from Lucy and Steve.

"Well, actually, I've been better. I just had a threatening phone call on my brand new BlackBerry that no one even knows the number of yet. It shook me up a little."

"We saw you on TV the other night. Was this about the terrorist case?" Steve asked.

"I don't know. The caller just told me to mind my own business, only not that politely. I'm sort of uneasy. Earlier this week I was hit on the head in my office parking lot. And besides Luis Corona's case, I've got another very sensitive case."

"Listen, Mary, you're beating yourself up. You need some R and R. When was the last time you got to the gym or made time to jog?" Lucy asked. Lucy had turned into a fitness nut after her last baby.

"You're right about that," I said. "But with my own practice, I really need to take all the cases that I can. I have to pay my office expenses and keep up my house payments. I'm my only support."

"What about Carlos? We really liked him when we went to dinner last month," Lucy said.

"We're still together, but I'm busy and he's busy. It's a struggle."

"He's a keeper, Mary. Don't blow it." Lucy was about to go into her lecture on the beauty of married life. Fortunately, the impatient waiter interrupted. Steve and I ordered burgers and fries. Lucy gave us a dirty look and ordered a salad.

Steve reached across the table and patted my hand. "Did you talk to the police about the assault? What did they say?"

"They're investigating. It was probably just a robbery gone bad."

"What about the phone call?" Steve asked. "Did you check the caller ID?"

I handed the phone to Steve. "It was a 213 area code. Where is that?"

"That's Los Angeles, but with cell phones it could be any-one anywhere." Steve pulled a notepad out of his pocket and wrote down the number. "I'll turn this over to one of our in-vestigators, and see who the number is registered to. You need to be careful. See if anyone is following you."

As soon as the food arrived and the waiter, who had in-formed us his name was Brad, left us with the usual, bon ap-petit, I turned to Steve.

"Lucy, I hope you don't mind if I talk a little law stuff and pick Steve's brain."

Lucy nodded.

"I need to find a way to contact Luis Corona. I went to see him at the Dade County Jail because he was some relative of a friend of Carlos's family in Argentina. The feds took him away before I could give him any help. He's being held in some secret location. He needs a lawyer. I thought maybe you had some way to get me through to him, or at least find out where he's being held."

Steve frowned and drummed his fingers on the table. "I can try, but I think it's a lost cause. We're taking our orders from Washington. The Guantanamo prisoners are being handled by them. The prisoners charged with terrorist crimes are unrepresented by counsel, and they're being held indefinitely without charges being filed. It's not like anything else in our justice system."

"My God, no charges? No lawyers? I guess I've been so preoccupied with building my practice that I haven't kept up with these issues. When will they be tried and where?"

"No one is certain. There may be military tribunals set up. It's very hush-hush. The Justice Department in Washington won't share information with any of the U.S. Attorney's Offices. I have never seen anything to compare to this in my years in this office."

"Maybe they haven't taken him to Guantanamo yet. Maybe I can still meet with him."

"Don't count on it," Steve said.

"If I can't talk to him, I can't find out if this is just some awful mistake. I spoke to his family by phone. They sound like really nice people. I feel terrible that I was less than helpful when I did see him. I was repulsed by thinking I was representing a terrorist. I'm ashamed of thinking like that."

"Don't blame yourself. Homeland Security wouldn't have let you have enough time to fully interview him, anyway. I'll make some discreet inquiries, but don't hold out a lot of hope. Don't repeat this. A lot of guys in my office are appalled by this situation, this operating outside the justice system."

Steve's cell phone rang. He glanced at a text message coming in, and stood up. "Girls, I gotta run. I'm needed in court. You sit here and get caught up. I'll pay the bill on the way out." He shoved the last of his burger in his mouth and loped out of the restaurant.

Lucy and I looked at each other. Then we both spoke at once.

"I'm glad we get some time alone," Lucy said.

"I really need some downtime with a friend," I said at the same time. We both giggled and suddenly I felt like we were back in elementary school whispering secrets to each other on the playground.

"Mary, I'm worried about you. You never take a vacation, even when you were working for Frank. I've offered you my grandmother's house in Vermont so many times. When will you take me up on it? Just go up there and chill. The summers are wonderful."

"I appreciate the offer. Maybe someday, but not right now. I remember when you used to go up there when we were kids. You always wanted me to come with your family even then, but we were always going to my grandparents in North Carolina. You know they moved back there when we were little. They didn't like Miami, so we went there. And then to balance things, Dad insisted that I spend two weeks of the summer at the Jewish Institute Camp in Georgia."

"It must have been hard for you growing up with two religions. I never knew why you didn't just pick one instead of splitting yourself into two segments," Lucy said.

"How could I do that? I couldn't choose one parent over the other. I love them both, so we kids just rolled with it all. In a way, we felt special. We celebrated, and still do, every holiday."

"Well, I must admit I did envy you getting presents for everything, Chanukah and Christmas, while I was just a dull Presbyterian."

"That's one reason I'm taking things slow with Carlos. His family is Catholic and our backgrounds are different."

"Steve and I liked him. He's easy to talk to, and great looking. He's definitely a hotty."

"Oh, so you noticed that?" I laughed.

We gathered our handbags and jackets and walked out of the restaurant together.

"I wish you lived closer to us," Lucy said. We like living on Miami Beach. I thought you'd live there too. It's where we were raised."

"I know. I miss you, too, but the Gables isn't that far away. I like it there. I fell in love with South Dade when I went to the university. It has no tourists, and it looks so tropical. The Beach has changed. It's so congested now. I hate seeing where our old house used to be."

"Come over soon and see our kids, please, Mary." Lucy hugged me and we went our separate ways.

CHAPTER TWENTY-ONE

Back at the office, I went through my notes from my interview with Liz and the papers she had sent over. I added notes of my meeting with Jason. Jason appeared determined to go full-steam ahead with his investigation. He scared me. Liz could lose her judgeship and even her law license. She was counting on me and I had no plan.

I read everything again. The big question mark was the cases Jason said Liz had dismissed without reason. There was no mention of those cases in her summary of cases she had handled. Either Liz was lying to me, or someone was signing her name on orders.

A large manila envelope in my in-box drew my attention. The name of a court reporting firm was printed on its front. I found the transcript of the trial Liz had conducted with Joe as defense counsel. It was voluminous. I scanned the pages quickly for objections and decisions by Liz. It did seem that Joe had gotten more objections sustained than the prosecution had received, but none of them looked like favoritism. I decided to have Catherine read the whole transcript and give me notes on any evidence of fawning or favoring of Joe.

I glanced at my watch. It was after four o'clock. I didn't want to talk to Liz at the courthouse. I called her cell phone, but only got the voice mail.

I glanced down at the file and saw her home number and dialed it. Liz answered after a couple of rings.

"Hi, Mary. Is anything new?"

"Not exactly, Liz. How are you? I didn't expect to find you at home."

"I came home early. I just couldn't concentrate with this thing hanging over my head. I picked up when I saw it was you."

"I met with Jason today, and it may be necessary for you to be interviewed by him, but don't worry. I'll stall that for a while, and we'll have plenty of time to prepare you. Meanwhile, Jason said that you had dismissed a lot of drug cases with no hearings, and early in the cases, sometimes even after the arraignment. You wouldn't have done that just to lower your case numbers, would you?"

"Good heavens, no. My division has always been very efficient, and I'd never play the system like that. I don't know of any cases I ever dismissed like that."

"I didn't think so, but I had to ask. Here's what I want you to do. Get a complete printout of the dispositions of the cases in your division for the last few months. Then we can pull the files and see what these orders look like. It may be that someone has been manipulating cases assigned to you. When you have the list, Catherine and I will go to the clerk's office and view the files. Do this as soon as possible. Oh, and order the printout yourself. Keep your staff out of this."

"Do you suspect one of them?" Liz sounded almost hysterical.

"It's a possibility," I said. "The list you sent to me contains only the cases in which you actually sentenced a defendant. We need the official printout from the clerk's office. That should show all of your closed cases."

"Okay, Mary, I'll get on it first thing tomorrow. I'll go in early before any of the staff arrives."

I hung up and looked over the notes again. I needed to know more about Jack Carillo. Carlos must know something about him. He took me to a party at Jack's house.

I dialed Carlos and left him a message to call or come by the office. Just in case he showed up, I brushed my hair and put on fresh makeup and a spritz of Obsession cologne.

Lucy was right. Carlos was definitely a hotty.

CHAPTER TWENTY-TWO

I spent the next hour catching up with mail and drafting motions in two D.U.I. cases. Catherine came in to say she was leaving, and that Carlos had just called that he was on his way over.

A few minutes later, Carlos clumped into the office and folded his tall frame into the chair across from me. He was in his jeans and construction boots, which he propped up on the end of my desk. He looked macho and I must admit it turned me on.

"What's up?" he asked.

"Thanks for coming over. Are you on your way home?"

"Eventually, but I have to stop at my parents first."

Angelina and J.C. live in a condo in one of the most glamorous high-rises in the Grove. They have the penthouse, which is a whole floor. The elevator opens directly into their own hallway. They moved there after their kids were out of the nest. Carlos had shown me where he grew up. It was in what used to be horse country in the southwest part of the county, before housing developments sprung up on every piece of ground.

"How come you have to stop at your parents? Is everything okay with them?"

"Oh, yeah, I just have to talk to them. I have to fire Marielena's daughter, so I need to give them a heads-up."

"You mean your aunt's daughter works for you? Marielena is the worst busybody. How come you let her daughter work for you?"

"I don't know. It's family, and she needed a job."

"What's her position?"

"She's supposed to be my realty agent at the condo. You know, man the sales office. For the last few years these things sold themselves. In fact, for the building in Fort Lauderdale, we held a lottery. That's how many buyers there were. I didn't think she'd get in much trouble, but now people are screaming to move in, and she can't handle it. She doesn't know how to talk to people. I told you about this."

"Yeah, but you didn't tell me your cousin was mucking things up."

"She is. She insulted a couple of the buyers and she just can't handle things, so I gotta fire her. I might get sued by the buyers. I've never been sued."

"All right, Carlos, we'll sort this out. Right now I need to ask you about Jack Carillo. You took me to his house on Star Island, to that party. I need to know some more about him."

"You're not his lawyer, are you?"

"No, but he has something to do with a case I'm working on. How well do you know him?"

"We went to high school together. I see him from time to time at the Yacht Club. When he bought that house, he hired me to renovate it. It's not the kind of work I do anymore. Haven't since I first started the business, but he was an old friend so I agreed. It was a messy job. He kept changing the plans."

"What about his drug-dealing reputation?"

"What about it? Why do you think I know anything about that?" Carlos was clearly annoyed.

"Well, is he part of the Mafia drug dealers?"

"How should I know? You mean the Cuban Mafia, don't you? Do you think I hang around with that group of people?" Carlos began to show his Latin temper.

"You took us to a party at his house. I just thought you'd know something about him. Don't be so sensitive," I said.

Carlos stood up. "I never thought you were one of those Anglo bigots who thinks every Cuban is a drug dealer. I have no information to give you for your case."

Carlos tramped out of the office, slamming the door. I was too surprised to go after him. Oh great. Now I had the two cases from hell, and I just lost my boyfriend.

CHAPTER TWENTY-THREE

I left the office after Carlos's tantrum and went right home. Sam was glad to see me at a normal time for a change. While he chowed down his dinner, I found a beer in the fridge. I thought about Lucy's healthy diet and decided not to order the pizza I craved. I opened a can of tuna and turned on the TV. It made good background noise to drown out Carlos's words. How could he think I was a bigot?

Something on the TV caught my attention. The reporter was doing a feature on Miami as an international center. "While Miami does not have full foreign embassies like New York and Washington, Miami does boast the largest number of foreign consulates of any city with less than five million in population. Many nations post consul generals in South Florida, with their offices and homes located throughout the area. Central and South American countries in particular find this helpful, since many of their citizens visit, live, or work in South Florida."

I smacked myself in the head. Why hadn't I thought to locate an ambassador or consul from Argentina? When a foreign national is arrested, they always call their embassy. At least that's what they do in the movies. Luis probably never had the opportunity. I wondered if Miguel Corona had made such a contact. I needed to follow up on this in the morning.

I spent a restless night worrying about the fight with

Carlos, which was really a one-sided fight, — all on his part. At two a.m., I wandered into the kitchen and gave in to chocolate chunk ice cream. Then I slept.

At six a.m., I was wide awake and decided to take Sam for a run before the heat of the day enveloped us again. More of Lucy's guilt trip. The humidity was draining and the thermometer read eighty degrees already.

We ran several blocks up to the Miracle Mile. Starbucks was open. I got a double espresso, a glass of water, and the morning *Herald*. We sat down at a table. Sam lapped up the water. I sipped my espresso and opened the paper. The headline in the Metro section leaped from the page.

ALLEGED DRUG DEALER MURDERED, MANSION BURNED

Jack Carillo, recently arrested and indicted on numerous drug and money-laundering charges, was found shot in the back of the head in the smoldering ruins of his Star Island mansion.

A call to the Miami Beach Fire Department was received at nine p.m. last night. The first responders found a blazing inferno. Arson was immediately suspected. Firemen found chemical residue throughout the first floor.

The mansion was the residence of Jack Carillo, who was found in a second-floor bedroom. The medical examiner arrived at the scene as soon as conditions were safe for entry. Initial tests showed Carillo was dead before the fire began. No medical signs appeared to show that he had been asphyxiated by smoke inhalation. Further examination found two bullet holes in the back of Carillo's skull.

Police and the state attorney have refused to comment on possible suspects. The investigation will continue with assistance from special police and fire investigation units. The medical examiner will perform a full autopsy later today.

I sat staring at the paper. Then I grabbed Sam's leash and raced home. I jumped into the Explorer, threw Sam in the back, and drove directly to Pinecrest to Carlos's house. As I pulled into the driveway, Carlos was getting into his Escalade. I leaped out of my SUV, waving the paper and my arms to stop him from driving off.

"What is the matter with you?" Carlos yelled. For a minute, I thought maybe he was still mad and was about to run me over. He idled the motor and got out of the car.

"Did you come over early hoping to catch some of my Cuban Mafia friends?"

Sarcasm dripped from him like the morning humidity.

I handed him the paper. He spread it on the front of the car, and we read the article together.

He looked up. "I can't believe Jack is dead. I'll call his parents and see if I can be of any help. Thanks for letting me know." When he finally looked at me, I saw tears in his eyes.

The lack of sleep, the shock of the article, and seeing Carlos's emotional reaction shook me. "Look Carlos. I didn't ever mean to hurt your feelings yesterday. Please, forgive me. I love you. You should know, there's been a Jewish Mafia in Miami Beach for years. Myer Lansky died in Miami. I wouldn't mind if you brought all that up. None of it reflects on you or me. It's just part of the landscape."

"What did you say?" Carlos asked.

"I said there is also a Jewish Mafia and —"

"No he interrupted. The love part. You've never said that before." He put his arms around me and we stood there together while the next door neighbor gawked at us.

CHAPTER TWENTY-FOUR

I walked into the office an hour later. Catherine was at her desk getting the messages from the voice mail. There was one from Liz and one from Jason.

I returned Jason's call first. This time I was put through immediately. Probably not a good sign.

"Hello, Mary. Thanks for returning my call so promptly."

"Of course, Jason. What can I do for you?"

"I think it's time to bring your client Judge Maxwell in for questioning. Since she's represented by counsel, I am duty bound to tell you that we are going to go visit her and ask her to come in voluntarily. Of course, she has a right to have you present while we talk to her."

"And suppose I refuse to allow her to talk to you."

"Well, I have several options. I could subpoena her to appear before a grand jury. Then she won't have access to her lawyer. I could arrest her as a material witness or she could make an appointment and come in here and talk to me. It's up to her."

"Jason, what has changed from yesterday that is causing you to jump like this?"

"Did you see this morning's paper? I'm sure you know that Jack Carillo has been murdered."

"Surely you don't believe Judge Maxwell is involved in that."

"Listen, Mary, I'm going to share something with you that can't go any further. Jack's lawyer made a deal with me yesterday. Jack was about to become a cooperating witness and name the head of his organization. Before we could talk to him, he was dead and his house was torched. Right now, everyone is a suspect. That's what has changed. Let me know what your client decides." Jason hung up.

My phone rang immediately. Catherine answered and announced that Liz was on the line again. I hadn't even had a minute to think how much to tell her.

"Mary, I'm sorry to bother you again, but I really am so nervous. Is there anything new?"

I was used to lots of phone calls from my clients. Part of being a criminal defense attorney is also being a psychologist, a life coach, and a sympathetic ear.

"You're not bothering me at all," I said. "As a matter of fact, I just spoke to Jason a minute ago. Do you know that Jack Carillo has been shot?"

"No, I didn't know." Liz drew in her breath. "Is he a — alive?"

"No, he was shot and his house was burned down. He's quite dead. Jason is moving this investigation along. We may have to go in to see him next week. If we don't go voluntarily, he may subpoena you. Please, let me do the worrying for you. How are you coming on the list of closed cases?"

"I can't stop worrying. I ordered my case audit last night, and it was delivered a little while ago. Jason can't believe that I'm involved in Jack's death, can he?"

"Who knows what prosecutors think? See if you can get the list together by Monday and send it over by messenger."

"Why can't I just e-mail it to you?"

"Because then it will become a document that has to be given in discovery. You're probably seeing numerous motions in court regarding what is now known as E-Discovery. Let's keep everything as quiet as possible right now."

"Of course, you're right. I guess I've stopped thinking like a lawyer or a judge and started thinking like a defendant."

"You hired me to do the legal thinking, Liz."

CHAPTER TWENTY-FIVE

While I finished the phone call, I searched for embassies and consulates on the Internet. Under Argentina, there was an embassy in New York, and one in Washington, and a consulate in Miami. The consul general's name was Philipe Marquez. A further search turned up the name of our ambassador in Buenos Aires, Francis Miller.

Francis Miller? I couldn't believe I had just read that name. I knew him, as did everyone in Miami. He was a devout Republican who had been in Congress for umpteen years and was finally defeated by a young energetic woman. His full qualifications for the job of ambassador were that he was out of a job and had donated and raised lots of bucks in the last presidential campaign. None of that was important. What was important was that he and J. C. Martin were fishing buddies. I had met Miller at a dinner at the beach condo in April.

Catherine got me the phone numbers for the embassy in Buenos Aires, and for the consulate in Miami. I tried the local one first. A friendly voice told me that Señor Marquez was in Washington until Monday morning. When I explained that this concerned an Argentine citizen who had been arrested and was being held in an unknown jail, she promised to give this top priority. I gave her all the information that I knew.

Next I called the American Embassy in Argentina. Ambassador Miller had left for the weekend. I spoke to his assistant and asked that Miller be reminded that we had met through J. C. Martin. That was the magic door opener. The assistant took a full report about Luis's arrest. Then he said that Miguel Corona had actually phoned there some days ago complaining about the arrest.

"What action did you take?" I asked, already knowing the answer.

"We explained that we would look into it, but we had other pressing matters."

"I hope these pressing matters do not take precedent over my phone call." I said.

"I will share all of this with the ambassador first thing Monday morning," he said.

As I hung up, I surmised that the pressing matters were Miller's weekend vacation plans. I just love seeing our government in action.

So now I had an idea about what to do next with Liz's case, and a start on finding Luis. Now if only I didn't have the "family" dinner tomorrow night with two sets of parents with about as much in common as a pride of lions and a litter of wildcats; both of the feline species, but likely to tear each other to pieces.

Just as I was finally getting settled at the computer to draft some motions, Catherine hurried in. She dropped a phone memo sheet on my desk and announced that Detective Jim Avery was in the waiting room.

I glanced at the phone memo. It was a message from Steve. His investigator had found that the cell phone number that had called my BlackBerry was assigned to Beverly Hills Financial Services and had been reported stolen the day before the nasty phone call. The location of the theft was alleged to be Miami International Airport.

"What does Avery want?" I asked.

"He wouldn't say; just said he needed to talk to you again about the incident in the parking lot."

"Okay, better bring him in. Just what I need, a police interrogation. Oh well, it's probably good training for my mother's questions tomorrow night."

Jim Avery strode into the office. He was dressed in jeans and a tee shirt with the police logo on the front. He looked very different than when he was dressed in the standard plain-clothes attire. The shirt showed off his muscles and suntan, and the jeans, well, they showed off how tight they were. The head injury must have dulled my senses or I would have noticed his good looks the last time we met.

"What can I do for you, Detective?" I stood up and extended my hand. He grasped it firmly. Maybe it was my imagination, but I thought he held the handshake a little too long.

"We've arrested two kids involved in a robbery and assault a few blocks from here. I was wondering if you would view a lineup and see if you recognize anyone?" he asked. He seated himself in one of the chairs across the desk from me, but not before he scooted the chair to the side of the desk, almost next to me.

"Will they be totally dressed in black and will the lineup take place in a darkened room?" I asked.

"Of course not. Sometimes victims think they haven't seen anything and then a lineup triggers a memory."

"I understand that, but in this instance, I never viewed anything. The perp was behind me and it was pitch black out. I can't even say if it was a man or a woman. I really think this would be a waste of your time and mine."

"Have you had any other problems since the assault? Anything that would help us investigate further?"

I glanced at the memo from Steve. "Well, yes, as a matter of fact, I got a threatening phone call the other morning.

The strange thing was that it came in on a new mobile phone that I hadn't even used yet. I asked a friend at the U.S. Attorney's Office to look into it. There was a number on the caller ID." I handed him the phone message.

"What did the caller say?"

"To keep my ass out of other people's business."

"Someone must have noticed you have a cute one." He smiled, but it was more like a leer.

"This is a professional visit, isn't it?" I asked. I stood up, hoping this was a signal for him to leave.

His face turned red as he stood up too. "May I take this information with me?" he asked. I'd like to follow up on this. There have been a number of phone thefts at the airport lately."

"Help yourself. On your way out, ask Catherine to make a copy of this for our records," I said as I opened my office door.

I hadn't even had time to calm down from Detective Super Stud, when Catherine buzzed that she was leaving to go to her kids' school for an assembly, and she had just seen Carlos drive into the parking lot in his Corvette.

In a minute, he walked into the office. He was in a gray business suit and blue tie. He looked amazing. This was certainly my day for sexy male visitors.

"I take it you were not out climbing around on a construction site," I said.

"Good guess," he said, and leaned over and kissed me.

My first inclination was to grab him and throw myself across the desk, but you never know who else might come barging in here next.

"I'm here for two reasons. I just talked to the lawyer who sent me this letter." He dropped the piece of paper in front of me. From his expression I assumed it contained anthrax.

"Then I went to my office where I fired my cousin and met with two outraged condo buyers."

"Why did you talk with the lawyer yourself? You have legal counsel of your own. How many times do I have to tell you not to handle legal matters like that without me around to protect your interests?" I glanced at the letter which was threatening a class action lawsuit by a group of buyers who were demanding to get out of their contracts at the new condo building.

"I'm not stupid, Mary. I know how to conduct myself with scumbags like that."

"Of course, you're not stupid. You're a brilliant developer and an outstanding builder, but you are not a lawyer. What did you say to this guy?"

"I told him to take his lawsuit and stuff it; that I wasn't scared of his stupid threats, and that if I wanted to, I could break his jaw."

"I'm sure that calmed the situation. I'll call him. You said you stopped by for two reasons. I hope the other one is less stressful."

"I had a great idea about tomorrow night."

"I hope it was that we leave unexpectedly for Tahiti, and skip the dinner."

"No, but you said the dinner was at the Ocean Inn. I booked us a room there. We can check in after lunch, have a relaxing afternoon, a little fun on the beach, a little fun in our room. Then if the dinner gets too nerve wracking, we can escape to our room, and we won't have to drive back to Miami after drinking many bottles of wine."

"It's a brilliant idea, Carlos, but what would I do with Sam? I can't just leave him alone for that amount of time."

"I know that. I got it covered. Marco would love to keep him at his house for the weekend. He and Catherine and her boys are going to have a barbecue over there, so Sam will get to play with the kids. He loves that."

"So Marco and Catherine really are having a thing? Is Marco married or, I guess I should ask, is he divorced?"

"He's divorced. He's been single for two years. He has a five-year-old son who he gets on weekends. I guess that's why they're having a barbecue over there. You and Catherine seem to like taking turns playing Mother Hen to each other."

"What do you mean?"

"Here you are trying to protect her from Marco, and last week, she stopped me on my way in to see you, and hinted around about what my intentions were with you."

"Catherine and I have become pretty close. We're friends as much as work colleagues."

"You still haven't answered about tomorrow. What about my idea to stay at the inn?"

"It's great. I might be able to get through Saturday night," I said.

CHAPTER TWENTY-SIX

We dropped Sam off at Marco's house early Saturday afternoon. Marco lives in a cute stucco house in Westchester, an old neighborhood near the Palmetto Expressway. At one time it was predominantly Jewish. Now it is heavily Hispanic. In both instances it's an affordable neighborhood for young couples. The small houses are well kept.

"Marco, I took you for a cool guy who would live in a bachelor pad in some condo," I said.

"Yeah, well, this house belonged to my grandparents. They left it to me. After my divorce, I was glad to have it, paid for, free and clear. Alimony and child support kicked in," he said. "Don't worry about Sam. He'll have a blast playing with the kids."

It was a gorgeous sunny day as we left Marco's, perfect for a picnic. But as we got closer to Fort Lauderdale, the sky turned into a stormy gray ceiling. The first drops slapped the windshield of the Escalade as we drove under the portico of the inn. So much for an intimate walk on the beach.

Our room overlooked the ocean. It was furnished in a quaint island décor, wicker furniture, an iron headboard on the slightly small bed. It might have been romantic with the rain pelting the sliding doors to a small balcony. Unfortunately, the mood was repeatedly broken by a group of Brazilian tourists next door.

It was Brazilian shopping time in South Florida. Hundreds of tourists invaded every June. Winter was beginning there, so they took in the sun, the sand, and the discount stores, departing at the airport with copious bags and boxes. The rain must have kept them in, and they must have had thirty kids with them. The screeches of laughter and the boom box music made it hard to converse, let alone engage in any other activities. Finally, Carlos turned on a ball game on the TV, which he beamed up loud enough to hear the announcer.

I settled on the bed with three weeks of *Florida Law Weeklies*. These are the advance sheets which publish the latest cases decided by the Florida Supreme Court and the five Courts of Appeal. If a lawyer doesn't keep up with these, she can look pretty stupid in court. Like everything else in Florida, events cause cases to change the prevailing legal theories at breakneck speed. I was particularly looking for lawsuits involving contracts for new condos. It was evident that I would have to defend Carlos sooner than I had imagined.

At five o'clock, I showered and began getting ready for The Dinner. I washed my hair and blew it dry for once. I had brought two complete outfits, including shoes. The last thing I needed was Mother or Angie critiquing my appearance.

"What are you doing? I thought the dinner reservation was for seven," Carlos said.

"It is, but I have to decide what to wear, and my parents are always fifteen to thirty minutes early." I held up a pantsuit and a flowered sundress.

"Oh, great. My parents are always thirty minutes late. Someone should have told them six thirty," Carlos said.

"I'll be dressed and take my parents into the bar. Maybe I can get them relaxed, as in drunk, and they won't notice the time ticking away," I said. "Which outfit do you like better?"

"Which one has a low-cut top?"

"The sundress."

"Wear it, so I'll have something good to look at." He pat-ted me on my butt as I slipped on the dress.

I was waiting in the lobby when my parents walked in at six forty. Mother looked like an ad for Ralph Lauren. She was wearing white pants and a red jacket. Her blonde hair, which was beginning to show some grey at the edges, was pulled into a twist. She looked, as usual, like a beautiful WASP. Dad looked like Miami Beach in the old days in green plaid slacks and a green sport coat. I guessed the green jacket was in recog-nition of the Masters Golf Tournament, the pinnacle of Dad's TV viewing year.

"Mary, where's Carlos?" Mother looked around the lobby, frowning. She was sure I had wrecked her party.

"He's getting dressed. I forgot to tell you, we decided to take a room here, so we wouldn't have to drive back to Miami tonight."

"Smart idea," Dad said. Why didn't you think of that, Hope? I hate driving late at night."

"Then I'll drive, Abe. I have my Sunday Bible class in the morning. I like your hair, Mary. You should do it like that all the time."

"I never have the time. Come on, let's go sit in the bar and have a drink while we're waiting," I said. I steered them to a table in the bar

"Where are they? It's ten of seven, already," Dad said.

"Seven is when we're supposed to meet. It's not even seven yet," I said. I'll get us some hors d'oeuvres and drinks. What would you like?"

"I'm hungry," Dad said. "See if they have chopped liver. They'll call it pâté, and a tall Scotch and water."

"I'll have a glass of sherry, dear."

I moved to the bar and put in our orders. Carlos was at the table when I returned. He gave Mother a hug and a kiss. She gave him a smile and a pat. I could see she was delighted with his greeting. He looked yummy in a blue sport shirt and navy slacks. He and Dad shook hands and eyed each other.

The drinks came and we made small talk that grew smaller as the minutes ticked by.

"Do you think they had an accident?" Dad said at seven fifteen.

"Abe, it's traditional for Latins to arrive late," Carlos explained.

"Well, that's a strange tradition. I'm really getting hungry." Dad was beginning to grumble — not a good sign — but maybe they'd understand why I was cautious about our differing backgrounds.

A minute later Angie and J.C. swept into the bar.

"You're early." Carlos grinned as he hugged both of them.

Angie air kissed me on each cheek. "Mary, you look delicious, and these must be your parents."

Mother and Dad stood up and Angie air kissed each of them. J.C. kissed Mother's hand and shook hands with Dad.

"Hope you're ready to eat. I'm starved," Dad said.

"But we haven't even had a drink yet," Angie said.

"You'll have one at the table," Carlos said as he steered them toward the dining room. "We'll lose our reservation if we don't get seated."

Mother was examining Angie's attire. She was dressed in a long black skirt and a sheer ruffled off-the-shoulder blouse, which showed off her two diamond necklaces and long diamond earrings. She wore several bangle bracelets that jingled as we walked. J.C. was in his Yacht Captain mode in white pants, navy shirt, and navy blazer.

"I made a reservation for six people. Hope Katz," Mother told the maître d'.

The maître d' checked his book and led us to a rectangular table in the corner.

"No, I specifically asked for a round table, near a window," Mother said.

"Never mind, Hope, let's just eat," Dad said.

"No, I want what I requested" Her eyes narrowed and she pursed her lips. Her stubborn streak was on display.

"Ah, I see where Mary gets her persistence. I'll take care of this," Carlos said. He took the maître d' by the arm and walked him away from our group. We stood in silence watching Carlos gesture and talk.

In a minute, he returned. "They're readying the round table in the private dining room for us. It'll be ready in a minute," Carlos said.

We were led into a room to the side where we had a view of the ocean and a round candlelit table. Mother smiled. "Thank you, Carlos. How did you do that?"

"I just pointed out the condo tower I was building down the street and asked him how he'd feel if I gave each new occupant a letter telling them not to dine at the Ocean Inn, as they were known for tainted seafood." Everyone laughed.

"How much did you give him?" I whispered.

"Shhh," he said, and whispered back, "Twenty."

J.C. had the wine list open and was in discussion with the sommelier. "I have ordered us a wonderful red wine from Chile and a white from Italy, so everyone can have a choice."

"So how's your golf game, J.C.?" Dad asked.

"Actually, I've never played golf," J.C. said.

"Oh, I guess that's why Carlos doesn't play," Dad said. He looked as if he had just smelled something rotten. "What do you do with yourself?"

"You mean for recreation? I have a boat and I go out fishing as often as I can. We have a place over on Marco Island. I keep the boat over there. That's why we go back and forth so much. Carlos has brought Mary over there."

"It's really lovely," I said.

"Maybe you'd like to go out fishing sometime, Abe," J.C. said.

"Thanks, but I couldn't. I get seasick."

We were saved by the waiter who was waiting expectantly for our orders. This took up some time, thankfully, while everyone asked what someone else was getting and the waiter recited the five complicated specials. As soon as the waiter finished his spiel, Dad ordered his usual, steak well done and baked potato with everything.

Angie had numerous questions about how the vegetables were prepared. She gave specific instructions that none were to be sautéed and there was not to be a hint of butter. She further asked for a sample of two of the low-fat salad dressings so she could decide which seemed the least fattening. I saw mother roll her eyes. I was quickly losing my appetite.

"Just a salad and a simple grilled fish for me, red snapper," I said, and hoped I could stomach it.

"Sounds good for me too," Mother said.

Carlos and J.C. ordered pastas with various seafood. They loved to eat, and the tension of the evening didn't seem to bother either of them. The waiter brought a basket of rolls and butter. Dad grabbed for the basket and helped himself to two before passing it. The uncomfortable silence was thicker than the butter.

Angelina, a born talker, interrupted the silence. She turned to Mother. "Do you play cards, dear? There must be a lot of games at your retirement center. I love bridge and gin myself."

"No, I never have liked cards, and it's not exactly a re-tirement center. It's a planned-development community."

"Well, what do you do with yourself all day?" Angie asked.

Here we go, I thought. In another minute they'll be claw-ing each others eyes out.

"I teach Bible classes, at Sunday School for children, and every Tuesday for adults," Hope said.

"How do you handle all that? I mean, Carlos explained to us that Abe is Jewish and you're Christian. I hope I'm not bringing up a sore subject. I'm just curious."

"I teach an ecumenical class. I wrote the curriculum my-self. So my students learn about various religions and how they relate to each other."

"That sounds so interesting. I'd like to learn something like that."

Mother smiled and relaxed. "Why don't you come up to Boynton Beach one Tuesday morning and come to class. Some of us go to lunch afterward, and I'd be pleased if you'd join us."

"I'd enjoy that. Thanks." Angie actually looked pleased.

"I also write a little poetry and I play tennis on Thurs-days," Mother said.

"Well, I can see where Mary gets her intelligence. And how you stay so slim. Have you ever tried Pilates? It's won-derful exercise."

"I went to a class once. I really meant to try it again."

"Good, maybe you would be my guest at the studio in our building. We have classes twice a week."

I couldn't believe it. These two were becoming girlfriends. They pulled out their calendar books from their purses and began making dates. The waiter poured another round of wine. Everyone had quickly drained their glass as soon as the first round was poured. Carlos ordered two more bottles.

I turned my attention to Dad and J.C. Dad was regaling Carlos and J.C. with stories about how he and Uncle Max had learned the grocery business as teenagers working at the store. I had heard the stories a thousand times; how they made deliveries by bicycle around the Beach. They would tell the little old ladies that the bill was a bit higher than what they had already paid. They collected three or four more dollars and put them away to jointly purchase a car. Dad was dying to get a car in order to impress Mother, whom he was seeing on the sly after they met on the beach one weekend. It all went well until customers called to complain that Katz's prices were too high and they would have to shop with the competition. That ended the secret quest for the car, but Grandpa Katz relented and bought them a Dodge a couple of months later.

J.C. was laughing heartily. No one seemed to notice that the food still hadn't arrived. Carlos poked me. "Our dads have made a date to play in each other's poker games. See, you had nothing to worry about. They're getting along fine."

The food finally arrived. Everyone dug in while the waiter poured more wine. Carlos signaled for another bottle.

When the coffee was served conversation began again. The coffees were as diverse as the group. Mother and Dad had decaf, Angie ordered café con leche, a blend of coffee and scalded milk, I opted for cappuccino, and Carlos and J.C got the high-test Café Cubano. This is a drink that is so strong it is served in a thimble-sized cup and is guaranteed to keep most Anglos awake for a week. I knew it would have no effect on Carlos, who could drink three cups and fall asleep in the car.

"I want to thank you for going to the hospital with Mary when she was accosted," Mother said.

"Don't mention it. We were all worried. I hope someone

would do the same for my daughter. Celia is so far away, and so is my younger son and my grandchildren. All of them are in Argentina," Angie said.

"I guess I am lucky that William and Jonathan and their kids are close by," Mother said.

"And that you already have four grandchildren. I only have two. I've given up on Celia. She's my wild girl. She's even wilder than Carlos was."

My ears perked up. "How wild was he?" I asked. Dad leaned forward and looked at Mother with the I-told-you-I-didn't-trust-him look.

"Well, he did nothing but play around at the university. His professors said he was a brilliant architect in the making, but he quit in his third year."

"I didn't know that," I said, glaring at Carlos.

"But he did what he wanted. Started his construction business. He did so well that he never even dug into his trust fund."

"You have a trust fund? I didn't know that, either," I said.

"He probably didn't want to tell you. You know his ex-spouse tried her best to get at it. It makes you a little gun shy," J.C. said. "We're proud of Carlos. The only help we gave him in getting started was to arrange some bank loans. You know I sit on the boards of a few banks."

"I didn't know that," Mother said. "Mary had us worried a few times when she was an undergraduate. Especially when she brought home that baseball player."

"Oh, yes, we were worried," Dad chimed in. "Announced that they were engaged. But then he was drafted by the Red Sox, and he was out of Miami before the next day dawned."

Carlos stared at me. "I didn't know that," he snarled.

"Getting back to grandchildren, Carlos is my last best hope for some who live in Miami," Angie said.

"I want more, too, especially from Mary. You know daughters are supposed to be different from sons, closer to family. But that doesn't seem to be holding true yet," Mother said.

"Maybe that will change when they settle down. Can you imagine the gorgeous children Carlos and Mary will have?" Angie asked.

"Why are you talking about us like we're not here?" I said, but no one bothered to listen.

"Maybe Mary will stop getting herself in these dangerous situations with those criminal clients of hers, if she has kids waiting at home," Mother said.

I turned to give her a dirty look. She was sipping the last of her wine. I saw that her hair had come loose and was falling around her face, which had turned a strange crimson color. I realized that she was sloshed.

"You know what would be nice?" Angie asked. "A November wedding. The weather is cooler and the holiday dresses are so attractive."

"Okay, this is getting out of hand. Who said anything about a wedding?" I realized I was shouting. Everyone stopped talking and looked at me. Then they started in again, as if I wasn't there. The four parents were all talking at once.

Carlos saw the anger creeping up my face. He took my arm. "This is why we have the escape room upstairs," he said. He guided me out of my chair. As we exited the dining room, he gave the waiter his credit card, signed the bill, and pushed me toward the elevator. No one noticed that we had left The Dinner.

CHAPTER TWENTY-SEVEN

I was having a strange dream that the alarm clock was ringing and I was unable to find it or move my arms. I realized the
phone was ringing. Carlos grabbed it, while I fumbled to see
my watch. It was not eight o'clock yet.

"Okay, we'll leave right away," Carlos was saying

"What is it? What's wrong?" I tugged at his arm.

"Here, better tell all this to Mary." Carlos handed me the
phone. It's Marco. Don't panic."

Marco's voice sounded far away. "Mary, we have Sam at
the vet. Catherine remembered that your vet is Doctor
White. That's where we are."

"What has happened?" I was on my feet searching for my
clothes.

"Sam was barking to go out real early. I let him into the
backyard. A few minutes later, he was at the back door and he
was having trouble walking. I got him inside and he looked
like he was going into shock. His eyes rolled back. I called
Catherine, and she called Dr. White. He met us here at the
clinic, and he's looking at him right now."

"Oh, my God, we're on our way. I'll call from the car." I
slammed down the receiver. Carlos was throwing our clothes
into our overnight bags.

We were on the road in fifteen minutes. I couldn't stop
crying.

Carlos drove down the turnpike at ninety miles an hour. Thank goodness, it was early Sunday morning with very little traffic. Dr. White's clinic was near downtown Miami. We were there in less than thirty minutes. I was out of the car before Carlos could stop.

Catherine opened the front door. "It's going to be okay, Mary. He's coming out of it."

I rushed into the exam room. Sam was on the metal table. His eyes were closed, but when he sensed that I was there, he wagged his tail. It made an off-beat drumming noise on the table.

Dr. White was half dressed in jeans and what looked like a pajama top. "It was a bufo toad, Mary. You know how poisonous they are. I've told you over and over, don't let a dog out unattended at dawn or at twilight when those damn things are hiding in the shrubs. Sam must have gotten hold of one and got a mouthful of that poison. If he were a smaller dog, he wouldn't have made it, but these big guys dilute the poison enough to come around. They got him here fast. I've washed his mouth out thoroughly and poured a lot of milk down him to absorb the poison. His vital signs look good."

Marco was as pale as the cotton swabs lying on the table. "I'm so sorry, Mary. He had such a good time last night. We all loved playing with him. I would never have let him out, but I didn't know."

I was still too shook up to answer, but Carlos patted his arm and told him it wasn't his fault.

"You can take him home in a few minutes, but keep an eye on him. If he has a seizure, call me right away," Dr. White said.

Carlos carried Sam to the car and the week from hell was finally at an end.

CHAPTER TWENTY-EIGHT

Monday morning I awoke to the sound of thunder and gusts of rain. I rolled over and reached for Carlos. Instead, I touched something warm and furry. I opened my eyes and looked into Sam's eyes. He had crawled onto the bed and wedged himself between us. He looked perfectly normal, but he must have been scared after being poisoned or scared of the thunder or both.

I got up quietly and left my two guys sacked out. By the time I dressed and gulped down some coffee, Carlos and Sam walked into the kitchen.

"I've got to get to the office early and hunt down the embassy people to help me find Luis. Then I've got to formulate some plans for my other case," I said.

"The case you can't tell me about?" Carlos asked. "Go ahead. I'll feed Sam and walk him."

"Call me if he doesn't seem A-okay, and please, don't hassle with the attorney about the condo tower. Just fax me a copy of the standard contract that the buyers signed. I'm pretty sure no one will be able to sue you."

No lights were on in the office. I was in before Catherine. I put in a call to Ambassador Miller's office. It was almost eight o'clock here. Argentina is at least two hours ahead of us, so I was sure he'd be there.

"I'm sorry, ma'am, Ambassador Miller is not here at the moment. Would you like to leave a message?" the clipped voice on the other end of the line asked.

"I left a message on Friday. Does the ambassador actually work there? I am calling about an Argentine citizen who has been wrongly arrested, and spirited away by federal officers here in Miami. His parents are well-known citizens. Before this turns into an international incident, you better have Miller return my calls. I may have to have a press conference today if I don't hear from him." I slammed down the phone. Media threats usually get some action.

Catherine arrived while I was trying to reach the unreachable Mr. Miller. She was standing in front of me as I hung up. She looked foggy and a bit undone, her hair in tendrils around her face, and her jeans wrinkled and sagging.

"Are you losing weight?" I asked.

"A little. Is Sam okay? I can't tell you how sorry I am about the toad incident. Oh, I just answered a call from Mr. Marquez's office. His assistant said that they are working on the Luis situation, and that Luis's parents are flying in to Miami today. They were in touch with him, and thought it would be better if they were here in town."

"Sam is fine. When are the Coronas arriving, and how can I reach them when they get here?"

"He didn't say, but I'll try to find out all the details. The assistant just said to tell you that as soon as they get more information about Luis, they'll call you."

At ten o'clock, a messenger arrived with a thick packet of papers from Liz. She had listed every closed case on her audit for the last six months. A note was attached. She had worked over the weekend to list all the cases. She wanted to know what else she could do to help me prepare her case. All I could think of was to pray, if she was into that.

The list was very long. Either Liz was the most productive judge in the courthouse or something or someone was manipulating her assignments.

Catherine interrupted to announce that State Attorney Jason Jones was on the phone. I picked up, but fear was making my voice sound hesitant and squeaky.

"What's it going to be, Mary? Is Judge Maxwell coming in voluntarily? I'm in the process of readying subpoenas for a grand jury session," Jason said.

"I will be bringing her in to meet with you, but I have some scheduling conflicts. I have to be in court on a federal case, and I may be called into trial also. As soon as I can get free of this schedule, we'll set an appointment."

"Well, don't drag your feet too long. I'll cut you a little slack, but patience isn't my best trait." Jason hung up abruptly.

"Okay, Catherine. It's time for another field trip. Forward the phone lines to your cell phone, and let's go," I said.

Catherine grabbed her ever-present backpack and we piled into my SUV with Liz's file, yellow legal pads, and a laptop computer and headed for the courthouse.

CHAPTER TWENTY-NINE

The clerk's office covers two whole floors of the criminal courthouse. I explained to Catherine that we were going to request every file of every closed case on the list Liz sent over. There were so many that the normal procedure for viewing case files was not going to accommodate our accomplishing this task.

Ordinarily, you fill out a slip of paper with the case name and number and your name and phone number. Then you wait while a clerk fetches that file from the thousands shelved by numbers. If the case is fairly old, it has to be brought from storage. It would be impossible to get fifty or more files with that procedure. By the time we were able to look at half of them, Liz might be serving a prison sentence.

I would have to call on my friendship with the elected clerk of the court. It was eleven o'clock by the time we arrived on the seventh floor. The morning hubbub in that office had subsided. Two clerks are assigned to each courtroom. One clerk does courtroom duty while the other sits in an assigned cubicle answering phone requests and processing paperwork. Clerks unassigned to a particular courtroom division pull files needed in court and reshelve cases coming back from the courts.

By the time we arrived, clerks were already in court and

the rest were busy doing their office work. I approached the reception desk and asked to see Mark Epstein.

"Please tell him Mary Magruder Katz is here and needs to speak to him," I said.

A few minutes later, Mark came through the swinging gate marked "No admittance. Court Personnel Only."

Mark had been in the clerk's office for some years, and had been elected chief clerk four years ago. It wasn't the career he planned. He was a star baseball player at the University of Miami the year they won the College World Series in Omaha. He was scooped up by the major leagues and was so good that he played for the Red Sox in the same year he was drafted. Two years later, he blew out his knee. Surgeries never repaired it enough for him to play again. Eventually, he came home to Miami and ended up in the courthouse.

Mark was my college boyfriend. By the time he returned to Miami, I was in my last year of law school, and I was more interested in my career choices than in boyfriend choices, especially a boyfriend who had left town without a backward glance in my direction. As they say, timing is everything.

"Mary, what a great surprise. How are you?" Mark asked. He gave me a hard hug.

I introduced him to Catherine and explained that I needed to have a kizillion case files pulled. "I can't tell you the reason. Attorney-client privilege. I wouldn't bother you, but I couldn't think of any other way to get a look at this many files." I said.

He pulled two visitor passes from the pile on the receptionist's desk and handed them to Catherine and me. He took each of us by the elbow and walked us back through the swinging gates to the file room area.

"Let's see what we can do," he said.

I produced the list of file numbers and handed it to him. He went to a red phone and called over the loudspeaker for three workers.

"This is a long list, Mary, but for you I'll do what I can."

In a few minutes three young kids arrived. "These are summer interns doing their high school community service," Mark said. "I'm going to assign them to help you. Girls, pull some carts out and start looking for these files. When you get ten or so, bring them to the conference room, so these ladies can start looking at those files while you locate some more."

"This is very nice of you. I didn't mean to tie up your conference room. We'll try to do our work quickly," I said.

"Stop in my office on your way out." Mark walked us to the conference room and left us there. I noticed that he was limping.

The first files were delivered in a few minutes, followed by a full cart of files a short time later.

"This isn't as hard as it sounded," one of the interns, whose name badge said Lena, told us. "All the files are from the same division, so it won't take us that long. Here's my cell phone number. Call when you're done and we'll take all the files back."

"Lena, please, don't discuss this with anyone. This is very confidential. Here's my card. I might need an intern sometime soon, so call me," I said, hoping that three high school girls had better things to gab about than files in the courthouse.

We began the task of looking for the final orders in the case files. We listed the case number, the name of the defendant, and the disposition of each case.

A few of the cases had been settled by a plea agreement and sentencing. A few more had gone to trial and were noted

NG, meaning not guilty with the jury verdict attached to the back page of the file. A few more showed conviction at trial and a sentencing order signed by Liz.

The bulk of the cases were dismissals. Some were dismissed after a perfunctory boilerplate motion by a defense attorney. The orders were also boilerplate, saying only "Motion to Dismiss, Granted," and signed by Liz. No legal or factual reasons were given for the decision to dismiss. Some contained a similar order of dismissal at the arraignment. All of these cases were drug related, including a few that were charged with money laundering.

Many different attorneys were involved in the cases. One firm was involved in eleven of the cases, but different attorneys from that firm were attorneys of record. The rest were from a variety of offices including the office of the public defender.

"There doesn't seem to be a real link as to the attorneys. What are we missing here?" I asked Catherine. "Let's make copies of some of these orders so I can go over them with Liz."

Catherine began pulling orders from files and utilizing the copy machine in the back of the conference room. "Mary, all of these files have a disposition sheet on the back of the file and they're all signed by Judge Anne Ackley. Why is she the one to sign them all?"

"I guess it's her job. She's the chief judge of the criminal court, but I'll ask Liz."

I looked down at the file in my hand. It contained one of the dismissal orders. Then I looked at the five orders Catherine had just copied. Liz's signature was exactly the same; none bigger or smaller, all slanted exactly the same. I doubted that I could sign my name repeatedly without some little variances. Maybe this was something important.

I looked at my watch. It was two o'clock. "We've missed

lunch. Let's get out of here and eat. We've earned a real sit-down meal," I said.

Catherine rang for Lena and we packed our laptop.

"Remember, Mark told you to stop and see him on the way out," Catherine said.

"I'd rather not open up old closed doors. I'll send him a thank-you e-mail."

CHAPTER THIRTY

We loaded the car and walked across the street to a cafetería, the kind of place famous in Miami. The walk-up window on the side dispenses Café Cubano and is jammed every morning. Inside there are a few tables and a counter to place an order. The simple menu consists of Media Noches, a specialty Cuban sandwich of ham, cheese, and whatever else is leftover. There were also toasted paninis and fresh fruit.

By this hour, the tables were empty, and one worker was mopping the floor. We sat down at a corner table and in minutes were biting into the toasty delight of a sandwich rich in cholesterol and calories, the perfect combination to de-stress any attorney.

"Was Mark Epstein your boyfriend? Wait'll I tell my kids. I think they have his baseball trading card," Catherine said.

"Was, is the operative word. It was a long time ago."

"I don't know. He looked like he was ready to go back in time," Catherine laughed.

"Please, don't mention Mark to Carlos. He has a big jealous streak. While we're asking nosy questions, what's with you and Marco?" I asked

"You're not nosy, Mary. I really like being with Marco. He's kind and funny. It's been a long time since I've had fun evenings. I try to spend all my spare time with my boys. They never see their father. He gives me no help at all."

"I haven't asked you about your divorce, or much else, but I have wondered. And I definitely have wanted to ask you about your interest in wolves."

"You've been great not to ask, but I feel very comfortable now about telling you what I went through. I guess from my résumé you know that I graduated high school in Daytona, and went to Volusia County Community College where I got my paralegal certification."

"Sure, I read that," I said.

"Before that, I went to at least six other schools. My dad was in the army and we moved a lot. One of the best places was Seattle. That's where I learned about wolves. I always loved animals and with us moving so much, it was too hard to get a dog, so my mom found out about Wolf Haven outside of Seattle, and I fell in love with the place. In the summer, I trained to be a volunteer, and I spent every minute I could working with the vets and the field workers. People who breed wolves as pets and then abandon them or give them up, send them to the haven. Some are found injured and are unable to return to the wild, so they end up at Wolf Haven too.

"They are the most intelligent animals and they really won't bother people if they're left alone, but they aren't dogs and they can't be treated like they are. I've never forgotten those great days and everything I learned from the animals. I tell my boys about my time there. The pictures and calendars remind me of a good time in my life."

"I guess that's why you and Sam get along so well."

"About Brady, my ex, we met in Daytona. He was a me-chanic and amateur race car driver You know Daytona has the big five hundred race, and lots of car jockeys hang around there. We got married after a few months. I thought he was exciting, but excitement goes away fast when babies come along and money is a big problem.

"Then he got a chance to work at the track in Homestead. That sounded exciting, like a new life. We sold our trailer and bought an RV to live in, packed the two kids, and arrived with enough money to eat for a week. Brady worked at the track and I tried to get a job, but the only wheels we had was the RV. I hated Homestead. It looked like a bombed-out town, even eight years after Hurricane Andrew."

"What a nightmare," I said.

"Tell me about it. But that's not the worst. I woke up one morning and found a note from Brady. All his clothes and tools were gone, along with the fifty bucks I had in my purse. But I'm a survivor. I sold the RV and with the money, I bought a used Honda Civic and drove out of Homestead with my kids and all our worldly possessions crammed into that little car. I drove up U.S. 1 until I came to Coconut Grove. It looked so pretty, flowers blooming and narrow curvy streets. I took the rest of the money and rented a garage apartment on Bird Road. The old lady who owned the house knew someone looking for a legal secretary. I got the job in a law firm on Bayshore Drive, put the kids in school, saved my money, and moved to a better apartment, and the rest is history, as they say."

"I can't even imagine being that brave. Did you ever connect with Brady again?" I asked. I snuck a glance at Catherine expecting to see a sad expression. Instead she was smiling.

"Oh, sure. Six months later, one of the attorneys where I was working helped me get my divorce. The office investigator found Brady in Fort Lauderdale, living with some bimbo. He's two years behind in child support. Every so often, I go to the state attorney's office. You know they have a child support division. They haul him into court, threaten jail, and I get a few hundred bucks. It's funny. I never really missed him. Once I got us settled, I just felt peaceful."

"You deserve a medal, like Mother of the Year. I admire you, Catherine."

"So you can see why Marco is such a part of my happy new life. He seems like everything Brady wasn't, but I'm never rushing into any permanent arrangement again."

"I hear you. I'm scared of 'forever' too."

CHAPTER THIRTY-ONE

The cell phone rang on the way back to the office. Catherine covered the phone and told me it was Liz.

"Tell her to come over after work tonight. I need to go over the information we found in the court files."

As soon as Catherine disconnected from that call, the phone rang again. This time she handed it to me. It was Señor Marques, not an assistant.

"Ms. Katz, I am delighted that Luis has an attorney ready to work on his case," he said.

"Thank you. Do you have any news?"

"I am working with our embassy in Washington. We have filed a formal request for information about Luis's location. Our government in Argentina is considering filing a petition in Congress seeking their help. Honestly, I am at the end of my ability to find Luis. Here's what I'm considering. Luis's parents have arrived in Miami. What would you think of calling a press conference to appeal to everyone and anyone to come forward with information regarding Luis's detention?"

"Who would be giving the press conference?" I asked.

"I would be there and lay out the facts that we know. Mr. and Mrs. Corona would be there to answer questions about Luis, and you would be there to discuss any legal matters. If the timing is right, maybe we can smoke out the federal authorities before it's too late."

"I think it's a great idea. I even suggested that I might call a press conference in the last message I left for Ambassador Miller, not that he returned any of my calls. I was thinking of filing a Writ of Habeas Corpus in the federal court. Maybe this is the time to do that and produce it at the press conference," I said.

"Habeas corpus means bring me the body, doesn't it? I thought that was only used in cases where a person is already sentenced, like in a death penalty case."

"You are exactly right about its meaning. It means produce the body of the person. It's what we call an extraordinary writ, and what better place to use it, than in a case of a wrongful arrest."

"I'll set the wheels in motion for a press conference for tomorrow afternoon. We could be the lead story on the evening news and be in plenty of time for the morning papers. You get your petition ready. Shall we hold it here in my office?"

"Why not in front of the federal courthouse?" I asked. We may as well pull out all the stops, if we're going to find Luis before he's locked away at Guantanamo. Where are the Coronas staying?"

"They are at the Ritz-Carlton not far from your office. You're in the Grove, correct?"

"Yes, I'll go to meet them before the press conference."

I was on the edge of my seat and gripping the steering wheel of the car as we drove into the office parking lot. I jumped out and raced inside to begin drafting the petition. I needed to finish it before Liz arrived for our meeting. The life of a criminal defense attorney may be nerve wracking, sometimes gut wrenching, but never, ever dull.

CHAPTER THIRTY-TWO

Liz arrived at five thirty. Catherine had already left for the day. I was proofreading the habeas corpus petition at the computer. I looked up to see Liz standing at my desk.

"You startled me," I said. I jumped up and came around the desk.

"I can see that. You never even heard me come in and call your name. You know that's not really safe. Anyone could come in here and attack you. You need some better procedures, like locks and an intercom after five o'clock," Liz said. She plunked down on the sofa and looked at me expectantly. "Anything new?"

"Catherine and I spent a good part of the day in the clerk's office going through the files in your division that were closed without any plea or sentencing. There were many files like that, with orders of dismissal."

"What? That can't be right."

"Well, we made copies of a number of the orders so that you and I can go over them." I pulled the pile of orders out of my briefcase and spread them on the coffee table in front of us.

Liz picked up one and read it, then another and another. She frowned. Then she began rereading each one. She shook her head and looked up. "I have no recollection of any of these case names or these orders."

"Your name is in the heading of each order right below the case number, and your signature is on each one."

"I see that, but there must be some mistake. Honestly, Mary, this just isn't my work no matter what these papers say."

I could hear the panic in Liz's voice. She sounded like my five-year-old nephew when he fell into a sewer opening and was trapped, but that's another story. Trapped! That's what was happening to Liz.

"Liz, let's talk about your signature on these orders. Is that your signature? I noticed that your signature on each order is exactly the same, none bigger or smaller. They almost look like carbon copies."

"It's my handwriting. Oh, wait. I have a signature stamp."

"You what? You have an ink stamp with your signature?"

"A lot of the judges have them. When you sign a few hundred orders a week, it saves time and it keeps you from having hand surgery."

"I guess I'm kind of surprised that you would have such a thing. You just lectured me about safety. How safe is it to have your signature floating around?"

"Well, like I said, I'm not the only one to have a stamp. Ann Ackley is the one who told us to get them. She suggested it at a judges' meeting. Why would our administrative judge suggest it, if it wasn't safe?"

"I don't know. Who has access to this stamp besides you?"

"My staff, especially my bailiff. She uses it on the agreed orders that the lawyers send in. She opens the mail and if there's an agreed order that doesn't require anything but a signature and sending copies back to the attorneys, she moves it right along."

"What kind of orders would those be?"

"Oh, agreeing to a continuance of a hearing or agreeing

to extra days for discovery or agreeing to take a deposition in another city, things like that."

"I also noticed that every closed case had a disposition sheet signed by Judge Ann Ackley as the administrative judge of the criminal division. What are those sheets for?"

"I guess they're so Ann can see if the cases are moving along timely. I think they're just boilerplate. She probably doesn't even read the files. You know the courts love to make paperwork."

"Do you and Judge Ackley get along well? Please, don't think I'm snooping. I'm just trying to get a whole picture here."

"She's been a good friend to me. You know she was one of the first women on the bench in Miami. She gave me a lot of help when I was first elected. She's really a fun person. And since both of us are single, we go out for a drink after work sometimes."

"Liz, Judge Ackley has a — how can I put this, a strange reputation. You know they call her Annie Oakley instead of Ann Ackley. Some of the lawyers say she has an extensive gun collection, and there are rumors that she has a gun with her on the bench. There are also stories about her and some of the cops who testify in cases in front of her. That she's a little too friendly to be objective."

"That's a whole lot of gossip, Mary. Several judges have concealed weapons licenses. We aren't always in the best situations. Many of us have had death threats. As for Ann's boyfriends, those are her own business."

"Liz, don't you see that someone is setting you up? The state attorney thinks you're helping out drug dealers. All these orders have your signature. Add in the Jack Carillo case and everything points to you. If you're not involved, then you need to open your eyes and see that someone is using you."

Liz stood up and paced over to the window and back. "I can't believe that the people I work with everyday could be using me." She began to cry.

I had my fill of tears and sobs for the month. I hate to yell at a client, but sometimes it's the only way to reach them.

"Liz, shut off the waterworks and sit down here. I need your objective thinking now, if I'm going to help you," I said. "Jason is chomping at the bit to subpoena you to a grand jury if I don't produce you for questioning voluntarily. He's issued an ultimatum. What are you going to tell him? That you signed all the orders, but you didn't know you signed them? Or that you ordered the murdered informant to have his deposition taken?

"We need an action plan. If you can't give me some help here, I can't dig you out of this hole by myself."

Liz sat down and wiped her nose. She looked like a helpless child.

"Now, listen to me carefully. Someone is using you. This is an unpleasant reality. I need you to think like the great judge that you are. I see three possibilities: Judge Ackley, who has access to case assignments and dispositions; your bailiff, Gladys, who has access to your signature and your orders; and Joe Fineberg, who is a defense attorney and has access to — well — your chambers and condo."

Liz's face turned a bright red. "It can't be Joe. We never discuss any cases, his or mine, and he never comes to my chambers. We meet outside of court. Ann could fix cases all by herself. She has access to everything in the criminal courthouse." Liz drew a deep breath.

"Do you honestly think it could be Gladys? After all the years we've worked together?" Liz asked.

"Tell me everything you know about Gladys's personal life." I pulled my yellow pad closer and got ready to take notes.

"I wrote it all in the papers I sent you. She's a local girl. Graduated from Hialeah High School and Miami-Dade College. She dated here and there until she met Billy Martinez. They lived together for a year and got married two years ago."

"How well do you know him? What's their relationship like?"

"I met him at the wedding, and he's been to a few courthouse parties with her. He's very good looking and Gladys adores him. She's so proud of their new house.

"He took her to South America with him to visit his family and she told me it was a business trip for him. He's originally from Colombia. She asked for the time off to go on the trip."

"When did that trip take place?"

"Let me think. It was eight months ago, right before I moved back to criminal."

"What kind of business does he have?"

"I think he imports Colombian artwork and accessories, and he exports some American products. Oh, he also plans shopping trips for South Americans who travel here."

"This wouldn't be the first time that an import company was importing more than artwork," I said.

"Oh my God, Mary. Are you saying that he's dealing? Just because he's Colombian doesn't mean he's a drug dealer."

"Of course not. Not to sound trite, some of my best friends are Colombian. Well, two or three, and they're lawyers. It's very possible that he and Gladys are the key to this mess. We need to test this theory. I think I know a way to do this. Let me work on it, and I'll call you as soon as I have things in place. Meanwhile, I'll give Jason a date to bring you in to his office, but I'll try to put it off for a week."

"Can't you tell me what you're going to do?"

"Not yet. In the meantime, be careful. Don't discuss the investigation with anyone, and keep your eyes open."

CHAPTER THIRTY-THREE

The next morning I was up at six. I finished the petition in Luis's case by ten, and checked in with Catherine at the office where everything was under control. I told her to call Jason and explain that I couldn't arrange my schedule for his questioning of Liz until the middle of next week.

"He'll see the press conference about Luis on TV and know that I'm not conning him about being busy," I said.

I washed my hair and tried to tame it with a product called "Frizz Me Not." Not that it would help much. The weather called for intermittent showers and the humidity enveloped me in waves of mist, promising to turn my hair into a frame of frizz. That's the thing about Miami. It's great for your skin and shit for your hair. Why in the world had I suggested holding the press conference outdoors?

I was on the way to the Ritz-Carlton to meet Luis's parents when my cell phone rang. It was Carlos.

"How's it going?" he asked. He sounded distracted.

"I'm on my way to meet the Coronas. What's up with you? You sound funny."

"I don't feel funny. I'm at the office and I just got served with a class-action lawsuit by fifteen of the condo buyers. It says I have thirty days to answer. I am pissed."

"Okay, don't panic. Fax the papers to the office and the

contract that I told you to bring me. I'll look everything over tonight after the press conference. Everything will be okay." I closed the cell phone and gave myself a slap on the head. Just what I needed. A protracted civil case involving my boyfriend.

The phone rang again immediately. It was Catherine.

"Mary, I'm putting Mr. Marquez through to you. It's about the press conference."

"What now? Okay. Put him on. Señor Marquez, I'm just on my way to see the Coronas. Is there some change of plans?"

"*Buenos dias*, Ms. Katz. I'm concerned about the rain. Maybe we should hold the conference in my office."

"It's a little late to call all the media again, isn't it?"

"Well, that's another thing. No one seemed too interested in attending. They all just said they'd pass on the information."

"Who did you speak to?"

"I had my secretary call the *Herald* and the local TV stations. She left messages with the receptionists."

"Leave it to me. I'll head over to my office. You need to get through to the actual city desks and newsrooms and to all the Spanish radio stations and Univision and the other Spanish newspapers and CNN. If you don't mind, call the Coronas and tell them I'm delayed."

I clicked off and called Catherine back to tell her to look in my Rolodex for all my media numbers. After the Lillian Yarmouth case, I had obtained a number of private contact numbers for news-hungry reporters. When Catherine and I finished on the phone, a good crowd would be assembled outside the courthouse, and the grieving family might look even sadder with a backdrop of rain.

By the time I got to the Coronas' hotel, it was almost time to leave for the courthouse. Miguel and Maria were a well-dressed couple in their fifties. I assumed Maria's elegant dress and jewelry came from one of their boutiques. Their worried demeanor was evident.

"Mr. and Mrs. Corona, I'm sorry I've been delayed. I'm Mary."

"I am so glad to meet you in person, Mary," Miguel said with a slight bow.

Maria nodded. She was clutching a handkerchief. Between the rain and the crying clients, I was beginning to feel like the victim of a dripping water torture.

"Exactly what are we to do at this meeting of reporters?" Miguel asked.

"Just tell them what a good boy Luis is, and how worried you are that no one knows where the government is hiding him or why. Just be yourselves and be honest. I'll explain the papers I'm filing to try to force the feds to produce Luis, and Mr. Marquez will explain how upset the Argentine government is about Luis's treatment. Hopefully, this pressure will bring us the answers we need."

"This is good. Also I spoke this morning to J.C. Martin. He is going to try to get through to Ambassador Miller. I told him you have had no luck."

I eased the Coronas out to my car, and we made our way to the federal courthouse for our one o'clock press conference. The rain began as soon as we hit the freeway.

By the time I pulled up to the nearest access point at the federal courthouse, it was not just raining. The skies were dropping a tropical deluge. I handed Miguel one of my large black umbrellas reserved for pre-hurricane sprints from car to court.

"Wait for me under the porticos in front and look for Mr. Marquez, but don't speak with any media people until I get there," I said.

Miguel and Maria hurried up the steps. I saw no cameras or reporters gathering.

I left the car at the closest parking lot, grabbed my second-class umbrella, and jogged back to the courthouse. My carefully planned white suit was now mud spattered and my once blow-dried hair was dripping down onto my blouse.

One lonely TV remote truck pulled up as I reached the front steps. It was from the local Fox News affiliate. No others were in sight. As I mounted the steps, I felt a tug on my elbow. A very young-looking guy holding a reporter's pad was staring at me. He looked like a boy on the first day of school, scared but expectant.

"Ms. Katz? You're Mary Katz, right? I'm Harlan McFarland, from the *Herald*. Our regular courthouse reporter, Roberta Nowack, sent me over. She's tied up covering a trial or something. She apologizes for not getting over here herself. I know she promised you earlier she'd be here but—" His voice trailed off.

"Harlan McFarland? Is that your real name? It's like a little poem." I couldn't believe I had just said that. Harlan looked like he might cry. "Just a little joke," I said, making matters worse.

"It's really my name. My grandfather's name was Harlan and my mother insisted on it in spite of our last name. It's okay. I get worse comments all the time."

"Well, Harlan, it looks like you've got a clear field for a singular story. I don't see any other print media here."

"Gee, that's great. I'm a summer intern. This'll be my first story. I'm covering for *El Nuevo Herald* also. I speak fluent Spanish."

"Okay, let me take you over and introduce you to Miguel and Maria Corona, the parents of Luis Corona, who the government has kidnapped and taken into hiding. Here's a copy of my habeas corpus petition."

I handed him the papers, introduced him to Miguel, and went to speak to a very well-dressed gentleman who had to be Mr. Marquez. At least he had been well dressed. At the moment his water-splotched suit pants were dragging on the ground. He looked as angry as the thunderclouds that were spewing lightening flashes as they hovered overhead.

"Señor Marquez, it's so nice to finally meet you in person," I said.

"I told you we shouldn't have held an outdoor conference," Marquez said, forgetting what I expected would be his old-world manners. No hand kissing and bowing today.

"Well, I was wrong. Sorry. But look, a few more newshounds are arriving." I pointed to a woman and two men approaching with cameras.

Altogether there were five reporters, representing one Argentine paper, the *Herald* kid, the local TV station, a courthouse blogger, and good old CNN. The Coronas, Marquez, and I lined up shoulder to soggy shoulder and began to address the motley group.

"I am Philipe Marquez, consul general of the Argentine consulate here in Miami. Thank you for coming here today in spite of the weather. We are greatly disturbed about the arrest of Luis Corona last week. Luis is a young man of spotless reputation, a citizen of Argentina, who was traveling to Miami to purchase a business here. He was arrested when he arrived here by plane. He has not been charged with a crime, has not been afforded a hearing to set bond, and worst of all, no one knows where he is being held. As a representative of the government of Argentina, I have orders to find this young man and see that he is returned to our country. I must say that we are shocked that Luis has been afforded none of the rights that Americans constantly state their constitution mandates.

"Luis's parents have traveled here from Argentina. This is Miguel Corona, the father of Luis, who will speak to you now on behalf of his wife, Maria, and himself."

Miguel stepped forward and began to speak. His voice was unsteady. It was clear that he was fighting back tears. "I am Miguel Corona. I am here with my spouse to implore the members of the press to help us find our son. I beg the government or any citizen who knows where our boy is to please let us know that he is all right. We have heard rumors that he is being treated as a terrorist and may be on his way to Guantanamo or some other country.

"I sent Luis to the United States to purchase a store. We own a group of boutiques in Buenos Aires and its suburbs. That was Luis's only purpose in traveling here. He is a good Catholic boy who attends Mass with us every Sunday. Your country has made a terrible mistake." Miguel's voice trailed off. I stepped next to him and took his arm. I could feel his body shaking.

"I am Mary Magruder Katz," I said. "I am Luis's attorney. I saw Luis briefly at the Dade County Jail two days after his arrival in Miami. He was removed from the jail by government agents while I was present. I was unable to gain any information regarding what charges are being lodged against him or where he was being taken. That is the last anyone has seen or heard of Luis.

"This afternoon I am filing a petition seeking a habeas corpus hearing before a federal judge to seek the release of Luis Corona. It is outrageous that an innocent person arriving in our country is spirited away by our own government. Luis has been afforded none of the safeguards that sets our justice system apart from most other countries. Any person on our soil who is arrested has a right to know what he is accused of, and within hours, to have a hearing before a neutral magistrate to set conditions of release.

"I join the Coronas in asking anyone who can give us information regarding Luis's whereabouts to come forward."

Mr. Marquez stepped forward again. "My government wishes to resolve this matter peacefully and quickly before we are forced to seek international help in this matter. Are there any questions?"

The CNN reporter called out immediately. "Ten days ago another Argentine citizen was found murdered at a downtown hotel. Is there any connection between these two matters? The murdered man had in his possession documents from a group called the Army of Allah."

Mr. Marquez answered quickly. "I have been investigating whether the murder victim was an Argentine. We have been unable to match his fingerprints with any on file in my country. We do know this much. The passport he used actually belonged to a gentleman in his seventies who died over a year ago. There is no relationship to Luis Corona at all."

I remembered reading about the murder at the Floridian Inn, but I was startled to hear this new information about the identity of the victim. Could our government actually have been linking Luis to some scumbag who could be from anywhere? What kind of paranoia was gripping this country?

"Any other questions?" Mr. Marquez asked.

Harlan McFarland raised his hand. As he did so, he dropped his notepad on the wet pavement, scooped it up, looked embarrassed, and asked, "What kind of agents removed Luis from the Dade County Jail? Where did they say they were taking Luis?"

"Good question," I said. "They never identified themselves, but they looked like the Secret Service people you see on TV. They were busy shoving me out of their way and weren't answering any of my questions. However, the desk sergeant did say that the feds were the ones who were coming to get him, and that he thought they were accusing him of trying to blow up a plane."

I heard laughter behind me and realized Miguel was actually chuckling. "What's funny?" I whispered.

Miguel stepped forward. "The reason I laugh is because Luis was the poorest science and chemistry student in the history of his academy. These were the only subjects he totally failed. When I addressed his poor work with him he told me that he couldn't stand to touch the various components in the laboratory. He said the smells made him nauseous and dizzy. I don't think he would be a candidate to blow up anything."

Miguel continued to chuckle. Soon the reporters joined him and right then the rain stopped. When I looked out over the street, I saw the beginning of a rainbow.

CHAPTER THIRTY-FOUR

I left the Coronas with Mr. Marquez and sped back to the office. I couldn't do anything else for Luis except hope that someone would respond to the press conference; someone who wasn't a crackpot with some misinformation.

Time was running out for Judge Liz. I had to put my plan in motion before Jason decided to convene the grand jury. My plan called for inveigling Mark Epstein. Without his help, I couldn't get my plan off the ground.

"How did it go?" Catherine asked.

"Wet and wild," I said. "I need to work on Liz's case right away. See if you can get Mark Epstein on the phone and hold off on anything else for a while."

"Okay, but here're the papers Carlos sent over. He's being sued."

"I know." I grabbed the papers and put them on the side of my desk.

Catherine buzzed the intercom. "The secretary said Mr. Epstein is unavailable at the moment. I left a message."

"Unavailable. Since when did he become so damn important?"

"I told you, you should have gone in and thanked him when we were at his office. You can't control the wind, but you can adjust your sails."

"What does that mean? Did you get that from Marco?"

"Well, yes. He said his grandmother always said it. It means you never know when you'll need something from someone so act accordingly," Catherine said, and clicked off the intercom.

I thumbed through my Rolodex and found Mark's private office number. Thank God, I never clean out my Rolodex. Mark picked up on the second ring.

"Is this unavailable Mark Epstein? This is Mary Katz, the humble attorney," I said.

"I saw the message, Mary. I figured if you wanted to talk to me, you could have called yourself without the help of your secretary. You also could have stopped by to see me the other day after I practically turned my office over to you. What favor do you need now?"

"I apologize. Can I come and see you in the morning? Yes, I really do need a favor. I'm kind of in a mess. Please."

"Okay. I guess so. Could you come around noon? My morning is crazy tomorrow."

"I'll see you at noon," I said. This wasn't going to be easy, and I hate begging, especially where an old boyfriend is concerned.

I really wanted to go home and get out of my wet clothes; especially my soggy sagging panty hose, but I knew Carlos would want to hear that I was working on his lawsuit.

I pulled the papers back to the center of my desk and began to read the complaint. The first thing I noticed was that the lawyer who was representing the plaintiffs was Henry Cumberland, one of the underlings in Frank Fieldstone's office. My old fiancé strikes again. I was surprised that Carlos hadn't noticed the name of the firm.

The lawsuit was fairly simple. Fifteen disgruntled buyers were suing to get their deposits back due to the delay in the completion of their condos. They also sought interest compounded from the day they paid the deposits, and punitive damages for triple the amount, plus court costs and attorney fees. They claimed each had been injured in various ways; paying rents to stay in their current homes or losing income on renting the new condos or other sundry costs.

Next I turned to the standard contract that each buyer had signed. I flipped through the pages until I came to the paragraph I hoped was there. "In case of disputes between buyer and seller for any reason, buyer agrees that the filing of any lawsuit in any jurisdiction is waived, and that the sole remedy shall be binding arbitration."

This was a piece of cake. None of them had any right to sue, so this lawsuit would be dismissed as soon as it walked into a courtroom. At least I would have one happy client. Thank goodness it was the one who currently occupied my bed.

CHAPTER THIRTY-FIVE

I phoned Carlos and told him not to worry about the lawsuit. Then I left for home. Sam did his usual greeting, dancing circles around me and running to the cupboard where I keep his dog chow.

I poured his food, which he devoured in the time it took me to remove my shoes and the soggy panty hose. I was as ravenous as Sam had been. I picked up some carryout pasta from Papa Luigi's on my way home, which I ate right out of the cardboard container.

I carried my glass of red wine into the bedroom and dropped the rest of my clothes onto the floor. It felt very warm in the bedroom. My first thought was that the air-conditioning was broken. This is a disaster in June in Miami. My air conditioner repairman's number is the first one on my speed dial.

I checked the register. Cold air was tumbling out. I pulled up the window shade I hadn't bothered to open in the morning and saw the problem. The bedroom window was pulled open as far as it would go. Rain had come in and saturated the window sill and floor. I couldn't have left the window open. Sam certainly couldn't open the window, as bright as he is, especially since I leave the bedroom door shut. Otherwise Sam spends the day frolicking on my bed.

I shut the window and went into the bathroom. That's

when I saw the writing on my mirror. In bright red, it said "BITCH, MIND YOUR OWN BUSINESS. YOU'LL GET HURT. WATCH OUT!" I saw my twenty-dollar lipstick lying on the side of the basin. My first thought was, couldn't the writer have used their own lipstick?

CHAPTER THIRTY-SIX

By the time the Coral Gables Police arrived, I was dressed in jeans and had downed the rest of the wine, but my hands were still shaking. Police Lieutenant Fonseca was photographing the mirror.

"How do I rate a ranking officer?" I asked.

"Everyone on patrol is busy, so I came myself. I'm the shift commander." He bagged the lipstick in an evidence bag. "I noticed in my computer on the way over here that we answered a call here a few months ago when your house was vandalized. Is there somebody who is pretty angry with you?"

"Actually, the break-in was last February. It was someone I knew, an old boyfriend."

"Why didn't you report that to us?"

"I really didn't want to prosecute. Let's just say, I took care of it myself. I doubt that he'd risk breaking in again."

A loud knock on the front door startled me. Then I heard, "Mary, it's Flako."

Flako is Marco's head Pit Bull. I called Marco before I called the police. I let Flako in. He's a huge man, imposing enough to scare away the meanest bad guy. The "Flako" nickname, which really means chicken, is the Pit Bulls' idea of a joke.

"Marco said to tell you he's sorry he couldn't get over here himself. He's following some wandering spouse for another client. Wow," Flako said as he followed me into the bathroom. "Hi, Fonseca. Glad you're here to file a report."

"I was just asking Ms. Katz if she had any thoughts about the perp. What else are you involved in these days? Any angry clients?" Fonseca asked.

"I was part of a press conference this afternoon. I have a client who's been seized by the government. I'm trying to find out where the feds are hiding him," I said.

"Oh, I saw that on CNN a little while ago. You represent that terrorist?" Lieutenant Fonseca frowned. For a minute, I thought he was about to tear up his report. He stood staring at the paper in his hand.

Noises in the living room stopped the conversation.

"Mary, where the hell are you? What's going on?" The angry voice of Carlos filled my little house.

"Carlos we're back here. Calm down. Everything is okay," I called to him.

"Ay, who did this?" Carlos said as he burst into the bathroom, which was now filled to capacity with large male bodies.

"That's what we're trying to find out, sir," the officer said. "Now if everyone will step into the bedroom, I'll try to finish my investigation."

"This does it, Mary. Tomorrow I'm having a burglar alarm installed here. If you won't move in with me, then you must have more security here. Do not argue with me." Carlos's face was turning the color of the lipstick writing.

"I do not need or want an alarm here. I have Sam."

"Sam is a wimp. Where was he today?"

"He couldn't get into the bedroom. I keep the door closed."

"Well, he tried," Flako said. He was pointing to the outside of the door. "Didn't you notice this?"

I came over to see what he meant. The door had claw marks all over it. Some wood splinters hung precariously. The white paint was barely visible.

"I guess I saw it, but I was pretty tired when I walked in and Sam had already begun his handiwork on some other occasions," I said. "See, Carlos, he did try to protect the house."

"That's not protection. He does that when you and I are in the bedroom and he wants to join in."

"Let's discuss this later," I said. "The lieutenant wants to finish his work."

"Try not to touch the window frame or glass. The fingerprint tech will be over first thing tomorrow to see what we can get, but with that rain it probably won't amount to much." Lieutenant Fonseca packed up his goodies and started for the door. "Oh, and don't erase the writing or touch the mirror either."

Flako followed the officer to the front door. Carlos put his arm around me.

"Mary, you can't ignore the things that have been happening to you. First you were accosted at the office, now this. I feel responsible for getting you involved with Luis. I want you to move into my house until this case is resolved."

Before I could answer, Flako returned. "Fonseca told me that if the feds are involved in scaring you off of Luis's case, there is very little the local police can do. I think he was a little scared."

"Okay, boys," I said. "I'm not moving out of my house, and I refuse to believe that my own government would be threatening me. I am staying right here and now I am going to sleep, so everyone clear out. Carlos, I know you care about my safety, but I will be fine. Sam is good protection, and I'll keep him right here during the night."

"This is against my better judgment, but at least take this

and keep it with you." Carlos reached into his pocket and pulled out a small revolver.

"Do you have a concealed weapons license for that?" the lawyer part of me asked. "Were you going to use that tonight?"

"You seem to forget, Ms. Attorney, Florida is one of the few states where you can chase away an intruder and still shoot him as he runs. A man's home is still his castle in this state," Carlos said.

I reached out and took the gun. I felt Carlos was safer without it.

CHAPTER THIRTY-SEVEN

The fingerprint tech arrived while I was still downing my morning coffee. She did her work quickly, covering the bedroom and bathroom with the dust used to pick up the prints. She took a complete set of my prints to eliminate them from anything she could retrieve.

"I don't think I've got much of value here, but we'll see. Sorry, I've got to rush on, six more scenes to get to this morning. Busy night last night," she said.

"Can I clean up this mess?"

"Wait 'til this evening in case we need to look this over again."

I was glad not to deal with it. I had too much work at the office, and I was still facing my meeting with Mark at noon.

At eleven I left the office and made a stop at the local deli. Maybe I could soften Mark up with an offering of food. Sandwiches, potato salad, and cookies were packed in a cooler bag, and my last-ditch plan to help Liz was whirling in my brain as I arrived at the courthouse.

I was sent directly back to Mark's office when I checked in. I tapped on his closed door and walked in. Mark came around his desk and took my arm. He led me over to the sitting area and pointed to his sofa. I opted for the straight chair next to the sofa.

"I brought lunch. I thought maybe I was using up your

lunch hour." I began to spread the contents of the deli bag on the coffee table in front of the sofa.

"That was very thoughtful of you. This looks like the picnics we used to have by the lake on the campus. Remember?"

"Sure." I grabbed a sandwich and took a bite, but for once I wasn't hungry.

"Mary, so many times I've wished we could go back and do everything over. I have missed you." Mark covered my hand with his. I dropped the sandwich.

"Look, I'm sorry if you got the wrong impression about my visit to your office. We can't go back in time. We're both different people now."

"I know you cared about me, Mary, and I know I hurt you when I left, but I didn't have a choice. I missed you and I still do."

"I'm going to say this one time. Yes, I cared about you, and yes, you hurt me, but it was all for the best. You had to do your baseball thing. I had to do my law school thing. I still want to be your friend. Can't we be friends and forget the past?"

"I guess so. Is it true that you have a boyfriend? I saw your brother William last week He said you were seeing some rich Cuban builder."

"He's half Cuban, and we are together. I am really happy, and I know you'll meet someone great. Are we friends?"

"Yeah, we're okay, but why are you here?"

"I have a giant favor to ask. I need your help, but everything I'm going to tell you is in strictest confidence. Can you promise?"

"I don't know. What's this about?"

"I have to know that you won't discuss this with anyone. It's about a client."

"Well, now my curiosity is kicking in. Okay, I can keep a secret."

"Judge Liz Maxwell is being investigated by Jason Jones's office. He thinks she's involved in fixing some drug cases. I know she's innocent, but someone is using her to dismiss cases on her docket. The informant in the Jack Carillo case was murdered after she ordered his deposition to be taken, so that just added to Jason's suspicion."

"Maybe she is involved. This sounds very serious. Why are you coming to me?"

I took a deep breath. "I want you to create a fake case file, a drug case, and file it in Liz's former criminal division. Liz was moved to family court while the investigation is ongoing, so this whole charade will be even more difficult. Once the case is filed, I want you to call Liz's bailiff, and tell her to come and pick up the file, that the file is confidential and needs to be kept in Liz's chambers."

"Mary, this is a nutty scheme. You and I could both get in deep shit by doing such a deal. I could lose my job and you could lose your law license. And how do I explain to the bailiff why a confidential file should be kept in the chambers of a judge who isn't even presiding in criminal court? And what do you expect to happen? Are you trying to catch your client in a criminal act?"

"Of course not. I know Liz isn't involved. It's her bailiff, Gladys, that I expect to catch, along with her import-export husband. I think Gladys will send a dismissal order to your office as soon as she's had time to discuss the case with her husband."

"And how does the bailiff accomplish this order without Judge Maxwell seeing it?"

"Believe it or not, Liz has a signature stamp that Gladys is allowed to use. She says Judge Ackley told her to get a signature stamp. Do you know if other judges use signature stamps?"

"No, I didn't know that. I wonder if any of our clerks use

those stamps for judicial orders. This could open up a whole bunch of problems. But Jason will have a stroke if this thing backfires and we've used fake filings that appear to have come from his office. Only the prosecutor can file criminal charges. Maybe this will make everything worse for your client."

"Come on, Mark, think about it. You'll be doing a public service. Getting rid of a bad apple in the court system. You have to run for election again, and the bar might even give you an award."

The suggestion of an award to a former athlete used to receiving yearly trophies turned on a light in Mark's eyes. I watched him turn to the credenza behind his desk where his Rookie of the Year picture and plaque looked back at him. What could sound better to a former jock who has to run for office every four years than a brand-new award.

"Where do we start? How do we create this file?" Mark asked.

"We need the charging document. You know, it's an information, not an indictment, because it's filed by the state attorney. You know what they look like. And we need a discovery packet. I'll do the writing. We'll identify the defendant as a Colombian citizen. That should send up a flag for Gladys to go running to her husband. We can include the name of the murdered informant and Jack Carillo."

"I'm not following you. Who are they and what do they have to do with this?"

"The informant was murdered after Liz set up his deposition, and Carillo was murdered after he agreed to identify who else was involved in the drug ring. If they're both involved in our made-up case, Gladys and her husband will make their move to end the case. That is, if my theory about them is correct. The dismissal order will come back to your office. Then you and I will go in to see Jason with Liz on Monday."

"Oh, no, I'll help you with the file. I'll get it delivered to the bailiff, but I'm not going to go with you to see Jason. Next thing you know, he'll arrest me. My messenger will deliver the file to the bailiff. I don't want her coming to pick it up. That would really look strange."

"Okay, okay, do it your way and you don't have to go with me to see Jason. Let's just get started making up the file. Pull out the charging document from another file so we can trace some of the signatures and get the language right."

"Now you've got us facing forgery charges too. You really owe me. Let me know if you ever get rid of the Cuban guy you're dating."

"Half Cuban," I said, as Mark planted a very friendly kiss on my lips.

CHAPTER THIRTY-EIGHT

I left Mark's office with that great feeling you get when you're waiting for a special gift. Like the night before Christmas when you're sure you're getting a new bike. I was sure that I was about to catch a drug dealer and free Liz from disaster; well, almost sure.

Catherine had a list of messages waiting for me. The first was from my brother Jonathan. Jonathan was the oldest of the three of us. He was my hero from the time I took my first steps. William was two years younger than Jonathan and only seventeen months older than me. William was the typical middle child, always trying to keep up with Jonathan, and always vying for attention that was being usurped by me, the baby.

I looked through the other messages. There was one from Liz. "Just checking in" was the message. I'm sure Catherine had listened to her nervous chatter and boiled down the real message.

The third message was from a male who refused to leave his name. He said he would keep calling, but would only speak to me. Catherine's note said he spoke in a whisper and sounded paranoid or crazy. I get a lot of calls from strange people who want to sue the government for putting radio waves in their brains. One caller wanted to sue NASA because "they had spirited him into outer space and allowed aliens to give him a medical exam." I threw away the message from the whisperer.

The fourth message was from the assistant to Ambassador Francis Miller. "We want to assure you that the ambassador is in communication with the State Department about Luis Corona, but we have no new information." I wondered if Francis Miller ever spoke to anyone directly other than the president.

I returned Jonathan's call first. He was still my hero.

"I just called to tell you great job on your press conference. That was a very good *Herald* article."

"Yeah, the reporter is just an intern. I guess he was thrilled to get on the front page of the local section," I said.

"Mother and Dad probably won't tell you, but they were really proud of you. They think you've been very brave defending someone so unpopular."

"I don't feel brave, just angry that Luis has all but disappeared after his arrest. Why won't our parents tell me that they're proud of me? That makes me angry."

"They've got this thing about women getting married and nurturing kids. I guess they think if they reveal that they like what you're doing, that'll just encourage you to put off a family life. You should try to talk to them, not to me. Not to change the subject, how is the new BlackBerry working out?"

"Yes, you are changing the subject and you know it. I'm actually getting to like the calendar part of the BlackBerry. It does help to keep my schedule straight, which Catherine likes. But I had a strange threatening phone call right after you guys gave me the phone. No one even knew the number yet. Where did you buy it?"

"I didn't. William bought it. It was really his idea. He just added my name and told me he was having it delivered to you at the office as a surprise. What kind of threatening call? Maybe it was a wrong number."

"Don't worry about it. I'll call William."

I hung up and dialed William. He was in a client meeting, so I told his secretary to check his calendar and see if he could meet me for a drink after work. After a short wait, she came back on the line. "I interrupted him and he said to meet him at the bar at the Hyatt at five thirty. He's going to a dinner meeting down there tonight."

I punched in 5:30, Hyatt in the BlackBerry just as Catherine buzzed me.

"That guy, the whisperer is on the line. I can hardly hear him. He says he's got to speak to you."

"Okay, just what I need, another psycho," I said as I pushed the button for the front phone line. "Mary Katz here. How can I help you?"

"Ms. Katz. I have some information I think you're looking for."

"Can you speak up a little? I can hardly hear you. I didn't catch your name." I realized I was talking louder to encourage him.

"I can't give you my name. I need to see you in person. It's about Luis."

"When are you free to come to my office?"

"I can't come to your office. It's too risky. We need to meet somewhere where no one will recognize me."

"I'd rather you'd come to my office. How do I know I'm not walking into a dangerous situation."

"You just have to trust me. Please, I want to help Luis."

"Well, I'm going to be at the Hyatt Hotel downtown this evening. Can you meet me in the parking garage by the elevator to the hotel?"

"I could get there by seven."

"How will I recognize you?"

"I'll recognize you. I saw you on TV last night."

The line went dead. I realized my heart was pounding. I opened my desk drawer and pulled out Carlos's gun. I slid it into my purse. I'd have to make William watch me from a distance in the garage, just in case he had to identify my body.

CHAPTER THIRTY-NINE

The bar at the Hyatt was noisy with the chatter of lawyers on their way to dinner, and convention goers on their way to who-knows-what. Somehow, when people come to meetings in Miami, they keep remembering the tourist slogan, "Miami, The Rules Are Different Here." Ever since those TV ads, visitors test the theory by drinking too much, buying drugs, and/or having sexual hookups with just about anyone. Then they complain about the unsafe environment of the city. At least that's what they tell their spouses back home in Kansas or Ohio, when they call home for bail money.

I spotted William at a corner table holding onto the chair next to him so it wouldn't get grabbed off by anyone. We exchanged hugs, and I plunked down in the chair. Two daiquiris were on the table.

"To what do I owe this sudden yearning for a sibling get-together?" William asked.

"A couple of things. Carlos is being sued by some of the buyers of his new condo project because he hasn't met the closing date established in the contract. You're the dirt lawyer, so I was hoping you could look over the contract and tell me if I'm on the right track. There's an arbitration clause that says they can't go to court, just to arbitration."

"Sure, I'll be glad to look at it. These contracts can be

tricky, so he may not be out of court entirely. The whole family really likes Carlos."

"Even Dad?"

"Dad will never like anyone who steals his baby girl, but he recognizes how happy you two are together."

"Sure, when we're not arguing. I really want to talk to you about something else. Please don't think I'm not grateful for your gift of the BlackBerry. I'm starting to get very mellow with it, but I need to know where you bought it."

"Is it broken?"

"No, it's just that the day after I got it, before I even had a chance to use it, I got a nasty phone call. I didn't think anyone even knew the number. I wouldn't think much about it, but it seems to be part of some other threats I've been receiving."

"I got it at that electronic shop on Flagler Street right by the courthouse. I was thinking about how you needed it after I saw all those scraps of paper in your purse the last time we were at Mother and Dad's. Someone in my office said they had some great bargains at that shop, so I went there. I guess they mainly do exports, but they do sell to the locals. The owner waited on me. He was very knowledgeable. When he heard what you'd be using it for, he went to a lot of trouble finding just the right model and features."

"What was the owner's name?"

"Let's see. I still have his card in my wallet. The shop is EXPORTS 'R' US, and the owner is Guillermo 'Billy' Martinez," William said as he passed the card over for me to see. "See it says 'everything electronic.' I should have remembered the owner's name. It's the same as mine, sort of."

I gulped and reached for my daiquiri which I downed in two swallows. Gladys's husband owned that shop.

"Did you give him my name?"

"Sure. He needed all your information. I filled out the forms for him. Name, occupation, home and office addresses. You know, for the billing and the warranty. Is anything wrong?"

"I'm not sure. Don't worry about it."

"Do you know this guy?"

"I'll tell you all about this when I finish with a case I have right now. Listen, you can do me a favor. I have to meet some guy who won't give me his name. He says he has information about Luis. You know, the Martins' friends' son from Argentina. The no-name guy is going to meet me in the parking garage. I'm a little uneasy. Could you just watch from a little distance, until I see what's up?"

"Mary, are you crazy? You can't go meeting strangers in a garage. Luis is the terrorist suspect, isn't he? Why did you agree to such a meeting?"

"I have to find Luis. This is our first good lead. Just stand there until I give you a signal to go away, or if he's a nut case, I'll just leave and run right over to you. It'll be fine."

"You're leaving yourself totally unprotected. You could be kidnapped."

"I'm not unprotected." I opened my purse so William could see Carlos's gun.

William slapped himself in the head, and I realized how much he looked like Dad.

CHAPTER FORTY

At five minutes to seven, I walked to the parking garage under the hotel. William walked a safe distance behind me. I was still stunned about Billy Martinez being the person who knew all about me. Gladys knew Liz had been coming to my office. Billy got a windfall opportunity to harass me when William walked into his store. I felt certain that all the threats were coming from Gladys and Billy, and not from anyone involved in Luis's arrest. I also felt certain that Gladys was the one who was setting up Liz.

I looked over at the garage elevator and saw a beefy older man looking around at the few passersby still in the garage. Rush hour was over and the evening crowd had already arrived so foot traffic had slowed. The man looked like a cop with his short hair and muscular build. I moved slowly toward the elevator.

The man smiled as I approached. "You're Mary Katz, right?"

"You're the man who phoned me?"

"Of course. Please, I'm not here to hurt you in any way. Look, here's my card."

I glanced down at the card, while still trying to keep my eye on Mr. No-Name. But here was his name, Sergeant Jim O'Malley, Federal Corrections Officer, South Florida Region.

"You're a prison guard." I breathed a sigh of relief and realized my hand holding the card was shaking.

"Yes, and my meeting you and giving you the info about Luis could cost me my job. I'm only a few years from full retirement. I'm gambling that you'll keep my name out of this."

"Does this mean Luis is still in Miami-Dade County?"

"He was as of three o'clock this afternoon."

"Where is he?"

"He's in the South Dade Detention Facility in an isolation cell."

I glanced over at William who had started toward us. I signaled him by shaking my head. He frowned and retreated around a corner, but I had the feeling he was still waiting for shots to ring out.

"How do I know this isn't some trick just to keep me from locating Luis?" I asked.

"Well, you don't. You just have to trust me, I guess. Look, I'm the only officer on the day shift who is allowed access to Luis. There is one other officer who has the three to eleven shift. During the night, no one is allowed into the isolation area. Every day the feds question the kid for hours. He's not allowed to shower or exercise. I feel sorry for the kid. He's a mess. Spends most of his time, when they aren't hassling him, in his cell crying. When no one's around, he and I talk — mostly about his family and how sick he feels."

"Do you speak Spanish?"

"Sure. We all had to take conversation classes, so I can talk to him, and he knows a lot of English when he's not too nervous to remember it."

"What made you decide to risk so much to contact me?"

"I saw the press conference on TV. Rumors are that they're trying to decide where to move Luis. A few days ago the rumor was that they were going to send him to Egypt for further interrogation. That usually means torture. Then yesterday the lieutenant told me that they were waiting for transport to Guantanamo, which could be in the next couple of days. That's why I had to contact you. It don't seem right to me."

"Sergeant O'Malley, you've done a wonderful thing. I will never tell anyone where I got this information, not even Luis's parents. I just pray that I'm not too late. Just remember, if you ever need legal help, it's yours for free."

"Geez, I hope I never have to take you up on that."

O'Malley looked around and then walked away. I stood staring at his card as William popped up beside me. I noticed that he was perspiring heavily.

CHAPTER FORTY-ONE

I rushed back to the office and drafted an emergency motion for a restraining order to keep Luis from being moved from the local detention facility. I still hadn't received any answer to my petition for habeas corpus, not even notification as to which judge it had been assigned.

I closed up the office and proceeded back downtown to the night depository for filing emergency federal motions. I was exhausted, hungry, and I noticed I had ripped another pair of panty hose. I fervently wished that the courts would finally convert to electronic filing. Then I could have filed my motion right from my home computer while wearing shorts and flip-flops instead of shredded panty hose.

By the time I pulled into my driveway, all I could think of was food and bed. Instead I was greeted by a police car parked in the swale in front of my house. Now what?

I stepped out of the car and saw that Detective Avery was getting out of the police car.

"Hello, Detective, what are you doing here?"

"I hope I haven't caught you at a bad time," he said.

"They're all bad times lately. Why are you here?"

"I have some information I wanted to give you."

"That's what telephones and e-mails are for." I didn't even try to hide my annoyance.

"I felt this was important enough to warrant an in-person

visit, and to give you a warning. You know I haven't dropped
the investigation into your assault. You told me you'd keep in
touch if anything else occurred out of the ordinary, but you
didn't bother to let me know about the break-in at your
house. Fortunately, we cross reference cases and victims with
the suburban departments. Were you aware that a print was
lifted in your bathroom that matched that of a guy our narcotics unit has been watching?"

"No, I didn't know that. I haven't been home much lately.
I guess I haven't checked my home voice mail in a while."

"The print belongs to a Colombian national. Our narcotics boys are investigating a tie to the victim found murdered at the Floridian Inn. That's why I came all the way out
here tonight. You may be in danger. Maybe you need to ask
the Coral Gables Department to put a watch on your house."

"I thought that murder victim was from Argentina.
What's he got to do with a Colombian suspect?"

"Turns out he wasn't an Argentine at all. He was from
Colombia."

"I'm sorry I've been rude, Detective. Thank you for being
concerned and coming over here. Do you know the name of
the guy whose fingerprint was a match?"

"I probably shouldn't tell you. I'll get in trouble if I screw
up the narcotics unit's investigation."

"I'd really like to know. I'm involved in a high-level investigation, myself, involving an elected official. I can promise you, your name will never come up."

"Well, okay, his name is Billy Martinez."

I gulped but tried hard to keep my face expressionless. I
also realized I was keeping a lot of names confidential. I
needed another file in my BlackBerry.

CHAPTER FORTY-TWO

I walked into the house without remembering the mess in the bathroom. It was a shock to walk into the bathroom and read the threat on the mirror again. Between the lipstick letters I could see my own face, which looked unusually pale. My nerves were stretched thin.

I changed into shorts and flip-flops, packed a bag with clothes and makeup for work, grabbed Sam and his food, and headed for Carlos's house. It was after ten when I drove into the driveway in Pinecrest.

Two other cars were in the circle in front of the house. I decided to knock instead of just barging in. Carlos opened the door. He looked startled.

"Mary, are you okay?" he asked.

Sam didn't wait to be invited in. He rushed into the hallway and headed to the living room. I heard him bark his angry low bark.

"Carlos, get that animal out of here. He's scary," a high female voice said.

"I'm sorry to barge in without calling. I decided to take you up on your offer to stay here for a little while, but I can hear that you have company," I said, as I tried to back out of the door.

Carlos grabbed my overnight bag from my hand and

pulled me inside. He led me towards the living room. "You know Marielena and this is Margarita."

Margarita was Carlos's ex-wife. I recognized her name at once. I glanced at Marielena, the Martin family busybody, who was grinning like an alligator. Margarita was prettier than I had imagined in a little girl sort of way. She had a round face and pouty lips. A handkerchief was balled up in her fist, and she appeared to be crying. Sniveling might be a better way to describe the noises she was making.

"I can see you're in the middle of a discussion. I'll just take my things up to the bedroom," I said. I watched Marielena's smile fade. "Then I'll feed Sam."

"They were just leaving," Carlos said. He took Marielena's arm and helped her up from the sofa.

"What about what I asked you?" Margarita said as she followed them into the foyer.

"I'll let Marielena know tomorrow, but this is absolutely the last time," Carlos said.

I heard the heavy mahogany front door close. Carlos came back with Sam at his heel. "Mary, I'm sorry. Let's get you unpacked."

"No, this was a mistake, just coming over here. I'll go back home." I grabbed Sam's collar. Carlos pulled me to him and held on to me. I couldn't move. I really didn't want to move.

"I want to tell you why they were here. Margarita keeps running up credit card bills and getting herself in a jam. Marielena and Margarita became friends when we were married. She brought Margarita over here to ask me to bail her out again."

"Again? You mean this has happened before?"

"Several times. I made the mistake of giving her a large sum of money in order to get her to divorce me. She keeps turning up like a bad peso."

"I think you mean penny. Doesn't she have a job?"

"She worked for Pablo Guerra's art gallery for a while. But she was so unreliable that he fired her."

"Why doesn't her family help her? Or Marielena?"

"Her family really can't help her. They have four other kids and they barely make ends meet. I suggested that Marielena loan her some money, but she claims that she barely gets by on her alimony. She's been divorced for years and soaks her ex real good. I guess that's her advice to Margarita too."

"Well, Carlos, put a stop to it; that is, unless you want her around."

"Of course I don't."

"Then get rid of her once and for all. I'm beat. I just want to sleep. I'll take the guest room." I stomped up the stairs.

CHAPTER FORTY-THREE

I actually managed to sleep until six the next morning when Sam woke me. He was pawing my arm.

I showered, fed Sam, and walked him. The neighborhood was peaceful and smelled of night blooming jasmine. The first light streaked the sky with a pink glow, a sign that it might not be raining today.

Carlos was in the kitchen when I returned. The smell of strong coffee filled the air. I sat down at the breakfast bar and gratefully took the mug of coffee that Carlos handed me.

"I am so sorry about last night," Carlos said. "I wanted you to stay here with me. I know you're having a tough time at work, and I wanted to make a quiet, safe place for you. Instead you got Marielena and her garbage. Margarita means nothing to me. She was like a bad dream in my life. I just hope you understand that."

"You're right about work being tough right now," I said.

"My business isn't going well either. I know how much your career means to you, because I feel the same way about mine. See, we do have things in common."

"Carlos, I can't worry about our relationship right now. I have to get to the office. Today is going to be important to Luis and to another important case. That's all I can think about now. If I can get through today, maybe we can have the weekend together. I'll come back here this evening. My house is still a mess from the break-in, and now I know who's harassing me and why."

Carlos put his arms around me. "Don't worry about anything. Just come home safe. I'll get someone over to your house to clean it up."

Reluctantly, I pulled away and got ready for a fearful Friday.

CHAPTER FORTY-FOUR

"You look terrible. Are you sick?" Catherine asked as I sprinted into the office.

"Thanks. What a confidence booster. No, I'm not sick. At least, not yet."

"Well, good, because the clerk's office at the federal court just called. Judge Martin Hammel will hear your emergency motion at nine thirty this morning. What emergency motion?"

"The one I wrote and filed last night after I met the whisperer downtown. I now know where Luis is. You can read the motion on my computer."

"That's great news. I can't believe the whisperer turned out to be a real informant. Which judge is Hammel? His name isn't familiar."

He's a senior judge, still handling half a caseload. He must be well into his seventies, but he's a great judge. He believes in the balance of power and he won't be pleased with the government ignoring the constitution. I'll grab Luis's file and get going."

"What do you want me to work on?" Catherine asked.

"Call General Consul Marquez and ask him to meet me in Judge Hammel's courtroom. Oh, and call Louisa Perez. She's the interpreter I use. Ask her to stand by in case I can see Luis this afternoon," I said. I was almost out the door when Catherine called out.

"Mary, what about Liz's case? You told me to have her here at noon today? I called her yesterday. Don't you remember?"

"Oh, I almost forgot. Double-check that she'll be here by noon. I've got to brief her about the fake drug case. And find out the name of that attorney who's suing Carlos. I can't even remember it. See if I can see him Monday afternoon."

"Don't take any new cases for a few days," Catherine said, as I slammed the office door.

Judge Hammel was already on the bench when I raced into his courtroom. He was in the old federal building that had once been the downtown Miami post office. It was built before air-conditioning, which means there are windows that beam natural daylight into the courtrooms. In the center of the building is an open courtyard with Spanish-style tiles. I always feel like I'm part of a movie set when I come to this courthouse, like *Twelve Angry Men* or *To Kill a Mockingbird*, except that I wouldn't have been in the movie. Women didn't practice law in those days.

"Welcome, Ms. Katz. We are here on your emergency motion to block the federal government from removing your client from this jurisdiction. I have also been assigned your petition for habeas corpus review. I can't address the petition this morning because the government hasn't been notified of that hearing," Judge Hammel said in his still-strong baritone voice.

"Thank you, Your Honor, for hearing me so quickly. I did file a copy of this morning's motion in the U.S. Attorney's night depository box last night."

A youngish looking man stood by the plaintiff's table. He looked uncomfortable. Probably hoping he wasn't putting his job in jeopardy. "Yes, Your Honor, Francisco Alito, assistant U.S. attorney for the government. Judge, I was sent over to cover this at the request of our Washington office, but only our Washington office is handling this matter. And they aren't present."

"Well, Mr. Alito, aren't you government lawyers fungible? Sort of like dollar bills. One's as good as another. You'll do for this hearing. Now, Ms. Katz, suppose you give me some background in this matter, and try to relax. If you clutch that piece of paper any tighter, it'll probably disintegrate." The judge smiled.

I looked down and realized the papers I was about to hand the judge were wrinkled and sweaty. "Judge Hammel, I'm passing to your clerk several cases that I believe show that Luis Corona is being falsely imprisoned. Luis Corona arrived in this country from Argentina three weeks ago. He has been held in secret since two days after his arrival. He has never been afforded a hearing to set conditions of release. He was entitled to that within the first twenty-four hours of his arrest. Further, he's never been charged with a crime and has no idea of the reason he is incarcerated. If this were the state system, he would be entitled to release on his own recognizance for the state's failure to file charges against him or to inform him of the reason for his arrest."

Francisco Alito was on his feet objecting. "Judge Hammel, this is a high-security matter. It shouldn't be discussed in open court. May we come sidebar?"

"Not right now, counsel. I want to hear the rest of Ms. Katz's argument. Please, don't interrupt." Judge Hammel turned back to me. I had piqued his curiosity.

"Thank you, Your Honor. Luis's parents, Consul General

Philippe Marquez of the Argentine consulate in Miami, and I have all been trying to locate Luis for the past weeks. I saw him for only minutes at the Dade County Jail before he was spirited away by the Secret Service or Homeland Security. I now have reason to believe that he is being held in isolation at the Federal Detention Center in South Dade. I also believe that he is about to be transferred to the Middle East or to Guantanamo for interrogation while still not being charged with any crime. I am asking the court to issue a temporary restraining order to stop this transfer so that I may interview him and argue my habeas corpus petition."

I turned to return to my seat when I saw Mr. Marquez. He was seated in the front row. Just behind him were Luis's parents. I returned to the lectern.

"Judge, I would like to point out that Mr. and Mrs. Corona and Consul Marquez are in the courtroom."

"All right, Ms. Katz. Thank you. Now Mr. Alito, what does the government have to say about this?"

"Well, Judge, as I said, this is a high-security matter," Alito said. "I must ask again for a sidebar."

Judge Hammel motioned us forward. "Mr. Alito, what is this about?"

"Judge, I'm in a peculiar position. Our local office is not privy to matters where there may be terrorist activity. Only Washington can make these decisions. I was told by my boss to appear here. He was directed by Homeland Security to have this hearing covered and to ask the court not to interfere in this matter."

"Interfere?" Judge Hammel's voice shook with anger. "Sir, I am not interfering. I am doing my job. If the day has come when the judicial branch has been supplanted by an agency of the White House, then we all better realize that our constitution is meaningless. But I don't believe that day has

come, so listen carefully. I am not letting Mr. Corona walk
out of jail. I am just placing a judicial hold on his being moved
from this county. This order will be in place until we have a
full hearing on Ms. Katz's petition. If Washington thought
this man was such a threat, why didn't they ask for a continuance of this emergency motion? It's obvious they knew of
the hearing since they asked your office to cover it. Now
everyone step back."

We returned to our places at the lectern. Judge Hammel
poured a glass of water from the carafe on the bench. I could
see that he was perspiring. I wondered if his health was ques-
tionable. It was rumored that he had suffered a slight stroke
a year ago. What if he wasn't around to hear my petition?

"Your Honor, will you be setting a date for the next hearing? May I request a date as soon as possible? My client is in
isolation and has been under interrogation for many days," I
said.

"Madam Clerk, I believe I was keeping next Wednesday
open. Is that correct?"

The clerk turned to the judge. "Yes, Judge, but that's the
day you have doctors appointments."

"Well, cancel those appointments. The hearing on petition for habeas corpus will convene at nine thirty on Wednesday morning. That gives the government plenty of time to
book a flight and be prepared for this hearing. My order restraining the government from moving Mr. Corona from
Dade County remains in effect until the end of that hearing.
Is this clear to both parties? And Mr. Alito, I don't mean to
kill the messenger, but if the government tries to spirit the
defendant — well, he's not a defendant — he hasn't ever been
charged. If you try to spirit Mr. Corona out of this country, I
will personally see that appropriate sanctions will be enacted.
It won't be pretty."

"Your Honor, I don't mean to press my luck, but may I also have an order allowing me access to my client immediately? I intend to see him at once for a full interview, which I have been unable to have, and I will need an order to transport him to court for the hearing on Wednesday," I said.

"I will make all that a part of my order." The judge motioned to his law clerk. Please, prepare the order for my signature before Ms. Katz leaves the building."

I rushed back to the Coronas and Mr. Marquez. We all shook hands and Maria hugged me.

CHAPTER FORTY-FIVE

I left the happy Argentines outside the courthouse after promising that I would see Luis that afternoon. I realized that Liz
was coming to the office at noon, so I needed to get back immediately, explain everything about the concocted case that
would lead to her bailiff, and still take the long ride to the detention center to see Luis. I promised Carlos that we would
spend the weekend together at his house, but with Friday
evening traffic, I'd be lucky to make it back there for a late
dinner. Catherine was right. I sure couldn't take any new cases
unless I was prepared to give up eating, sleeping, and sex.

I pulled into the office parking lot at eleven thirty and
saw that Liz's car was already there. I came through the back
door and buzzed Catherine to come into my office.

"All good news about Luis," I said as I showed her the
order.

"That's great, Mary. Guess who called while you were in
court? Well, you'll never guess. Ambassador Miller, himself,
not his assistant. He apologized for being so busy, and then
he said that he was unable to find out anything about Luis's
whereabouts."

"You didn't tell him anything, did you?" I asked.

"No, of course not. I just thanked him and said you'd
return his call when you had time."

"It's clear that he's in the pocket of the administration.

He must like his job a lot. I guess fear of losing it is more important than standing up for the constitution. I just wish he wasn't so buddy-buddy with Carlos's dad. How long has Liz been here? She's way early for our appointment."

"She got here about ten minutes ago. I explained that you were in court, but would be here by noon."

"How's she holding up?"

"That's the strange thing. She's sitting out there smiling like the Mona Lisa. She was even humming to herself a while ago. Maybe she's cracking up. Should I bring her in?"

"Yeah, let's get this over with, so I can get out of here and go see Luis. Let the interpreter know to meet me here at one. I anticipate a fight with the prison, even with Judge Hammel's order allowing me access."

Liz came bouncing into the office. She looked incredible. Color had returned to her face. She was dressed impeccably in a bright red suit. She looked ten years younger.

She took the chair across from me, smoothed down her skirt and leaned forward.

"Mary, I have something wonderful to tell you."

CHAPTER FORTY-SIX

Liz's Story Revisited

Liz had an uneasy feeling when Catherine called her to set another appointment with Mary for the next day at noon.

"What's this about?" she asked Catherine.

"I really don't know. Just that Mary's been working on your case and needs you to be here tomorrow." Catherine was elusive and evasive.

The courthouses were gossiping about the murder of Jack Carillo. Everyone seemed to know that his case had been in her criminal division. Liz dodged the questions from curious colleagues about her knowledge of Jack and possible suspects.

She jumped when her cell phone rang. Her heart did a flip when she heard Joe's voice. The craving to be with him grew as he spoke.

"Hey, honey, what are you doing in family court? When were you going to let me know that you moved? I came by your chambers early this morning and found grumpy old Judge Parsons. I felt pretty foolish," Joe said.

"Oh, Joe, everything is falling apart. I can't even discuss this with you."

"So it's not my imagination. You've been avoiding me. Have I done something wrong?"

"It's not about you at all. It's my own problem," Liz said. She felt tears welling up again. Her life seemed like one long crying jag.

"Liz, you have to tell me what's wrong. I have to see you. Lunch today. I'm not taking no for an answer. Meet me at your apartment. I'll bring lunch. We need to talk."

He clicked off.

The UDC calendar (uncontested divorce calendar) dragged on through the morning. Uncontested divorces often turned out to have unforeseen problems. They were supposed to be routine and quick: make sure the opposing spouse had been properly served, establish the residency of over six months through a witness furnished by the petitioner, take some simple testimony, and sign the order. This morning's calendar was extensive. Most of the litigants were unrepresented by counsel. More than usual needed the services of an interpreter. One woman had to redo her paperwork because she had forgotten that this was her fourth divorce, not her third. One woman was clearly pregnant, but had failed to have the father present to either establish or deny paternity.

Liz looked out at the sea of faces waiting expectantly to untie their marriages. Most were young and all of them looked unhappy. What a view of American so-called family values. She wanted to run out of the courtroom and into her own problems, but she knew better. She continued to grind out one divorce after another, barely hearing her own words spoken by rote as her mind wandered to Joe. Could he be using her in some way to help his clients? Maybe that's why Mary wanted to meet with her and why Joe was insistent on lunch today.

By the time Liz drove into the garage of her condo building, it was twelve thirty. She was thirty minutes late. Maybe Joe hadn't even bothered to wait.

As she slipped her key into her door, Joe opened it and pulled her inside. He held her close and kissed her. Then he pulled her into the dining room. She buried her head in his shoulder and held onto him as if she were drowning.

"Look, your lunch is served, Your Sexy Honor," he said laughing. "I stopped at Scotty's Market and picked up a feast."

Liz looked at her dining room table laden with food and wine. It looked like a celebration or a picture out of *Better Homes and Gardens*. She turned away from the food. She felt nauseous thinking about how she could tell Joe about the investigation. She had to confront this, even if Mary had warned her not to discuss it with anyone.

"I need to talk to you, but I don't know how to begin," Liz said.

"What's wrong, baby? Is Judge Marconi after you? He's such a putz. Well, I need to talk to you too. That's why I was looking for you this morning. Shall I go first?" He looked eager and excited.

"You can go first as long as it isn't bad news of any kind," she said.

"I'm hoping you'll think it's good news." He took her hand. "Janey and I have officially split. She and her mother left for the Dominican this morning, where she is going to obtain our divorce. I'll be able to ask you to marry me, and if you say yes, we can be married by the end of the month. Oh, please, say yes."

Liz looked into Joe's eyes. He looked like a young boy.

"Oh my God, you want us to get married?"

"What? This is a surprise? What do you think we've been

doing for months? I love you. Liz. Just tell me you feel the same."

Liz began to laugh. She had listened to one disgusting divorce after another all morning. Now she was hearing about one that had her heart soaring. "Of course I love you," she said.

"Okay, then. Let's plan a wedding. Oh, I forgot, what did you want to tell me?"

"Later," Liz said. She led Joe past the laden table and into her bedroom. Screw the state's investigation. She was never going to be alone again.

I couldn't imagine what Liz was about to tell me. Whatever it was, she was a different person.

"This is still confidential. Janey and Joe have split and he's asked me to marry him. I still can't believe it."

I tried to look pleased, but an unpleasant thought was forming in my lawyer's brain. What if Joe had been using Liz to fix cases and now he was marrying her to keep her from testifying against him. Spousal immunity jumped out at me like a line in a law school exam. But everything that happened in her case had occurred before any marriage occurred so it couldn't be protected testimony.

I realized that I hadn't responded to Liz's news. She was staring at me while I played legal theory in my head. "This is great news. Congratulations. You are positively glowing. I hate to spoil your mood, but we do need to talk about the investigation."

"Yes, of course, I didn't mean to take up your time. It's just that I am so happy that I hate to start thinking about the investigation again."

"Oh, Liz, you're not taking up my time. I'm happy that you have good news to share."

"Have you uncovered some new evidence? Will it make this thing go away?" Liz looked at me expectantly.

"Not exactly yet. I'm in the process of smoking out the people responsible for your problem. I have asked Mark Epstein for some help."

"Mark Epstein? The clerk of our courts? You mean he knows the state thinks I'm a drug dealer?"

"Liz, just listen, please. Mark is an old friend. Actually, he's an old boyfriend. His assistance will prove to be invaluable. He and I have manufactured a drug case, a file that will look like a new case filed by the state. It has references to the murdered informant and Jack Carillo. It looks completely authentic."

"Mary, have you taken leave of your senses? Are you trying to get us both disbarred? How can this help? I can't be a party to this."

"Why can't you listen to me? I thought judges always listened and then made up their minds. I'm putting myself on the line to help you. If you don't want my help, that's okay. I'll give you your file and you can find another lawyer." I stood up and began shoving papers into the file. "Take this out to Catherine. She'll make copies for my own file, which, by law, I need to keep."

I pushed the file across the desk. Liz looked at the file and then at me.

"Are you firing me as a client?" Liz asked

"I guess so. I can't help a client who refuses to listen."

Liz pushed the file back across the desk. "I'm sorry. I will listen to your whole presentation before I say another word."

"It's not a presentation. This isn't moot court in law school. This is an attempt to save your judgeship and your career. Now here's what's going to happen in the next few days, and by the way, Mark Epstein is putting his job on the line, too, all for you.

"On Monday, the clerk's messenger will come to your chambers with the file. He will hand it to Gladys and tell her it's been assigned specially to you because it relates back to the Carillo case. This shouldn't arouse any suspicion because normally cases are filed before the judge who has other related cases instead of being blind-filed.

"I feel certain that as soon as Gladys has a chance to show this to her husband, she will use your signature stamp to sign an order of dismissal. The messenger that delivers the file will tell her that only the judge and her staff should be allowed to handle the file, and if it needs to be returned to the clerk for any reason it should be delivered by hand, so no one else has access to it. I expect Gladys to return the file herself with the order of dismissal."

"What about Jason, the state attorney? Is he going along with this?" Liz asked.

"He will when I inform him of what I've put into operation."

"And when is that going to be?"

"Sometime on Monday. That's time enough to alert him so that Gladys can be arrested on the spot."

"What makes you so sure that she is the link to this whole mess?"

"Well, a lot of strange things have been happening to me since I started to work on your case. My brothers purchased a BlackBerry for me, and before I could even give the phone number to anyone, I got a threatening call. I found out that my brother purchased it from Billy Martinez's store. Billy waited on him and took down all the information on me, including my office and home address. My home was broken into and a threatening message left on my bathroom mirror. Billy Martinez left a fingerprint in my bathroom. Billy is also under investigation by the Miami P.D. narcotics unit. I learned that in strict confidence. I was attacked in the parking lot of my office a few weeks ago. I haven't any proof of who did that, but it probably was Billy or one of his guys. Didn't Gladys know that you were coming to see me?"

"Yes, I guess she did. She placed a call to you for me. She might have overheard my conversation. I'm so sorry you've been going through such scary things all because of me."

"I'm reasonably sure that Gladys knows that things are closing in on her and Billy. That's probably why Jack Carillo was killed. He was about to name names to the state in order to get a deal for himself. If I hadn't done something quickly, Billy might have split for Colombia, and maybe even taken Gladys with him. Once Gladys sees this fake file with more links to the Carillo case, I think she'll act quickly to keep anyone else from making a deal with the state, like the fake defendant in the case."

"What if this doesn't work?"

"Then there'll be an extra file sitting around in your chambers and Gladys will inform you that you have a new criminal case."

"I'm sorry I jumped all over you before. Just one more thing. I'd like to be present when and if Gladys is arrested. I want to confront her myself."

"I'll see what I can do. I need you to report to me if you see the file come in or if Gladys does anything suspicious. Keep your eyes open on Monday. Now you better get out of here and start planning a wedding."

CHAPTER FORTY-SEVEN

I watched Liz drive out of the parking lot. I put my head down on my desk. The next thing I knew Catherine was shaking me.

"Mary, wake up. Are you okay? The interpreter is here ready to go with you to interview Luis. I brought you a sandwich. You need to take the time to eat something."

Catherine pushed half a sub under my nose. It looked great: turkey, ham, cheese, tomatoes. I rubbed my eyes and took a couple of bites. There just wasn't time to worry about lunch. I shoved the sandwich back in its wrapper. Louisa Perez was seated next to Catherine's desk.

"Louisa, you look great."

"Well, you look like hell, Mary. You're downright skinny."

"You can never be too thin. Isn't that what they say? I'm so glad you're free to go with me this afternoon. I've told Catherine what a great interpreter you are. I think you're a frustrated actress. You always capture the spirit of what you're interpreting, even the tone of voice, the hand gestures, and the facial expressions."

"Yeah, well, you're right. I do community theater in little Havana. The *abuelas* love me, especially when I sing the old Spanish songs. Catherine is going to bring her boys one Sunday. Maybe you'll join them."

"Absolutley. As soon as I get my life back. I'm frazzled," I said.

The ride down to the federal detention center was actually pleasant. We turned off the highway and down a city street that became a two-lane road. Soon we were in the Redland, the last farming community in the county. We passed tree farms, nurseries, and fallow tomato and corn fields, waiting for replanting in the fall. Here and there the fields are interrupted by housing developments. The small houses appear planted in rows just like the tomatoes.

"Louisa, have you ever been down here to pick strawberries in the u'pick'em fields?" I asked.

"Of course, my whole family always did that every winter, and how about those great strawberry milkshakes? The little stand is still down here somewhere."

We turned again down a narrow road. If you didn't know the prison was there, you'd never notice it. It's set back from the narrow road on a dirt lane of its own that is easy to miss. I missed it while Louisa and I gabbed. I made a U-turn, almost putting us in a ditch, found the turn, and soon we were at the high electric gates. I spoke to the guard through a voice box announcing attorney visit. He was in a tower overlooking the gates that he activated from his lookout.

The gates swung back revealing a vast parking lot where we left the car. After a walk of about two blocks, we arrived at the main gated entrance. Families of inmates were lined up outside the gate. It was a regular visiting day, which meant a long wait to finally get to our interview. The sun was hot and the humidity was so heavy, it felt like you could touch it and taste it. Kids of all sizes played, running and laughing with the anticipation of seeing their fathers. Wives and girlfriends tried to corral them. Some of the women were dressed in revealing halters and tight pants. Elderly parents fanned themselves. One woman who had been leaning on a cane suddenly collapsed. "It's the heat," her husband yelled. "Someone help us."

I pushed my way to the front and told the guard I was here for an attorney visit. "An old woman just fainted. Please, can someone help her?" I asked.

The guard spoke into his walky-talky. "Send someone from the health center. We've got another crash case," he said. Then he opened the gate to let Louisa and me in.

I showed our IDs to the guard. "You'll go out in the next group," he said. "Get in that line." He gestured to a line forming on the lawn across from the administration building. Only a certain number of visitors are allowed into the buildings at one time, so the wait began for a group to be led out, so our group could advance to step two in the procedure.

Fifteen minutes later we were crossing the lawn and were admitted to the main building. We filled out paperwork: name, bar number, name of inmate, address, phone number, picture ID. We surrendered our briefcases, purses, and cell phones. The only items we are allowed to take into the visiting room are a pad and pen. The warden decided that lawyers could sneak letters out of the prison in their briefcases, so briefcases were put on the forbidden list.

Next we passed through metal detectors after removing jewelry, shoes, and belts. "They do a better job here than at the airport," Louisa said.

After redressing, we waited again for guards to walk us to the visitors' center.

"So far, so good," I whispered to Louisa. Just then a loud-speaker called "Attorney Mary Katz. Report back to the main desk."

The fat guard who had taken our paperwork was behind the desk. He smelled of cigar smoke and cheap aftershave.

"You're here to see Luis Corona?" he asked.

"That's correct. A copy of Judge Hammel's order is attached to my application," I answered.

"Well, I don't show that he's here. He's not on the roster."

"He's here. He's in an isolation cell. Look again," I said.

"He's not in the computer. You're holding up your group from being moved to the visitor building."

"He's definitely here. Judge Hammel's chambers called here and told the warden's office that I was to be allowed to see Luis." I could feel my face turning hot. Louisa put her hand on my arm. I guess she thought I was going to punch the guard.

"I said he's not on the roster," the guard said.

"Call the warden's office, now," I said. If I have to call the judge, he won't be pleased, to say the least."

"You'll have to wait a few minutes," he said.

"No, call there now. If we wait, it'll be time for another head count and we'll not be able to see my client. If you won't call, hand me the phone. I'll call."

"Be my guest." He dialed a number and handed me the phone.

A pleasant-sounding woman answered. I gave her my name and told her I was not being allowed to see Luis. I reminded her that the judge had alerted them that I would be here this afternoon. She asked to speak to the guard. I handed him the phone. He listened, then said, "Okay, okay." He replaced the receiver and said, "Come on, I'll walk you over there myself. No one tells me nothing. I didn't know we had guys who weren't on the roster."

We walked down a long sidewalk to the visitors' room. "The warden is sending for him. Just have a seat in one of the attorney rooms." The guard went over to the desk on a high platform where three officers stood watch over the families and inmates. He talked to one of the officers, pointed to us, and left.

Louisa and I settled into one of the attorney cubicles.
There was a table with four chairs around it. Glass windows
covered three sides of the cubicle. I knew we would be locked
in with Luis and would have to push a buzzer when we were
finished. If you are claustrophobic, this is not the profession
for you.

Some of my past clients have told me that the little rooms
are bugged and the feds listen to all conversations between
lawyers and their clients. I don't know if it's true or not, but
there aren't any other choices, so we keep our voices low and
try not to say more than is necessary. Since this was my only
chance to hear Luis's story, I would have to forget caution and
ferret out every fact.

A few minutes later, Luis was escorted in. He wore leg
irons and the guard attached him to a chair. For a minute, I
wasn't sure it was Luis. He looked very different than at our
first meeting in the Dade County Jail. For one thing, his head
had been shaved. He had several bruises on his face. He was
wearing a clean shirt and pants, but he looked like he had
lost a lot of weight.

"Luis? Do you remember me? I'm Mary, the lawyer who
came to see you a few weeks ago. I'm Carlos's friend. This is
Louisa. She's an interpreter, here to help you talk to me."
Louisa was speaking in rapid Spanish.

"Mary, thank God. I thought I'd never see anyone to help
me." Louisa translated swiftly. Luis began to cry.

"Luis, I'm going to get you out of here. We have a hearing before a federal judge next Wednesday. You have to hold
on until then. We've all been looking for you. Your parents
are here in Miami. I always knew we'd find you. Right now, I
need you to tell me anything you can about the time when
you were arrested, anything that the officers said to you, anything that happened on the plane. Even if it seems unimpor-

tant, it may end up being helpful to me. Now start by telling me about the plane trip."

Luis wiped his eyes on his sleeve. "My parents, they came to Miami? When can I see them? Are they very angry with me? They always think I'm going to screw things up. I guess they're right."

"I'll try to arrange for them to be able to visit, but I can't promise. No, they aren't angry. They're scared and worried about you. They love you very much. Now, please, try to tell me everything you can remember about the plane trip. We don't have a lot of time before the next head count, and that's when they'll make Louisa and me leave."

"Okay, sorry. I'll try to remember how it all was. Everything was fine. I went through security and got on the plane. We took off on time. The guy in the seat next to me, that's where everything started to go wrong."

"What do you mean? Was he talking to you?"

"I asked if I could buy him a drink. He just wanted a coffee. I had a couple of drinks. It's a long flight. We got our dinner trays, and I got some wine. I was telling him about some places that were fun in Buenos Aires and asking him if he had been to any of them. Then we started talking about the War on Terror, or maybe that was before dinner. It's hard to remember."

"That's okay. You can think about the way it all happened between now and the hearing. Did the man speak Spanish? Was he Argentine or American?"

"He was American, but he spoke good Spanish. We got into an argument. I told him I thought the United States was, well I guess I said crazy, to get in a war in Iraq, and that there would always be terrorists somewhere. He kept asking me stuff about what I knew about the war, and he got really angry when

I said that intelligent people in my country were laughing at the U.S. and its president. I didn't know he was one of them."

"What do you mean, one of who?" I asked.

"One of the guys that arrested me. But he looked just like any other passenger. I didn't know he was a policeman."

"You mean he was a sky marshal? You picked a fight with a marshal?"

"Well, it started to be a fight. I guess I pushed my fist in his chest once, but it wasn't like a fistfight."

"Okay, what else happened?"

"The flight lady came by and told me to stop shouting, so I quit talking to the guy. I guess I fell asleep for a while. When I woke up, I was just dying for a cigarette. I went into the bathroom, and I lit a cigarette. That's when everything went crazy."

"Didn't you see the signs that said 'no smoking'?"

"I guess so, but it's a long flight from B.A., so I lit up. Then an alarm went off. Someone pounded on the bathroom door. I opened it a crack, and that's when they dragged me out of there and threw me in the aisle."

"Who dragged you out?"

"I guess it was the pilot or the copilot and the guy in the seat next to me. They took me into the back of the plane and sat me on the floor, in the place where the attendants prepare the food."

"You mean the galley."

"I guess. Then they all started asking me questions. What was my purpose in flying to Miami? How was I able to start a fire? I tried to tell them that I wasn't starting a fire. I was just trying to have a smoke."

"How did you light the cigarette?"

"I had my lighter in my pocket."

"Didn't they take that away from you when you went through security?"

"No. It's in the shape of a pen. I put it in the basket with my other stuff, but they gave it all back, so I thought it was okay. I showed it to the people when they asked me how I started a fire. They took it then. Then they brought my carry-on bag from my seat and started going through it."

"Did they ask your permission to look through it?"

"No, they just tore it open and started pawing through it."

"Okay. What did they look at?"

"They pulled out the pouches with the money for my new shop. They asked what it was for and I explained that my parents gave it to me to purchase the boutique. I gave them the name of the woman who we were buying it from, but they didn't write it down or anything."

"What else was in there?"

"My shaving kit with my electric razor and some little bottles of shampoo and cologne. In the bottom of the kit they pulled out my little mustache scissors."

"How did you get the scissors through security?"

"What do you mean? I didn't do anything special. Do you think I was sneaking my mustache trimmer onto the plane?"

"No, calm down, Luis. I'm on your side. It's just that I had nail clippers taken away from me on a flight last year. It was in my purse, and security made a big fuss over removing it. I just wondered why they didn't take your scissors."

"I don't know. I took my little bottles out in the plastic bag, like I was told to package them. Everything else went through the x-ray machine, including my shoes and my belt."

"Okay, was there anything else the marshal pulled out of your bag?"

"Of course. They pulled out everything that was in there. Some magazines. chewing gum, and the white powder."

"What white powder?"

"Our housekeeper, Juanita, she put it there. She follows Santeria and the powder is to keep someone safe. She buys it at the bodega. I think it is just flour or talcum powder, but she wastes her money on it."

"What did the feds say when they found the powder?"

"I tried to tell them what it was. They said, yeah, yeah. We've heard it all before. They said they would send it to their lab. Oh, and they took my paper that said I had a reservation at the hotel. They passed that around and nodded their heads at each other. Then they handcuffed me to the back of the plane. I kept asking, what did I do? And they just laughed. The guy that I thought was a passenger, he said don't ask us stupid questions. I thought it'd all be cleared up when we got to Miami, but they took me off the plane in the handcuffs and took me to jail. I couldn't believe it." Luis was fighting back tears.

"Tell me about what they've been asking you since you've been here."

"They showed me the magazines over and over; the ones from my suitcase. They asked me why I was reading them."

"What were these magazines?"

"Just sort of graphics, maybe you call them comics. They were like funny stuff about a gang that blew up some places in Japan. Sort of like my video games. But the policemen here, they are cruel, hitting me across the face and blowing smoke in my face but they wouldn't let me have a cigarette, and they took away my clothes and played loud music in the middle of the night, and every day the questions, over and over, and Mary — I can't tell you some of these things they did." Luis buried his head in his hands.

At that moment, a guard appeared at the door. He unlocked it and walked in.

"I didn't buzz the buzzer. I'm not through yet," I said.

"Yes, you are. We're going into lockdown, and all visitors must leave right now," the guard said. He smirked at the three of us.

"I'm sorry, Luis. When we go to court Wednesday, I want you to tell the judge just what you've told me. Louisa and I will be there to help you. This will all be over very soon." I gathered up my notes and we were escorted through the maze of buildings and walkways once again. When we got to the first checkpoint, I stopped and asked the officer to connect me once again with the warden's office. I made it abundantly clear that no one was to question Luis any more without my being present.

"He is represented by counsel. A further violation of Luis's rights will most definitely trigger very expensive litigation and bring publicity that I don't think you or any of the government entities involved in this false arrest will want to deal with."

Louisa and I made our way to my car. It felt like being put in an oven when we got in. The leather seats burned through my pantsuit and panty hose. Sweat ran down my legs, but it was still a relief to be out of the prison. Even hot air is better than the air of oppression we had just left. I beamed up the air conditioner to high and hightailed it out of the parking lot.

I glanced at Louisa, who had her eyes closed and her head back against the headrest. I knew she was exhausted from interpreting without let up.

"Mary, I've never heard anything quite like what Luis just told us," Louisa said. "I've heard a lot of things in courtrooms and jail cells, but this is outrageous. How could they hold him without charges and with such flimsy evidence of terrorism? Why didn't they just charge him with disobeying airline rules or disorderly conduct?"

"I don't have a clue. I guess it's part of our current 'injustice system,'" I said.

We fidgeted through the stop-and-go traffic of Friday afternoon as the rain began once again. I turned on a CD of Anita Baker. Singing the blues seemed appropriate for our mood and the weather.

CHAPTER FORTY-EIGHT

By the time I delivered Louisa to her car at the office and turned south to Carlos's house, it was raining bullet-sized drops. The wind had picked up and lightning filled the sky. It was after seven when I dashed up the driveway and into the house.

The house was dark, and the only greeting I got was from Sam who had been sleeping in the kitchen. I poured his food and watched him scarf down his dinner. I couldn't imagine where Carlos was. I checked my cells but the only message was from my mother wondering why I wasn't answering my home voice mails.

The message light was blinking on the kitchen phone so I checked there thinking Carlos had left me a message.

A woman's voice came on. "Carlos, dear, I've had a call from an attorney who says there is a lawsuit against you by your condo buyers. He wanted me to join in the lawsuit, but I told him probably not since you gave me such a good price. So what's up with this? Call me."

I recognized the voice after a minute. It was Margarita. Carlos let her have a condo in his building? I shivered from the air conditioner or the rain or the thought that Carlos might be getting back with his ex-wife.

I was still sitting staring at the phone when I heard Carlos coming in from the garage.

"Mary, thank goodness you're here. You've heard the news?"

"What news?" I asked. I felt like slapping him and walking out.

"The hurricane, of course."

"What hurricane? This is only June. It's too early for a hurricane."

"Hurricane Alice. Haven't you heard the news today? I can see that you haven't. Hurricane season runs from June to December. They can come anytime. You oughta know that." Carlos hurried over to the TV on the kitchen counter and switched it on.

The familiar voice of Max Mayfield filled the kitchen. Ugly pictures of a great green blob with a red center flashed behind the Hurricane Center director. "We can't pinpoint where landfall will take place. At this time, the storm is lashing the outer rim of islands surrounding Hispanola. The outer bands are being felt in the Florida Keys. Winds are even picking up in the Greater Miami area. Landfall is predicted for Sunday or Monday, but this could be anywhere from the Southeast Florida coast to the Gulf Coast of Florida. We are advising residents of all of these areas to begin preparations now. This is already a category two storm."

Carlos lowered the volume. "I can't believe you didn't hear about this today. Where have you been? Hiding under a rock?"

"I've spent the last several hours locked in the federal prison with your cousin Luis or whatever he is to you, that's where." Then I did something I almost never do. I burst into tears.

Carlos rushed across the room and put his arms around me. "You're safe here. Please, don't cry. This house has impact glass windows and a generator. We'll be fine."

"It's just the last straw. I'm not crying just because of the storm. It's just everything; my clients, I can't relax for a minute. I was looking forward to this weekend, and then —"

"Look you're just exhausted. Mama brought groceries and water over this afternoon after she went to the store. There's nothing you need to do except take it easy."

I felt what I really needed to do was get a couple of my old clients out of prison to murder Margarita. I couldn't bring myself to tell Carlos about the phone call or how it made me feel. I forced myself to stop the waterworks.

"I can't just rest. I'm worried about my parents and my brothers' families and Catherine and my little house. I've got to go put up my hurricane shutters. The last one of these storms that I lived through was Andrew. I was in law school. We had just started classes when we had to evacuate the campus. My parents were living in Miami Beach, and they had to board up their house. They were supposed to leave. They didn't. I was living in an apartment in Kendall with my brother William. We thought we were in a safe place. My folks ended up being fine, but William and I spent the night in the hallway. All the windows blew out and everything we had in that apartment was either water soaked or blown away. There was no electricity for weeks. It was hell."

"Mary, we don't even know if this storm will come near us. We have time to close up your house. My parents' house was badly damaged, too, during Andrew, but we all survived. We went through many bottles of wine that night. So let's start a hurricane party right now." Carlos went over to the wine rack and pulled out a bottle, uncorked it, and put a full glass in my hand.

By the time I finished the second glass, I felt in control again. Carlos went outside to check on the patio furniture. I took advantage of his absence and erased Margarita's message from the voice mail. Then I felt much better.

CHAPTER FORTY-NINE

The next morning I was jarred awake by sunlight streaming in the windows. I listened for wind and heard none. The clock said nine fifteen. Carlos was still sleeping so I crept out of bed and went downstairs. I opened the French doors to the pool. It was a gorgeous perfect day.

I returned to the kitchen and snapped on the TV. The Weather Channel showed the green blob with the red center moving up through the Atlantic Ocean, far from Miami. The announcer was saying, "It's a woman's prerogative to change her mind. Alice changed her mind and took a northeastern turn. The storm is now riding through the sea, well away from land."

Suddenly the weekend looked like a winner. With sunshine and a refrigerator full of food, I called Catherine and suggested that she and Marco come over for a swim and a barbecue.

"Only if I can bring the boys," she said.

They arrived at three that afternoon. The boys brought an array of pool toys including a water polo ball. We all made fools of ourselves, diving and fighting in the pool. The adults were more raucous than the kids. Sam, who hates water if it's not in his bowl, circled the pool barking. All of us were relieving the fear that comes with the words "hurricane warning."

Later we sat on the patio in our wet suits as the sun set. The aroma from the grill filled the air. It was the first time in weeks that Carlos and I had been able to have time together that wasn't fraught with arguing or worrying about his work or mine.

When the first mosquitoes and the last daylight arrived together, we gathered up dishes and glasses and headed inside.

As Catherine began packing the car to leave, she grabbed my arm. "Mary, I'm so sorry. I forgot to give you an important message that came late Friday. Your motion to dismiss in Carlos's case is set for Monday afternoon at one thirty in front of Judge Preston. Are you prepared for it, or should I try to get it continued?"

Carlos walked up behind us. "Hell, no, I want to get this thing over with. Okay, Mary?"

"Sure, I can handle it," I said. I was plunged back into the world of worry. I tried to smile as I recalled that Liz's case might be coming to a head and I might have to get to Jason at the same time I was due in court for Carlos. Hurricane Alice was gone, but there was a storm brewing in my addled brain.

CHAPTER FIFTY

I opened the office at seven on Monday morning and finished two hours of solid work before the phone lines began to ring at nine. Catherine hurried into my office. "Liz is on the front line. She sounds excited or nervous or something."

"Hi, Liz, what's up?" I listened hard but heard only a thin whisper.

"Liz, I can't hear you? Are you okay?"

"I'm on my cell phone in my chambers."

I was able to make out that much. "Liz, take the phone into the bathroom, so you can talk above a whisper," I said.

A minute later I heard a door close and then Liz's voice, still low but audible. "I got in early and kept my eyes open like you said. A minute ago, I saw a messenger leaving the reception area. When I went out there, Gladys was putting something in her desk drawer. I asked her who just walked out of the office. She said it was a messenger with some files for court tomorrow, so I said, why are you putting them in your desk? She looked a little nervous. Then she said something about needing to look at them later to see if they were really on the calendar. I'm sure it must be the fake file. I'll try to get into her desk later, after hours."

"Okay, Liz, this sounds like we're in business. Keep me posted."

As soon as I hung up, Catherine was on the intercom. "Pick up the second line. It's Mark Epstein."

"Mark, is there news?"

"The die is cast, or whatever that saying is. My messenger took the file to you know where a little while ago. He called and reported that it was given to the bailiff. Please keep me in the loop on this stunt of yours. I hope you know that I've gone way out for you. I just hope I still have a job tomorrow."

"You will, Mark. If not, you can work for me. I'm beginning to need a full-time investigator. I'll bet with your famous name and face, you could get information from anyone." I tried to sound confident and upbeat.

"That job sounds like fun. It's a deal. You're as big a nut as ever. Glad you didn't become one of those stodgy lawyers."

As I hung up, I wondered whether Mark would actually expect me to hire him. Maybe this wasn't one of my dumbest ideas.

Carlos picked me up at one on the dot and we sped off to the civil courthouse downtown. He was dressed like a male model under the heading "Well-Attired Fashion Statement who Means Business": dark blue pinstriped suit, light blue button-down shirt, and a red tie. I had the urge to tell him to pull over and have a quicky in the backseat. The Ecalade was certainly large enough. I decided I'd better keep my mind on the hearing.

Judge Danforth Preston epitomizes old-school Miami, pronounced "Miama." His family came to Miami in 1927 right after the Big Hurricane. His great grandfather worked for the railroad but became wealthy developing what was once swampland. Danforth Preston had been a managing partner of one of the leading Florida commercial law firms. When it merged with a New York firm, he sought a judgeship and was promptly appointed by the governor. He is known as the best friend of big business. He's never met a Chamber of Commerce that he didn't want to join.

Normally, this wasn't the kind of judge I wanted to expose my clients to, but in this instance Carlos represented big business, or at least a big condo project. Some of the plaintiffs were also business types who had purchased their condos in order to flip them. Flipping has been very big lately. Speculators buy pricey condos at preconstruction prices and then resell them at a profit before the closing occurs.

However, most of the buyers in Carlos's new building were people who actually intended to use the condos, some as second or third homes. These were mainly foreign buyers from the Middle East oil countries or from Europe. A few of the buyers planned to make their condo their actual residence.

We entered the courtroom at one twenty-five. The judge was not yet on the bench, but the courtroom was almost full. Three surprises awaited me. The first person I spotted was J. C. Martin, Carlos's father.

"J.C., what a nice surprise," I said. What are you doing here? Did you have other business in the courthouse?"

"No, Mary, I wasn't doing anything and I know Carlos is concerned about the hearing so I thought I'd stop by and give you both some moral support." He stood up and gave Carlos a hug and gave me a big kiss.

Carlos and I moved to the defense table and I unpacked my files. "Does your dad have an interest in your condo project, or is he just bored?" I asked.

"Neither. He has a board meeting downtown later, so he's probably just killing time."

"I'm never quite sure what J.C. does," I said.

"Well, he has several investments in businesses, and he serves as a director of a bank and some other stuff, and he owns part of the cattle ranches in Argentina with my brother. He keeps busy."

The second surprise occurred a moment later when I turned to survey the people seated throughout the audience portion of the room. I assumed they were some of the condo buyers who were suing Carlos. I dropped my file when I saw who was in the back row. It was Margarita. Had she become one of the plaintiffs? I wished I hadn't erased her phone message.

"Carlos, why is Margarita here?" I asked.

"I don't know, but I'll find out." Carlos looked angry as he strode up the aisle.

I watched him gesturing as he spoke to Margarita, and recognized these were his "You've got to be kidding" gestures. He marched back to our table looking like John McEnroe after confronting a tennis umpire.

"It seems Margarita claims she left me a message asking about this lawsuit, and when she didn't hear from me she decided to attend the hearing out of curiosity," Carlos said. "She's such a liar."

"She wasn't lying. I got the message and I erased it," I said.

Carlos looked shocked. "You didn't tell me?"

"Well, we're even. You didn't tell me that Margarita was moving into your expensive condo tower. Don't I recall you saying that you had been considering taking one of the condos there yourself? How cozy."

We glared at each other. Then I turned away from Carlos and realized the attorney for the buyers had taken a seat at the plaintiffs' table. That was my third surprise. It was Franklin Fieldstone, my ex-fiancé and ex-boss. He had turned into Frank the stalker a few months back. I hadn't seen him since I had him ruffed up by Marco and his Pit Bulls.

Frank saw me staring at him. He got up and made his way

over to our table. I glanced at Carlos, who was already in a dark mood.

I stood up and took a couple of steps away from Carlos. "Hello, Frank. What are you doing at this hearing?"

Carlos must have heard the name Frank. He was beside me in a second with his hand on my shoulder.

"Carlos, this is Franklin Fieldstone. I don't believe you two have met," I said.

"Oh, we did meet, very briefly, only Carlos wasn't wearing his pants at the time, and as I remember, you weren't clothed either, Mary." Frank said.

"Why are you here?" I repeated. "Did you instigate this lawsuit against Carlos?"

"Don't be ridiculous. One of the attorneys in my office filed this suit. He was unavailable and asked me to cover this hearing for him."

"Oh, I'll bet. You just can't let go and accept that I don't want to see you or litigate against you or —"

Carlos squeezed my shoulder so hard that it hurt. "You are a coward and a bully, stalking Mary all of last February, even breaking into her house. I'd like to finish this fight here and now," Carlos said. I saw his fist come up. Just then the bailiff called the court to order, and the judge came through the door hidden in the paneling behind the bench and took his seat. I pushed Carlos back to our table and everyone was seated. "I think you dislocated my shoulder," I hissed at Carlos as I opened my file and tried to remember what I wanted to argue to the court.

"All right, folks. We're here on *Buyers at One Ocean Avenue vs. Carlos Martin Enterprises*. As I understand this case, the plaintiffs are seeking to be recognized as a class in their lawsuit. They are suing Mr. Martin, the builder of a condo tower, claiming that they have been injured due to Mr.

Martin's failure to meet the closing dates and dates for the occupancy of the properties. Am I correct, so far?" Judge Preston asked.

"Yes, Your Honor." Frank nodded his head like a bobble-head doll.

"Now, Mr. Martin has filed a motion to dismiss the lawsuit that we are to hear this afternoon," the judge said.

"Correct, Judge Preston," I said.

"All counsel identify themselves for the record," the judge continued. I see each side has brought their own court reporter. Isn't that a waste of money?"

"I am Franklin Fieldstone, managing partner of the Fieldstone Law Firm," Frank said. He made it sound like it was the Vatican. "I engaged my own reporter to be certain the record is absolutely correct."

"I am Mary Magruder Katz, of the Law Office of Mary Magruder Katz," I said. "I brought a court reporter because I couldn't get anyone from plaintiffs' firm to respond to my phone calls in which I tried to suggest that we split the cost of one reporter."

"I see," Judge Preston said. "Let's get on with this. May I have the plaintiffs stand, please, so I can get some idea of how many buyers are involved?"

I turned and saw eight people standing, including Margarita.

"Ms. Katz, it's your motion. Let me hear some brief argument." Judge Preston continued to look at the audience. Then I saw him smile. I turned as I made my way to the lectern, and saw J.C. smiling back at the judge

"Thank you, Your Honor. This will be very brief. You will see attached to the motion, a copy of the contract signed by each of the buyers at One Ocean Avenue. If you will turn to the third page, at letter K you will see a paragraph, which states that should any dispute arise between buyer and contractor/seller, the sole remedy shall be binding arbitration. Further, buyer waives any and all right to file a lawsuit regarding any disputes in any court of law or equity of state or federal jurisdiction.

"It's simple, Judge, the buyers have waived their right to litigate any dispute in any court. They are entitled to arbitrate their claims, and whatever the arbitrator decides is binding on all parties. Therefore, Mr. Martin asks this court to dismiss this wrongly filed lawsuit. If the buyers wish to pursue any misunderstanding with Mr. Martin, they should instruct their attorney to start the ball rolling for arbitration."

"Thank you, Ms. Katz. Do you have any counter argument, Mr. Fieldstone?"

"Yes, Judge." Frank walked up to the lectern. "Judge, there can be exceptions to the arbitration clause. If the seller knowingly misled the buyers by giving them a date for occupancy that he knew he could never meet, then the contract is null and void, and therefore the arbitration clause is gone with the rest of the contract."

"What do you mean I gave out a false date? Are you a builder? I don't lie to the people who buy into my buildings." Carlos was on his feet. His face looked like the red blob on the hurricane map.

I stood up and pushed Carlos back into his seat, no easy task since he's a big guy. Thank God I work out regularly at the gym. "Your Honor, my client apologizes for his outburst. He was shocked to hear his flawless reputation challenged in open court," I said. "The closing dates haven't even occurred yet, and they are different for each unit. The closings are staggered by floors, starting with the penthouse floors and then proceeding down. This covers a span of some three months, so even if this case could proceed, it couldn't be a class action. Each plaintiff would be impacted differently, and some might still be closing on their designated date.

"Each plaintiff would also have different damages. Some buyers weren't inconvenienced at all, because they were only going to occupy their units as a second home, a winter get-away. Winter is still months away. Others bought their units as an investment for resale. They would have to prove that they were denied making some profit. The few who bought their units to actually live in them would have to show that they had suffered losses by selling their previous home and having no place to live."

"Yes, I see your point, Ms. Katz. This case could never be a class action. The class is too diverse. Now what about the dates for the various closings? Mr. Fieldstone, are you aware that the actual date of the earliest closing has not even ar-rived yet?" the judge asked.

"The first closings are set for July fifteenth, but it's easy to see that this building will never be finished by that date," Frank said.

"Ms. Katz, when does your client think the first people can move into the building?"

"Let's ask him, Judge. He seems eager to talk." I gave Car-los the nastiest look I could muster. "Go ahead, Mr. Martin, stand up and answer Judge Preston," I said.

"Well, Judge, if we don't have any hurricanes, I can turn over the two penthouses by September. Those two have been sold unfinished with an allowance for the interior design. That's what those two buyers wanted. They are putting ex-tensive amenities into their units. The next floors will be ready in October and so on."

"Okay. Thank you Mr. Martin. First of all, I will dismiss this lawsuit based on the arbitration clause in the contract. Second, arbitration is not yet ripe because the contracted closing dates have not yet occurred. Ms. Katz, as the prevailing party, you will draft the final order, and I will entertain a motion for attorney's fees and costs. Mr. Fieldstone, you should have realized that an arbitration clause precluded your filing a lawsuit."

"Your Honor, my client wishes to be perfectly fair to the buyers. If any of these litigants can show us that they have been forced to rent housing because their units aren't ready in a timely manner, Mr. Martin will return their deposits. Of course, they'll never be able to duplicate the ocean views at One Ocean Avenue. Even lesser views are going for higher prices than their preconstruction price," I said. Carlos looked shocked.

"That's more than fair," Judge Preston said. "Anyone here who wants to take Mr. Martin up on his offer?"

No hands shot in the air. A few people shook their heads. Most were headed for the door. Frank hurried after them.

I packed my papers in my briefcase. Carlos was smiling his heartbreaker smile at me. It made me forget that I was angry with him.

J.C. leaned across the railing that separates the well of the court from the onlookers. "Good job, Mary. Carlos always tells us how smart you are. This was fun to watch."

Carlos shook hands with J.C. "Want to join us for a late lunch, Dad?"

"No thanks, son. I'm going back to Danforth's chambers. I happen to know he keeps a bottle of twelve-year-old Scotch in his desk drawer," J.C. said.

Now I knew why J.C. was sitting in the front row. I still think I'd have won this one anyway.

CHAPTER FIFTY-ONE

By the time Carlos dropped me back at the office, it was four o'clock. Catherine handed me a message from my mother. "Call me. It's important, but if your dad answers, just hang up and call back later."

"Did she say why the coded phone call?" I asked Catherine.

"No. I asked her if everything was okay. She said it was, but she sounded distracted."

I dialed her at once. She wouldn't have to go through such mumbo-jumbo, if she'd keep her cell phone on. She and Dad each have separate cell phone accounts. But she insists the cell is only for emergencies on the road. If she could donate her extra monthly minutes to me, I could talk for a year and never run out.

She answered at once. "Hello, Mary. Thank goodness you called while Dad is out working on the pool."

"Why is he working on it? Where's the pool guy?"

"He was here yesterday, but you know your dad. He thinks only he can keep everything running smoothly."

"What's with the secret code? Are we going to establish a secret handshake too?"

"Everything is not a joke, Mary. I am very worried. Dad is not himself. He's short of breath even after a short walk. Two of his golf partners have called me to say that they are worried about him. I've made two appointments with a cardiologist, and he's broken both of them."

"Maybe it's just his age catching up with him. What do you want me to do?"

"Can you talk to him? He listens to you. You have to get him to go to the doctor."

"Mother, he hasn't listened to me about anything in years. Jonathan and I tried to get him to redo his will last year. He's had the same one since I was in high school. He wouldn't listen at all."

"You're wrong. He went to Manny Goldsmith the next week and revised everything. He just didn't want to admit that he listened to you. Will you try?"

"Okay, I will, just as soon as I get through the next couple of weeks with these two cases. I'm up to my eyeballs in work right now."

"Don't wait too long. I'm very worried." She clicked off.

Before I could add my dad's health to my worry list, Catherine was buzzing me. "Liz is on the private line. She says she needs you right away."

"Yes, Liz, what's happening?"

Her voice was edgy. "Gladys asked to leave early. She said she had a dental appointment. She walked out with a big paper bag tucked under her arm. I waited a few minutes. Then I went out to her desk. I asked Patricia whether she knew where the case files were for tomorrow that Gladys had put in her desk. Patricia said she didn't know what I was talking about. She said the clerk was pulling the files for tomorrow. She asked why Gladys would have them. I told her that I wondered too."

Liz took a breath and went on. "Then Patricia said that she thought Gladys was acting very jumpy lately. Well, I went all through her desk. There weren't any files there. I'm sure that she took the fake file home with her. This is all really happening, just like you said. What do we do now?'

"Now I have to call Jason and get over to see him first thing tomorrow," I said.

"I think I should come with you, Mary. He wants to talk to me, and it's time I confront him. Besides if I'm there with you, he won't lose his cool and chew you out. I still am a judge, and his attorneys will still have to get along with me in court."

"I appreciate the offer. Okay, I'll call and ask to see him as early as possible."

When I left the office at six p.m., I had updated Mark about the file. I had also made the appointment with Jason for eight a.m. He was only too happy to accommodate me when he heard Liz would be with me. He was probably lining up a battery of questions that would cover Liz's life from kindergarten on. When he learned what we were up to, it might be doomsday instead of Tuesday.

I really wanted to go home to my own house, but I knew that I could be in danger there now that things were coming to a head in Liz's case. What if Billy Martinez detected that the file Gladys was carrying to him was actually a fake? What if he felt that the cops were closing in on him? Detective Avery said he was under surveillance. I didn't want my house torched like Carillo's.

I reluctantly headed for Pinecrest and Carlos's "starter castle." I was more eager to see Sam than to tangle with Carlos tonight.

Carlos must have sensed my mood because I gave Sam a hug and Carlos a "hi, how ya doin'."

"Thanks for the sizzling greeting. I know you're pissed with me about Margarita and the condo. I'm pissed with her showing up as if she were going to sue me, after Marielena's daughter gave her a great deal on that condo," he said.

"Listen, Carlos, I'm not an innocent rookie. Your cousin, who you fired, couldn't have given anyone a sweetheart deal without your approval. You can keep giving Margarita whatever you want. It's your money. You don't seem to see that she's trying to reopen your relationship. If that's what you want, you need to let me know. I'm not in the market for a threesome."

I put Sam's leash on him and headed for the door.

"Where are you going?" Carlos shouted over the excited whines and barks of Sam. It sounded like Sam and Carlos were both barking.

"I'm going to walk my dog. If I could, I'd go back to my house right now, but I'm pretty sure the house is still in the danger zone, so for now, we're stuck in the same house for another night. That doesn't mean we have to hang out. You can go do whatever you want," I said.

Carlos sprinted out the door right behind me. "I'll go with you," he said.

We started up the street past the row of immaculate megamansions, looming behind wrought-iron gates. Each one was illuminated by dozens of outdoor lights, which if turned off, could probably solve the energy crisis.

"Listen to me. I divorced Margarita years ago. She's like an out-of-control child. My life was a mess while we were married. Why would I want to go back to such punishment?" Carlos asked. "I'm sorry you have to put up with my home for another night. I've been trying to be supportive of your schedule, your stress, and your sarcasm. It's wearing thin. Why can't you tell me what's going on with the break-in at your house? Why can't you trust me a little?"

"It's not a matter of trust. It's a matter of client confidentiality. It's not even about trust when it comes to your ex-wife. I just think you don't see the stuff she's trying to pull on you." I turned Sam around and headed back toward Carlos's house.

"So you think I'm stupid. Just a dumb construction guy, and you are the smart lawyer. I know all about Margarita. She's unstable and I don't want to be blamed for sending her over the edge. Maybe I am stupid because I just don't understand why you can't realize how hard I've fallen in love with you, so much that I'm putting up with your constant pushing me away from you." Carlos turned and walked away, leaving Sam and me watching his fading figure as twilight turned to the darkness of a cloud-filled night.

Some time later I heard the Corvette revving up in the driveway. I had begun to fix a sandwich for dinner, but I left it on the counter, opened a beer, and stretched out on the sofa in the den.

At least Carlos could have thanked me for winning his case.

CHAPTER FIFTY-TWO

Sam woke me at six. He was licking my face, which must have caused the dream I was having of being kissed by Carlos.

I fed Sam, put him in the backyard, and went to take a shower. Carlos was in bed, a half-filled glass of Scotch on the bedside table. He looked like he was out for the better part of the day. I hurried to get ready to meet Liz and go to Jason's office where I would become a hero for fingering a drug cartel or a goat for faking a drug case.

For once the state attorney's office was fairly quiet when we arrived fifteen minutes early for our meeting with Jason. A few secretaries were busy booting up their computers, and a few attorneys were drinking coffee and trading war stories. No receptionist was in sight manning the entrance to the executive offices so we took seats in the waiting room.

We stared at the elevator waiting for someone to emerge to announce us to Jason. Instead, I was shocked to see Mark Epstein approaching us.

"Mark, what are you doing here?" I asked.

"I got your message that you were meeting Jason to tell him about our concocted case," he said. "Good morning, Judge Maxwell. I didn't know that you'd be here."

"I thought you said there was no way you'd go with me to see Jason," I said.

"I thought about it and I couldn't let you take his anger

all alone. He can be a horse's ass. Anyway, we're in this together, so here I am," Mark said.

We all looked up as Jason stepped out of the elevator, coffee in hand, newspaper under one arm, and bulging file under the other; probably his inquisition file for questioning Liz.

"Good morning Judge Maxwell and Counsel. You are a bit early. I'll be ready for you as soon as I round up my court reporter and Fred Mercer, our public corruption unit head. Mark, did you want to see me before I go into this meeting?" Jason said

"I am part of this meeting." Mark stood and shook hands with Jason.

"Jason, hold on before you call your troops together. The three of us need to talk to you. It's important," I said.

Jason frowned. "I still need to have Fred present. Follow me back to the conference room. You can be comfortable there. Fred and I will join you in a moment."

We entered the room, which was sparsely furnished. A large scarred wood table that had seen better days filled the room. Surrounding it were plain unpadded wooden chairs. A bookcase containing the Southern Reporter case law volumes covered the back wall. Other than the telephone on the end of the table, there was nothing else in the room. It looked like a larger version of an interrogation room at a police station. Jason certainly kept his pledge to be frugal with the state's money.

"He needs Fred to be a witness," I said.

"Maybe he thinks we're going to attack him," Liz said.

You could smell the adrenaline pumping through the three of us.

Jason returned with Fred Mercer in tow. Fred looked around the table and without even saying hello, he leaned his hands on the table and shook his head. "I'd prefer not to proceed without a reporter here, and I'll have to have each of you sworn in. I think I should warn you that you could be charged with perjury, if we later find that you have lied under oath," Fred said.

"Jason, I've come here with Liz and Mark to tell you what we have done to resolve these accusations you've made against Liz. You need to hear this now. We aren't here as adversaries. We are trying to help you find the perpetrators in a courthouse drug scheme. If you don't want to listen, we'll leave. The rest of the community may be more interested in hearing us out." I stood up and moved toward the door.

"Sure, Ms. Katz, we're all aware of how much you enjoy press conferences," Fred said.

"Thank you, Fred. Have a seat," Jason said. "I will handle this. There's no need to address Ms. Katz in that tone."

"Thanks Jason." I drew a deep breath.

I gripped the table and began. "I have made a complete study of Liz's cases in her criminal division and of all of her staff. I came upon a troubling fact. Liz has a signature stamp that her bailiff uses when working on her correspondence. Liz tells me that the stamp was suggested by Judge Anne Ackley, the chief of the criminal division. The bailiff, Gladys Martinez, is supposed to use the stamp only to quickly process agreed orders sent in the mail by defense attorneys and the state. I pulled every file that has closed in the last six months in Liz's division. I found a number of orders dismissing drug cases. Liz had never seen those orders or those cases. The signature stamp was used on all of those orders."

"That's just Judge Maxwell's excuse," Fred interrupted.

"Please, Jason, let me continue. You can see the orders for yourself and see that they are stamped and not signed. Gladys married Billy Martinez a short while ago. Billy runs an import-export business. He's under investigation and surveillance by the Miami Police narcotics unit. Not only is he suspected of importing cocaine, he also sells electronics in his shop. Some of them, or all of them, may be stolen."

"And how would you know that?" Fred interrupted again.

"Am I on trial here?" I asked.

"Of course not," Jason said. He had begun to take notes as I spoke. "I want to hear all of this, Fred. You can excuse yourself if you're in a hurry."

Fred grimaced but kept his seat. Jason nodded at me.

"My brother happened to go into Billy's shop where he purchased a BlackBerry as a gift for me. Unfortunately, he gave Billy my address, home and office, and other information about me. After that, I received a threatening phone call on the BlackBerry. The number of the caller came back to a cell phone stolen at the airport.

"Then my house was broken into, and a threatening message was left on my bathroom mirror. The police matched a fingerprint to Billy Martinez. Of course, Gladys knew that Judge Maxwell had made phone calls to me. Martinez wanted me to keep my nose out of his plan to go on fixing the cases of his foot soldiers. He had the perfect setup. If anyone became suspicious, everything would point to Judge Maxwell. That's exactly what happened. Liz was the one being investigated. Billy wanted me to be scared away from helping Liz."

"I understand your suspicions, Mary, but this doesn't prove to me that your client isn't also involved," Jason said.

"Exactly. That's why I took further action. I asked Mark Epstein for help. We fashioned a case file that would trigger Gladys to act. Mark and I designed a fake drug file. We wrote up an information and police report that mentioned the confidential informant who was murdered and also referred to

Jimmy Carillo. The clerk's messenger delivered the file to Liz's chambers, and gave it to Gladys. She was told the file was to be maintained in their chambers, that it was highly sensitive and, if it needed to be sent back to the clerk, it was to be hand delivered to Mark Epstein's attention.

"The messenger went to Liz's chambers yesterday and placed the file in the hands of Gladys. He had Gladys sign for it. As we expected, Gladys never told Liz about the file. Liz saw Gladys place a file in her desk drawer. When Liz asked her what file she was putting in her drawer, Gladys told her they were files for Liz's next calendar. Liz looked all through Gladys's desk later that day and found, surprise, no files, but Gladys left the office early with a big paper bag in her hand."

"Wait a minute. You and Mark cooked up a file? Did you use the office of the state attorney as the charging body? Don't you know how much trouble you two are in? You can be charged with forgery. Mary, you can be looking at discipline by the bar, and Mark, you could lose your job," Jason said.

"Shall I call our police liaison to come in?" Fred asked. He was pulling his cell phone out of his pocket

"Mr. Jones, I've had enough of this." Liz was standing. She struggled to remain composed. "I have come here with my counsel in good faith. I have done nothing. This young man, Mr. Mercer, is trigger happy, and I won't forget his attitude. Mr. Mercer, you have the opportunity to be a hero and take credit for ridding the courthouse of some disgusting influences. But I will call a halt to this interview right now if we aren't shown some respect. Secondly, I want a pledge that my name stays out of this in the press and in the courthouse rumor mills. I have no doubts about you, Mr. Jones, but I want a pledge right now from Mr. Mercer."

Liz stared Fred down with her best judicial look. Her statement sounded like an official order.

"Judge Maxwell, you have my assurance that if our investigation finds that you have played no part in this drug scheme, your name will never be mentioned, and should anyone else in my employ disregard my promise to you, they will be looking for another job," Jason said. He looked directly at Fred.

Jason looked down at the notes that he had made. He drummed his fingers on the table. No one said a word. We all sat waiting for Jason to say something. Mark broke the silence.

"I was leery of this plan of Mary's at first, but now that the file has taken the route out of the courthouse in Gladys's hands, and now that we know her husband's background, I truly believe this was Mary's only way to clear Judge Maxwell's name," Mark said. He smiled at me, and I immediately felt a gut-wrenching wave of guilt. Did Mark really believe in my plan or was this his way of trying to renew our relationship? I looked over at him and realized that wouldn't be the worst thing to come out of this. He still had that cute Brad Pitt look along with the muscles of an athlete, visible even through his Calvin Klein shirt.

"Where is this file now?" Jason asked.

"It should be arriving in Mark's office sometime today. Gladys will have to get the clerk to stamp the original order and give her copies. If she showed it to Billy last night, he's probably searching for the defendant in the various Dade County jails to find out what he knows about the informant and Carillo, and waiting for Gladys to give him the dismissal order so he can spring the defendant," I said.

"What happens when Billy finds out that this defendant isn't in any of the jails, or that he doesn't actually exist?" Jason asked.

"Then I may be screwed," I answered.

"I'll give you the benefit of the doubt. Mark, alert me at once if Gladys arrives at the clerk's office with the dismissal order. You'll need to stall her so that I can have someone ready to arrest her right there," Jason said.

"That shouldn't be hard. Half the lawyers in this town think my office is inefficient. Today we actually will be. It can take a lot of time to get someone to stamp the original dismissal and make the copies." Mark looked like he was really beginning to enjoy this fake file caper.

"I need to know if you intend to file a bar complaint against me," I said. "I may need to hire a lawyer."

"Let's see how this plays out. The most important thing is to stop the corruption in our court system." Jason gathered his notes and his bulging file that he had never opened. "Mary, I'll show you and Judge Maxwell out through my back entrance. It wouldn't be wise to have anyone spot you leaving this meeting. I'll get in touch with the head of the police narcotics unit. I need to know how far their investigation of Billy has gone. No sense in their office and my office working separately. I'm sure there'll be plenty of glory to share. On the other hand, it's always good to have someone to share the blame."

CHAPTER FIFTY-THREE

Liz and I were both quiet on the way back to my office. As she got out of my car, she turned to me.

"I want to be there if they arrest Gladys. I want to confront her. I still can't believe she'd turn on me like this."

"I know how disappointed you are, but you see all kinds of people in court every day. We live in the kind of society where every person is looking out for himself. Just be glad that we pieced this together before you ended up in a cell next to someone who you sentenced," I said.

"You mean you pieced it together. I would never have suspected Gladys. Just promise that you'll call me the minute you hear anything."

I returned to my littered desk to work on Luis's habeas corpus hearing set for Wednesday morning. Then I saw Catherine's reminder note taped to my computer screen. "LUIS Hearing Tomorrow A.M." I couldn't believe I had so few hours left to get ready for the hearing.

I called Luis's parents and prepared Miguel to testify at the hearing. I checked in with Señor Marquez at the consulate. Catherine and I prepared witness files and case law. The day was speeding by.

At three o'clock, Catherine answered a call and handed me the phone. "It's Liz. She sounds addled, but that's how she always sounds lately."

"Mary, Gladys just came in and asked to leave early again. The same dentist excuse. I stalled her for a few minutes by sending her on an errand to the equipment room. I told her as soon as she sets up some TV screens in the courtroom she can leave. I told her we're starting a trial tomorrow and the lawyers are going to show some videos. I'm leaving now for Mark's office. Will you meet me there?"

"Yes, I'll call Jason and Mark and alert them. Don't let Gladys see you when you get there." I slammed down the phone. Catherine called Jason while I talked to Mark. I ran to the car and prayed for light traffic. I hardly noticed that it was raining again.

CHAPTER FIFTY-FOUR

I broke my old record for speeding, and parked in a parking place labeled "authorized personnel only." A ticket was the least of my worries. I had several others in my desk drawer; a business expense that's part of being a trial lawyer.

Liz was waiting in the lobby. We called Mark's cell phone. He gave us instructions to use the freight elevator. His secretary met us and took us into his private office through a back hallway.

Mark came in a minute later. "Gladys just got here. I told her to wait; that I had a second file with the same defendant to send back to Liz. She thinks I'm processing the order in the file she returned. Here it is."

Liz and I looked at an order of dismissal signed with Liz's signature stamp.

"Jason is on his way over. He has Sergeant Morris with him from narcotics. He's supposed to have an arrest warrant ready," Mark said. "I'm going back out and check on Gladys."

Jason and a plainclothes officer came in the back door of the office as Mark went out the front. Maybe plainclothes isn't an accurate description. Morris was dressed like a drug dealer; tattooed arms, silk print shirt open down to his midsection, and enough jewelry to put any movie star to shame. He was clearly working undercover. We were introduced to Sergeant Bennie Morris.

Mark returned a second later. "She was on her cell phone. I overheard her leaving a message. I guess it was for Billy. She said something didn't look right. She's warning him, and I'm afraid she's about to bolt."

"Bring her in here. Tell her she'll be more comfortable. We'll make the arrest right now," Jason said.

Mark hurried out again. Sergeant Morris shook his head. "She won't be able to warn Billy. He's already split. We thought we had tight surveillance on him, but there was a slipup while I was getting the warrants. He's gone. His store is closed. He could be halfway back to Colombia by now, but that's okay. We've got the open warrant on him. Sooner or later they all surface."

We sat in a semicircle around Mark's desk, our heads turning toward the door, waiting for Mark to return with Gladys. After what seemed like hours, but was just a minute or two, Mark came in the door. He had his hand on Gladys's shoulder steering her through the door.

"Really, you'll be more comfortable in here. It's no trouble at all," Mark said as he came through the door.

"I'd really rather wait outside," Gladys said. She tried to move from Mark's grip. Then she spotted us. "Judge Maxwell, what are you doing here?"

Sergeant Morris stood up. "Gladys Perez-Martinez?" he asked.

Gladys turned a terrible shade of white. She had the same look that one of my clients had when he identified the body of his dead business partner at the morgue.

"Why are you asking?" Gladys said. She turned back toward the door, but Mark's large frame blocked her.

"Please, place your hands behind your back. You are under arrest for falsifying official court documents and for conspiracy to traffic in cocaine," Sergeant Morris said. He withdrew handcuffs from his pants pocket. He gripped Gladys's arm and deftly pulled her other arm behind her as the metal cuffs snapped. He pulled a form from under his shirt and placed it on the table. "Please have a seat here while we go over your Miranda rights form. "If you understand each line as I read it to you, please initial it and then sign your full name on the bottom of the form."

"How am I supposed to sign it with my hands in these bracelets?" Gladys asked. I glanced at Liz and saw that she was trying to choke back tears.

"You can sign it later. Do you understand the form? Are you willing to talk to me without a lawyer present?" Morris asked.

"I just want to tell you that my husband is not involved in anything that you say I've done," Gladys said.

Oh, great, I thought. This bimbo is destroying her own case. Then I told my lawyer brain to shut up. Gladys isn't my client, and she had nearly destroyed Liz, who is my client.

"If you mean Billy Martinez, you can quit worrying about him. He's long gone. We can't find him this afternoon. He's cleaned out your bank accounts and split," Morris said.

"I don't believe you," Gladys said.

"Here, be my guest." Morris handed her his cell phone. "Call your bank. Call his store. See for yourself."

"I can't very well call without my hands," Gladys said. "And I need my checkbook from my purse."

"No problem. I'll pull the checkbook out of your purse. You tell me the number, and I'll dial it for you." Sergeant Morris picked up the purse and allowed Gladys to look in it while he held it. She pointed with her chin at a leather book. Morris opened it and she read out a phone number. Morris let her watch him dial the number. He held the phone to her ear.

"This is Gladys Perez-Martinez. My account number is 8326061B. Can you please tell me what my balance is? — What do you mean the account is closed? When? But that's a joint account. I didn't give permission to close it. — What letter? I never gave my husband any letter. — I see." Gladys turned away from the phone the sergeant had held up to her ear.

"Shall I dial Billy's store for you? You'll just get the voice mail."

"No, don't bother."

"Do you want to talk to me without a lawyer? Better face it. Billy is probably halfway to Colombia right now. If you decide to tell us everything you know about this drug enterprise, maybe Mr. Jimenez-Jones here, the state attorney, will cut you some slack. You work for a judge. You know you're looking at a thirty-year-minimum mandatory sentence for the amount of drugs that have been involved. That's a long time for a young girl like you," Morris said. He looked over at Jason.

"If you want to proffer what you would be able to testify to in court, depending on the information you give us, we may be able to ask a judge to greatly reduce any sentence you receive," Jason said. "It's up to you."

"What about Billy? Does he get a deal too?" Gladys asked.

"Are you kidding? He has absconded from the jurisdiction. If you ask me, you better look out for yourself. Billy has left you high and dry. He took all your money too, as far as we can tell," the sergeant said.

"Well, I still have my house. It's in my name. I can use it to post bail," Gladys said.

"I don't think you get it. You're in real trouble here. My office is preparing the paperwork now for a forfeiture action. We believe your house was purchased with the proceeds from criminal activity, so your house will soon belong to the state," Jason said.

Gladys's face crumbled. All of her tough façade was gone. "I need to think. Please, can I think about this?"

"We'll give you a few minutes, but that's it." Sergeant Morris stood up. "We'll have you moved to the interrogation room over in the state attorney's building. You can do your thinking there. Mark, can you let us out the back way?"

Liz stepped in front of Gladys. "Can I have a minute with Gladys before you move her?"

I put my hand on Liz's arm. "I need to stay with you Liz, as your attorney. I don't want you subjected to any more accusations."

"We'll give you a couple of minutes, but this is our prisoner so I can't leave the room. I'll step over to the end of the room while you talk." Sergeant Morris motioned to Jason and Mark who stepped into the back hallway. Morris stood by the door, his arms folded over his chest. In his undercover drug outfit, he looked like a character from The Sopranos.

Liz pulled her chair up close to Gladys. I stepped in front of Gladys just in case she attacked Liz. I don't know any great defensive moves, but at least I could look threatening.

"Gladys, I thought I was more than just your boss. I thought we were friends. How could you have set me up? Were you deliberately out to get me?" Liz stared directly at Gladys, forcing her to look Liz in the eye.

"Listen, I saw what you are, an old lonely workhorse. Billy saved me from that. I love him. I love the excitement he brought into my life. I just tolerated you, Judge High and Mighty." Gladys looked away from Liz and turned to me. "What are you looking at? Trying to grab a new client? Why don't you both get out of my face so I can get on with this shit."

Liz turned and walked over to Sergeant Morris. "Get her out of here before you have to arrest me for battery," she said.

"Gladys, you definitely can never be my client, but if you could, I'd advise you to give up what you know. Maybe you can make a deal to save your house," I said.

"When they hear what I've got to say, they'll probably give me the house and the Miss America crown. Come on, Detective, I guess I'm ready to play *Let's Make a Deal*."

Sergeant Morris took Gladys firmly by the elbow and they moved out the back entrance. Jason started to follow them. I ran over to Jason.

"Can I listen to her statement, Jason? After all Liz has been through, I'd like to be able to assure her that there are no more accusations for her to deal with. I know you'll be stationed outside the interrogation room in your building. Please, let me stay there with you," I said.

"Mary, you'll have to be sure that nothing she says leaks to the press until we finish this investigation. You couldn't represent anyone she gives up. It'd be a clear conflict of interest."

"I know that, Jason. I'm only doing this for Liz. I hope you'll be informing the chief judge that Liz has been cleared entirely in this matter."

"As soon as we hear what Gladys has to say. If Liz has no part in this, I'll call Judge Marconi first thing in the morning."

"Not soon enough. I want you to call him at home tonight."

CHAPTER FIFTY-FIVE

While Jason and I walked over to his offices, I pulled out my cell phone and called Catherine. I told her Gladys was in custody. I also told her to call Carlos and let him know that I was working on a case and wouldn't be at his house until late evening.

"And Catherine, try to get him not to be so angry with me. Let him know that I'll be able to tell him everything very soon. You're great at smoothing over ruffled feelings."

"I'll do what I can, but Carlos has a lot of feelings to unruffle."

Jason and I went directly to the secure area just outside of the interrogation room on the sixth floor. We could see Bennie Morris settling Gladys into a chair across the small table from the glass window. We could see her and hear her, but she was unaware that she could be surveilled. Bennie removed the handcuffs and cuffed her left arm to the chair. She was signing the rights form as we got comfortable.

Bennie came out of the room. "I'm waiting for a court reporter. I'm going to get her a Diet Coke. I don't know why she's worried about the calories. Wait'll she starts dining on the prison menu. Can I bring you guys anything?"

"Coffee," Jason and I said together. I needed it to keep my eyes open for the rest of the day and night. I still hadn't finished my work on Luis's hearing.

By the time Bennie returned with a cardboard tray of drinks, the court reporter had arrived. Bennie let her into the room. We watched her set up her machine. Bennie also turned on a tape recorder. There weren't going to be any slipups in this confession, no suppression motions because of alleged threats or abuse.

Bennie went through the usual Miranda warnings again. He asked Gladys if that was her signature on the bottom of the form. Then the real questions began.

Was she married to Billy Martinez? How long had she known him? How long had they been married? Where did they live? When was the first time she knew that Billy was involved in drugs and stolen property?

"I knew from before we were married," Gladys said.

"And how did you first learn of this?"

"When Billy explained that he was going to make a lot of money with my help. He said we'd be living like movie stars, that he could introduce me to all kinds of great people."

"Weren't you worried about being caught?"

"Not really. He said we'd always be able to split to Colombia. He wanted me to be comfortable, so we took a trip to Colombia. He showed me some beautiful places where we could be safe. We met with some of the opposition forces who would hide us. They were a little scary. They had all these terrorist type of books and pamphlets, and they said they'd be in charge of the country pretty soon."

"When did you and Billy think up the plan to fix the cases in Judge Maxwell's court?"

"We never thought it up."

"What do you mean? Did someone tell you to do it?"

"Of course. Billy wasn't the head guy. He was kind of high up, but he wasn't the boss."

"Are you prepared to tell me who the boss is?"

"If I tell you, do I get a chance to keep my house?"

"I think I can arrange that, if we're able to get to the top of the drug ring."

"Well, I'm a little scared. She's gotten a lot of people killed."

"She? Is it Judge Maxwell?"

"Are you kidding? 'Miss everything by the book?' She raises a fuss about a traffic ticket. No way. She's not even that smart."

"Well, who then?"

"What kind of protection are you offering?"

"I wouldn't worry about that right away. The jail will keep you safe. If it becomes necessary later on, there are witness protection programs. We won't just cut you loose, especially if we need you to testify."

"The big brain was Anne Ackley. You know her as Your Honor. What a joke that is."

"Are you saying Judge Anne Ackley devised this scheme to use Judge Maxwell's division?"

"That's what I'm telling you. She thought up the whole thing, even sold Liz on getting her signature on a stamp. Good old gullible Liz."

"Did you meet with Judge Ackley yourself, or did your orders come through Billy? How did it work?"

"I met with her a few times and sometimes she'd tell Billy what I needed to do."

"Did she approach you first or Billy?"

"Billy already knew her before I met him. He put us together."

"You said a minute ago that you were scared because she had people killed. Were you talking about Judge Ackley?"

"Who else? You must be a little stupid. That's who we've been talking about."

"What people did she have killed?"

"Well, Jimmy Carillo for one. He was about to give us all up. Poor Jimmy. He was just in it for the drugs for himself. He didn't even care about the money."

"Who else?"

"The informant, Malaga. He was really playing on both teams. He worked for Ackley for a while and then he started working for the cops. Anne advised Liz how to set up the deposition. Liz was always asking Anne for advice. She even showed Anne the order bringing Malaga to the State Attorney's Office. Ackley would have liked to shoot him herself. She's good with a gun, you know, but it was too risky so she had one of her many boyfriends take care of it."

"Anyone else that you knew about?"

"I think she was involved with the guy who got offed at the Floridian Inn. Billy knew him. He was one of the rebel guys from Colombia. Billy and Jimmy met with him. Jimmy may have killed him. Jimmy was spooked. He thought everyone was an informant for the cops after what happened with Malaga turning on him."

"How long did Billy work for Judge Ackley?"

"I'm not sure. He introduced me to her as his boss. That was around the time we got engaged."

"Gladys, did it ever occur to you that Billy was one of Ackley's boyfriends? Maybe he married you to get to Judge Maxwell."

"So what. I loved him, and I'm the one he came home to." Gladys pounded her free fist on the table.

Detective Morris stood up and put his hand on her shoulder. "Calm down. I'm not here to hurt you. You rest a minute. I'll be right back." Morris left the room and in a minute was hurrying toward Jason and me. I was still in shock. Anne Ackley, the presiding judge of the criminal division, was a criminal herself.

Jason was on his feet. "We've got to get a warrant immediately, before Ackley flees. What time is it?"

I looked at my watch. It seemed like midnight. "It's five fifteen," I said.

"She may have left the courthouse already," Jason said.

"Maybe not. She's been presiding over that child abduction trial for the last week. She may not know what's going on," I said, "and she may be stuck in court tonight. I heard they were almost ready for closing arguments."

"Well, Mary, I will be able to tell the chief judge of Liz's innocence tonight. I'm going directly to him to sign an arrest warrant. I'll have my secretary call him to stay put," Jason said.

"And I'll call Judge Ackley's chambers and see if she's in court. If she is, I'll tell her bailiff to have her wait for me; that I need her to sign an arrest warrant in a murder case. Hopefully, we'll grab her tonight." Detective Morris pulled out his cell phone.

Jason left quickly. I sat transfixed, listening to Morris on the phone. "She's there in court," Morris said as he dialed another number. "I'm calling my partner to come pick up Gladys and take her to the women's jail. They'll process her, and I'm leaving word to have her kept in isolation."

"I guess I'll leave unless there's anything I can do," I said.

"You've done a great service, Mary. If you hadn't continued to investigate on behalf of Judge Maxwell, we might not have cleaned out this courthouse operation. We will probably need Judge Maxwell as a witness. Better alert her." Detective Morris shook my hand, which made all his jewelry shake and rattle.

CHAPTER FIFTY-SIX

I couldn't help laughing as I walked out of the State Attorney Building. I envisioned the incongruous sight of Bennie Morris in his drug dealer getup, getting ready to go to see Judge Ackley who really was a drug dealer, and Judge Ackley believing she would be signing a warrant for a killer's arrest, but being arrested herself because she is a killer. It was all too ridiculous. I couldn't stop laughing. People turned and stared at me for a minute, but then lots of nutty people walk the streets in the Civic Center, so nobody stared for long.

I approached the street where I had so hurriedly parked the Explorer. I saw the sign that said "authorized personnel only." I didn't see my car. I had left it so quickly that my first thought was that I might be on the wrong street, so I walked swiftly around the whole block, checking each "no parking" sign. Finally, it dawned on me. My car must have been towed. I sat down on the curb. It had begun to drizzle again. I tried to think of what to do or who to call. I was too exhausted to move. Suddenly, I looked up. A man was standing over me. I wanted to scream, but nothing came out of my gaping mouth.

"Here," the man said, "get yourself a hot meal." He extended his hand and dropped a five dollar bill in my lap.

"Oh, no, you don't understand," I said, trying to hand it back to him.

"I do understand. Everyone gets down on their luck some-time," he said and walked quickly away.

"Oh, great, now I looked like a homeless bag lady. I began to laugh again as the rain got heavier.

I pulled out my cell phone and called Marco. He always knows how to fix almost everything.

"Pit Bull Investigations." Marco was still in his office.

"Marco, it's Mary. I'm in the Civic Center on Twelfth Avenue and Fourteenth Street. Someone has towed my car away, or it's been stolen, but since I was illegally parked, it's proba-bly been towed. Do you know how I can get it back?"

"Geez, Mary, it's dangerous there. How do you get your-self into these things? I don't know about car towing, but Franco does. He knows everything about cars, including where the towing yards are. I'll call him. You stay there, and he'll come and get you. He's over in Little Havana, not far from you."

While I waited, I called Liz and left her a message. "You're cleared and you'll never guess who is getting arrested as we speak. I'll call you later with details."

Franco pulled up ten minutes later. "I brought cash and I know which lot is near here. That's probably where your car is. By the way, you look awful."

One hour later we had paid off someone named Cheeko who opened the padlocked yard. We walked past hundreds of cars and finally came to my red SUV that was now missing both its side mirrors.

"You're lucky to have your tires. These tow guys use this place as their own chop shop. Then they sell the parts." Franco watched me drive off after assuring me he'd be by in a few days with new mirrors for the car. I saw him walk over to the security guard. No doubt he was buying back my mirrors.

It was after seven when I drove into Carlos's driveway after stopping to pick up my files for Luis's hearing. Catherine had finished putting every paper in order and had typed all my notes.

Carlos came out the door before I could turn off the motor.

"Marco called me. Are you okay?"

"Aside from being mistaken for a bag lady and being given five dollars so I could get a hot meal while I sat on the curb without my car, after hearing that Liz — well, it's a long story that I need to tell you." Carlos opened his arms and I walked into them. For a minute all seemed right with the world.

"Carlos, it's safe for me to go home again. I need to see my house, but I want you to come with me. I can tell you everything now. Please, let's get Sam and all my stuff and go there now."

CHAPTER FIFTY-SEVEN

Carlos followed me home. We pulled into the driveway and Sam went wild pawing at the windows of the Explorer. I felt the same way. We ran into the house. I couldn't believe what I saw. The place was cleaner than it had ever been in the years I lived there. Sam and I ran from room to room. The bathroom that had been left with the ugly mirror message and the black fingerprint powder covering all the surfaces was spotless. There were fresh flowers in the dining room. The kitchen had been scoured. I opened the refrigerator and found a bag from Katz's Kosher Market brimming with goodies.

"How did all this happen?" I asked Carlos.

He smiled his sexiest smile. "So you're finally pleased about something. Marco had the place cleaned days ago. And your mother ordered the food and flowers delivered yesterday. I knew you'd be coming back here as soon as it was safe. Catherine called me this afternoon to say things were concluding in your super-secret case."

"You've been speaking to my mother?"

"Yes, she likes me. She thinks I'm a positive in your life."

"That reminds me. She thinks my dad isn't well, and he won't go to the doctor. I'm supposed to talk to him."

"She told me. It's all taken care of. My father noticed that Abe wasn't himself. Remember, they've been playing poker almost every week. Last week he walked my dad out to his car and he could hardly catch his breath, so Hope and Dad and I talked. Dad told your father that he wasn't feeling well, and he asked your dad to go with him to see Doctor Andreas. He convinced your dad that he was afraid to go alone. Then your dad said maybe they could both see the doctor, and they're going next week."

"I don't deserve you," I said. I pulled him into the bedroom. It didn't take a lot of pulling.

An hour later we opened a bottle of wine and filled our plates with the treats from Katz's. "I need to explain to you why this case was so important and so confidential.

"My client is Judge Elizabeth Maxwell. She was being investigated for allegedly fixing drug cases. Jason Jimenez-Jones believed that she orchestrated the murder of that informant and of Jimmy Carillo, but it wasn't Liz at all. Her bailiff, Gladys, and Gladys's husband were using Liz. Gladys was arrested today. She gave up the real boss of the operation. It was Judge Anne Ackley, the chief judge of the criminal division."

"My God, Mary. How did they find out that it was Gladys?"

"They didn't. I did."

"You did? How?"

"I sort of cooked up a trap and, lucky for Liz, Gladys walked right into it. I'm sure that everything that happened to me was done by Gladys's husband. Judge Ackley wanted me to keep out of the investigation. She gave the orders. So the break-in here and the phone threat had nothing to do with Luis's case. I'm so glad it wasn't the federal government, just a bunch of drug dealers."

Sam put his head in my lap and sighed. He appeared to be

listening to my explanation of why he and Carlos had both been neglected. Just as I stopped speaking, he raced to the front door barking. Then we heard a knock.

"I will go," Carlos said. He put his hand in his pocket as he went. I was sure he was fingering a gun.

Carlos opened the door a crack.

"Is Mary Katz here," a male voice said.

"Who are you and why do you want to know?" Carlos was speaking in his Al Pacino voice used for intimidating rival builders.

"I'm Jason Jones, the state attorney."

I went to the door when I heard Jason. He was showing Carlos his badge.

"What do you want with Mary?" Carlos was saying. His hand was still in his pocket.

"It's okay, Carlos. Come on in, Jason. What's wrong?"

"I'm sorry to come over here so late. I thought you needed to know what we found out when we arrested Anne Ackley."

"So you got the warrant in time to get her? Oh, Jason this is Carlos Martin, my uh — boyfriend. Carlos, you know who Jason is. We were just talking about you, Jason. You can tell me anything about this with Carlos here. I've finally been able to talk to Carlos about this whole case."

"When we got to her chambers, Judge Ackley was still in court. Bennie and I asked for her to come to chambers. We had a back-up unit down the hall. She walked in and Bennie said he had a warrant for her to review. She sat down at her desk, put on her glasses, and started to read the warrant. When she saw her name on it, she reached for her desk drawer, and got a gun half out of the drawer. Bennie was standing almost next to her. He grabbed his gun and pointed it at her head. She tried to get up, but Bennie was on top of her. She struggled. I ran around the desk, and between us we got her cuffed. The back-up boys came in, and we got her out to the judges' elevator and into the squad car in the garage."

"Someone could have been killed. So it's true that she has guns stashed everywhere," I said.

"I came over here for a couple of reasons. When we went to Judge Marconi for the warrant and told him about Gladys and how she used Liz, he was astonished. He claimed he never suspected Anne of being involved in anything. He was a little shakey when he signed the warrant. I wanted you to be able to tell Liz that she's been completely cleared of any wrong-doing."

"I'll call her tonight. Thanks for letting me know."

"That's not all. I was present while Ackley was interrogated. She said Liz was a fool. She also admitted that she was the person who accosted you in the parking lot at your office. She really hates you. Her exact words were, 'Liz was so stupid that she would have been the one arrested if it hadn't been for that smart-ass lawyer Mary Katz.' She said she'd see that you got paid back one of these days. I thought you ought to know. I need to know if you want to have us add an aggravated battery charge against her. It would mean that you would have to testify."

"Are you saying that Judge Anne Ackley beat me over the head herself?"

"That's exactly what I'm saying. She's not going anywhere for a long time, but I thought you better know how vindictive she sounds."

"We appreciate your coming here right away to warn Mary." Carlos said.

"There's one other thing before I go." Jason said. "You and Mark Epstein have done a great service to our justice system.

I don't want you to worry about any bar complaints because you used that fake drug case. On the other hand, never do that again."

"I wouldn't dream of it," I said.

"I do want to be sure that you and Mark get credit for ending this misuse of the courts."

"I don't need anything, but it would be nice if you arranged an award for Mark, a plaque and a little ceremony. He misses his days in the spotlight."

"We can arrange that. The media is all over this story already. Bennie and I told them that you and Mark and Liz were responsible for the apprehensions. I know I told Liz I'd keep her name out of this, but it seemed better to treat her as one of the good guys. Her name has to come out if we call her as a witness."

"Okay. I'll prepare her."

So finally Jason left and I was in my own house in my own bed with Carlos by my side and Sam huddled on my feet. Just as I was turning out the light, Carlos sat up.

"Mark Epstein? Your old boyfriend? What's he got to do with anything?"

"Never mind. All that's important is that you're here." I fell asleep in seconds.

CHAPTER FIFTY-EIGHT

The next morning I was awakened by my reliable alarm clock, Sam, who was pacing up and down the bedroom waiting for his morning chow. The clock said six a.m. I started my morning wake-up agenda on automatic pilot. Throw on some shorts, feed Sam, and start our morning walk. I was still feeling euphoric about Liz's case, and being back in my own house when I remembered that Luis's hearing was this morning. I hadn't had time to look over his file again, and I still had to call Liz before she left for work or read the morning *Herald*.

My phone call to Liz was made before seven. I knew I had awakened her. She sounded like she was talking from an underwater location.

"Mary, what's wrong now?"

"Everything is fine. I just need to let you know some new wrinkles before I leave for court. Gladys gave up the head of the drug operation and an arrest was made last night. It'll probably be front-page stuff in this morning's *Herald*."

"Who was it? Someone we know?"

"Better sit down. It's Anne Ackley. She was arrested at the courthouse last night."

There was a long pause. Then I heard a sob or a gulp. "Liz, are you there? Are you okay?"

"I'm here, Mary, but I'm not okay. This is like being run

over by a truck driven by my best friend. Are you sure it was Anne? Maybe you can help her."

"Liz, you don't get it. She gave all the orders for the drug ring. She set you up. It's possible that Billy Martinez was one of her many bedroom buddies. It turns out that she's the person who beat me over the head in my own parking lot. Jason wants to add charges of aggravated battery to the laundry list she's already facing. Now I need to tell you that you will be called as a witness at her trial. So will I. Jason told the media that you and I and Mark broke this case. He let them know that you're one of the good guys, so no one will believe any rumors about you being investigated. I know Jason promised to keep your name out of this, but this is the best way."

"Dammit. Every time I trust somebody and think they're my friend, I get screwed. Am I so stupid that my immediate world uses me as a doormat? First Gladys, now Anne. Maybe Joe will turn out to be a rat too. You can forget about coming to my wedding. No more Nice Girl Liz. I won't trust anyone again, ever."

Before I could ask if that included me, she hung up

"I take it you were talking to Judge Maxwell." Carlos had come into the kitchen.

"I can't worry about her anymore. I've got to get to court for Luis's hearing. If I don't win this petition today, Luis may end up as a Guantanamo prisoner for years."

"My parents and I will be in court to cheer you on and support the Coronas. I know you've done everything that you can do to free Luis. You're taking on the federal administration. My grandmother used to say 'no one can make the earth spin in a new direction.' Well, it made more sense in Spanish. Or maybe it was 'no one can make the earth spin sideways.' You know what I mean."

"Why aren't you going to work? You need to get your condo tower done."

"I can spare some hours. My foreman is on the job. It's moving along."

"Usually you have two other new projects on the table. What else are you working on? I've been so busy I haven't even asked you about your work."

"Nothing else is on the table. I'll talk to you about this when you finish Luis's case."

I dressed, grabbed my file, zoomed out of Coral Gables, and picked up Catherine at the office. I would have to worry about Carlos later. Right now it was going to be Luis Corona's moment of glory.

CHAPTER FIFTY-NINE

Catherine and I were rushing down the hallway to the court-room when I saw Harlan McFarland waiting outside the courtroom door. He had a cameraman with him.

"Ms. Katz, I'm so excited the *Herald* is letting me cover your hearing. Is there some reason why the feds haven't brought Luis to court? I figured I'd get the inside of this from you." Harlan dropped his notebook, picked it up, and dropped his pen.

The camera guy was pointing his camera at me and once again I was caught with my mouth gaping open.

"What do you mean Luis isn't here?"

"Just what I said. I asked the bailiff if there was any chance I could speak to Luis before the hearing, and he said you were in for a surprise The feds never brought him to the courthouse."

"Thanks, Harlan. This is definitely a surprise. The judge's order has been ignored."

Catherine and I hurried into the courtroom. I left Catherine unpacking our folders. I approached one of the security officers. "Would you please bring my client in? The hearing is about to start."

"He is not present, ma'am. I don't know anything about this." He turned and walked away.

I looked out into the audience and saw Señor Marquez, the Coronas, J.C. and Angelina and Carlos. They all looked expectantly at me. This was one of those times where I wished I was sitting in the audience, instead of standing in federal court with egg on my face.

Judge Hammel's law clerk entered the courtroom. Federal judges have law clerks to help them draft orders and do research. They are usually newly graduated attorneys with a lot of energy. The sign on the law clerk's desk said "Marcia Lu."

"Ms. Lu, I'm Mary Katz, Luis Corona's attorney. I have just been informed that he has not been brought to court this morning as Judge Hammel ordered last week. He also ordered that Luis not be removed from this jurisdiction until after the habeas corpus hearing today. He made that in the form of a temporary restraining order. Could you please inform Judge Hammel of this before he takes the bench, and could you see what you can find out about where my client is?"

Marcia Lu leaped out of her seat. She grabbed her pad and pen. "This is very surprising. I'll take care of this at once." She raced from the courtroom.

I walked back to the rail that separates the spectators from the well of the court and signaled to Carlos to come to the rail.

"What's wrong? You're frowning like you have a horrendous pain somewhere," Carlos said.

"I have a pain all right. The feds have pulled off a nasty surprise. They're hiding Luis somewhere. He's not here. I need you to prepare the Coronas." Someone tapped me on the shoulder. Ms. Lu was standing behind me.

"The judge is on his way into court. No one knows anything so far about your client's whereabouts. Here come the government lawyers."

We watched as three grim-looking attorneys marched into the courtroom pulling a cart with several files. Just then the bailiff called us to order as Judge Hammel took his seat.

"Hear ye, hear ye, all rise for the Honorable Judge Hammel. The District Court for the Southern District of Florida is now in session, God save this Honorable Court and the United States of America. Be seated. There will be no noise from the spectators or I'll clear the courtroom," the bailiff bellowed out his formal greeting.

I realized that Miguel and Consul Marquez were conferring in heated tones. Maria Corona was once again sobbing as J.C. tried to comfort her.

Judge Hammel looked like an approaching thunderstorm. "What have I been told? The petitioner, Luis Corona, is not present. I ordered this hearing and ordered that Mr. Corona be present. Where are the government attorneys?"

The heaviest of the three men got to his feet. "Your Honor, I am Michael Santini. I am a staff attorney in the Department of Homeland Security and at this time on loan to the Department of Justice."

"Well, Mr. Santini, that's a long title. Can you shed any light on why my order was ignored?"

"Yes, Judge. I can, but first I must request that we close this courtroom and clear it of any nonessential personnel."

"You mean it's top secret why you have disobeyed my order? All parties come sidebar with the court reporter. I want all this on the record."

We all trotted up to the bench, including Ms. Lu.

"Your Honor," Santini said, "Homeland Security under the Patriot Act has determined that all accused terrorists are to be held outside the United States. This takes precedent over all judicial orders. Accordingly, Mr. Corona is awaiting transport out of the country." Santini stepped back and smiled at the judge. He looked like he had just instructed a small child about better behavior.

"Young man, are you telling a United States District Judge that his orders carry no weight? Did you miss the constitutional law classes on the balance of power? I think we will hold an immediate hearing regarding the charge of contempt of court with which you are now charged. Do you need a few minutes to hire a lawyer to defend you?"

I looked away and stifled a laugh as Mr. Santini broke out in a copious sweat.

"Judge Hammel, please, don't kill the messenger. I don't make these decisions," Santini said.

"Well, who does?"

"I believe this one came from Deputy Marvin Golightly of the Justice Department."

"Ms. Lu, get that deputy on the telephone now," the judge said. "I'll be waiting for the call in my chambers." The judge left the bench his robe flying behind him like the feathers on an angry hawk.

We all turned to return to our tables. As I turned I was shocked to see Ambassador Miller entering the courtroom. Francis Miller had ignored all of my calls and those of Consul General Marquez. Now he strode down the aisle and took a seat next to J.C., who spoke to him while pointing to Miguel and Maria Corona. I watched Miller reach over and shake hands with the Coronas who looked decidedly unimpressed. I decided I better enter the fray before we were in open warfare with Argentina.

"Ambassador Miller, do you remember me? I'm Mary Magruder Katz. We met through J.C. a few months ago. I am Luis Corona's attorney. I hope you received my many messages regarding Luis's imprisonment."

"Yes, of course I remember you, and I've been receiving

updates on the situation regarding Luis. I've been terribly busy at my post in Buenos Aires, but I'm here now. What seems to be the problem?"

"The problem, Ambassador, is reaching an international stalemate." Señor Marquez joined the conversation. "Luis's attorney was given a hearing date almost a week ago to address the specious accusations against this fine Argentine citizen who has been held over three weeks with no charges filed against him. The judge ordered him to be maintained in this county until this hearing so that he and his witnesses could testify as to his false imprisonment. Instead, your government has spirited him away to some unknown place. They have violated the order of one of their own federal judges. Is this your idea of democracy?"

J.C. placed his hand on Miller's shoulder and fixed him with a piercing gaze. I realized that he looked exactly like Carlos just before Carlos goes into a full-out Latin rant.

"Francis, it's time for you to act. I expect you to use all of your considerable influence to get Luis brought to this courthouse," J.C. said.

"I appreciate your concern, J.C., but I think you are giving me more credit with our government than —"

J.C. interrupted. He increased his grip on Miller's shoulder. "With all of the money that you raised to put this administration in office for two terms, I would judge that you have more than enough influence. God knows, you hit me up for funds every time I answered my phone. The Coronas are highly influential in their country. Just suppose they felt that you were not the appropriate representative to be stationed in their country. Suppose they convinced their many friends that you were an impediment to future free-trade agreements. I really thought you were enjoying your appointment as an ambassador."

"Are you threatening me, J.C.?"

"Of course not, *mi amigo*, I'm just pointing out that which is in your own best interest. Perhaps you should go back to the judge's chambers and offer your help in locating Luis. I'm sure you can expedite his return to Miami from wherever he is now being held in violation of a court order." J.C. let go of the ambassador, who walked quickly to the bailiff's desk.

Miller talked to the bailiff for a minute, showed him some identification, and followed the bailiff out of the courtroom.

I returned to my table, and the long wait for news of Luis resumed.

Twenty minutes later, the court reporter and the security guards were playing some game on the court reporter's computer. The court clerk was repairing her nails. The bailiff was reading the latest copy of the *National Enquirer*, and I was going out of my mind.

Marcia Lu came bouncing through the door to the judge's chambers and sat down next to me. "Ms. Katz, Judge Hammel asked me to tell you that he has located your client. He's in Key West. He was supposed to be put on a government plane and flown out of the country last night, but the plane was unavailable. Someone is trying to make arrangements to return him here. We'll let you know when we have an exact time."

Mr. Santini came over to the table. "I believe I should be in chambers with the judge."

"The judge hasn't asked for you, but I'll convey your request," Marcia said as she bounced out of her chair and back through the door. She was enjoying the drama of the morning. I could imagine her relating the details to her law school friends who hadn't gotten such exciting jobs.

Ten minutes later the judge, Ms. Lu, and Francis Miller returned to the courtroom. Miller took a seat next to one of the security guards. He refused to look at anyone.

Judge Hammel looked at some notes in front of him. "Ladies and Gentlemen, Mr. Corona has been located at a holding facility in Key West. With the help of Ambassador Miller, who contacted the State Department, Mr. Corona will be flown out by helicopter within the hour. He will be returned to Miami-Dade County and then brought to the courthouse. His estimated arrival here is one thirty this afternoon.

"Now Mr. Santini, I see your displeasure, and I understand you are under certain orders here. I have spoken with Deputy Golightly, who has promised not to penalize you in any way. I am not assuming any outcome of the hearing to be held when Mr. Corona arrives. My original order stated that he was to be brought here so that I am able to rule on the petition for his release, and that he was to remain in this jurisdiction until the hearing was held. Key West is under the jurisdiction of this district of the federal court, so I suppose my order hasn't actually been violated, but I think we all know that he would have been long gone but for the dysfunctional government services.

"It's best that we recess this hearing until this afternoon. Mr. Santini, I want you to stay in close contact with your office to be sure that there are no more snafus." Judge Hammel exited before the bailiff could get the words "all rise" out, but we all stood anyway.

CHAPTER SIXTY

J.C. tried to organize everyone to go to the Bankers Club for lunch. I begged off. I was too nervous to think of sitting through a multicourse meal complete with drinks while staring at Francis Miller. Catherine was disappointed when I said we would use the time to reorganize our presentation. The Coronas, Phillipe Marquez, Carlos and his family, and Ambassador Miller trooped out.

Santini and his entourage remained at their table huddled over some papers. As Catherine and I looked over my order of witnesses, I realized there were some holes I had failed to fill. I strolled over to the government's lawyers trying to look ultraconfident.

"Mr. Santini, I suppose you have a copy of the lab report regarding the white powder taken from Luis's carry-on bag."

The two briefcase carriers looked at Santini, who stared back at them. Then they began to look through their files. They handed a paper to Santini.

"Actually, we only have the name of the lab technician here," he said.

"Oh, then you plan to call the lab tech this afternoon."

"Well, no, I just flew in from Washington this morning. I wasn't sure that would be necessary," Santini said.

"So you thought there wouldn't be a hearing because you knew Luis was on his way to Guantanamo. Isn't that correct?"

"I'm not on trial here. You can't cross-examine me." Santini began to sweat again.

"I think you'd better turn over the name of the tech to me now. I don't trust you to insure that you'll obtain the witness."

"It's really unimportant, but her name is Natalie Byron, Miami-Dade Crime Lab."

"What about the rest of the evidence taken from his bag?"

"It's being sent for. It should be here before the start of the hearing."

I stepped outside and began making calls. We had a few hours to pull together everything else we needed. I left Catherine in the courtroom eyeballing the Washington attorneys.

CHAPTER SIXTY-ONE

Promptly at 1:30, Judge Hammel returned to the bench. I still didn't know whether I had a client ready to testify.

"We are back on the record for the hearing on the habeas corpus petition filed in the case of *Luis Corona vs. the United States Government*. Lawyers for the government led by Michael Santini are present as well as counsel for the petitioner, Mary Magruder Katz. Ladies and Gentlemen, I have been informed that Mr. Corona is present. He has just arrived at the courthouse and the deputies are bringing him to the courtroom. He should be here in a matter of minutes."

I heard a sigh from the audience and knew it must be Maria. The door to the lockup opened and two men in suits escorted a man wearing a red prison jumpsuit, leg chains, and handcuffs into the room. Escorted is not the word. They dragged him in. His feet were hobbled together, and he looked too weak to walk even if he wasn't wearing leg irons.

I barely recognized Luis. He looked ten pounds lighter than when I saw him at the detention facility less than a week ago. His face had turned from merely pale to gray. The men stood at attention, holding Luis before the bench.

"Your Honor," I was on my feet in an instant, "my client looks ill. I need him to be a witness this afternoon. I need a few minutes to converse with him and he needs to be placed at the defense table. He also needs to have these chains removed."

One of the "escorts" shook his head. "Judge, we are responsible for maintaining custody of this prisoner. I cannot agree to removal of any of these restraints."

"Listen, this is my courtroom," Judge Hammel said. "I make the rules here. Mr. Corona is to be seated next to his attorney. The leg irons are to be removed. You can handcuff him to his chair. You may be seated behind him and Ms. Katz. A court interpreter will be seated on the other side of Mr. Corona. Is all of this clear?"

The two guys shook their heads, but they followed instructions and brought Luis to the table and went about unchaining and recuffing him. Then they pulled two chairs up behind us. They were so close that I felt one of them breathing on my neck.

"Your Honor, I need just a couple of minutes to explain to my client what we will be doing this afternoon. I can't interview my client with these federal officers blowing on my neck and listening in to privileged conversations. Can't they move back a little bit? They are treating this young man as if he were number one on the foreign enemies list. When you hear the testimony today, I'm sure you'll see how ridiculous this is. Right now I need to ask Mr. Corona if he's been given any lunch today." I turned to Luis who shook his head.

"When was the last time you ate?" I asked.

"I'm not sure," Luis mumbled. "Maybe yesterday or the day before. They've been moving me around a lot."

"Ms. Katz, I'm very sorry. I wish we could take the time to get your client fed, but I need to conclude this hearing this afternoon. We need to get started," Judge Hammel said.

Marcia Lu jumped out of her seat. "Judge, I'll be glad to go get Mr. Corona some coffee right now if that will help."

"Oh, *muchas gracias*," Luis said.

"Now, are both sides ready to proceed?"

"Yes, Judge, on behalf of Luis Corona."

"I may not be able to proceed completely this afternoon," Santini said.

"Well, better get ready, sir. You can send your two accomplices out to get whatever you need. This hearing will be finished this afternoon." Judge Hammel looked as if he might not make it through more than the afternoon. "Take a minute to speak to your client, Ms. Katz, and then we will begin with your evidence since you asked for the hearing."

Santini was on his feet again. It looked like he was going to object to everything from here on out. "Judge, that's backward. I'm supposed to be given the opportunity to show you why we cannot allow the petitioner to be released."

"You'll get your chance. I think I know how to conduct a hearing. I've been doing it since you were in grade school. Whenever you're ready, Counsel."

I turned to Luis and whispered as quietly as possible. "How do you feel? I need you to testify to everything you told me at the jail the other day. Do you think you can do it?"

"I'll do my best. I'm a little dizzy and I think I may be running a temperature, but I know this is my chance to get free."

"Good. I have other witnesses to call first, so you rest and drink your coffee. I'm going to get you out of here."

"I'm ready, Your Honor. We call Miguel Corona to the stand."

Catherine moved up the aisle to the center doors and led Miguel down the aisle. I had stashed Miguel and Señor Marquez in the hallway, so the government wouldn't complain that the witnesses had listened to everything in the court-room and were now tainted. But they hadn't even invoked The Rule. They hadn't even thought to complain that the witnesses were not sequestered.

Miguel gasped when he saw Luis. He stopped at our table and bent and planted a kiss on Luis's sunken cheek. Tears streamed down Luis's face. The escorts reared up out of their seats like race horses, but before they could complain Cather-ine took Miguel by the arm and delivered him to the witness chair where he was sworn in.

I began my questioning in what had become one of the most important hearings of my career. "State your full name for the record, please."

"Miguel Fabrecio Contes Corona."

"And where do you reside?"

"In Buenos Aires, Argentina, all of my life."

"Are you employed, sir?"

"Yes, my spouse and I own a chain of high-fashion bou-tiques featuring Argentine and other South American de-signers. That's my wife seated back there." Maria raised her hand.

"Are you related to Luis Corona?"

"Yes, of course, he's my only son."

"Now did you have an occasion to send Luis to the United States some weeks ago?"

"Yes, I did. We were in the process of purchasing our first store in the United States. I sent Luis to Miami to conclude the purchase. It was our intention for Luis to be in charge of this store."

"Can you tell us where this store is located?"

"Of course, it's the shop now owned by Paulina Morrero in Coral Gables. It's called Paulina's."

"How was Luis to conclude this purchase?"

"He was bringing a hundred fifty thousand in American dollars to Paulina as an initial payment. We were to pay her on a monthly basis every month for three years until the shop was paid for."

"Are you saying that Luis was carrying a hundred fifty thousand dollars in cash on the plane with him?"

"Yes. This is what Paulina wanted. She didn't trust bank checks. Many South and Central Americans don't really like banks, you know."

"Did you hear from Luis when he arrived in Miami?"

"No, we didn't. We were terrified. We called the Floridian Inn where he had a reservation and learned that he never arrived there. We called the Argentine consul in Miami, who started a search for him. Finally two days later, we had a phone call at five a.m. Luis told us he had been arrested and he didn't even know why. He said his money and all his possessions had been taken. Then they made him hang up. The nightmare for Maria and me began then and it goes on today."

"Why was Luis staying at the Floridian Inn?"

"We selected it for him. It's a good clean place. Many business people stay there. In fact, I have stayed there on occasion."

"Has Luis ever been arrested?"

"No, never. Once the police kicked him and some of his friends out of a club for making a disturbance, but basically, he is a good boy."

"Has he ever attended any Muslim mosques or training camps?"

"Muslim?" Miguel looked at me like I was crazy. "Luis goes to Mass with us every Sunday. He is a good Catholic boy. The only camp he ever went to was the summer camp in the mountains, but he was homesick, so we picked him up and brought him home."

This brought a chuckle from the spectators. I waited for the laughter to subside. "Has Luis traveled much out of the country?"

"He came with us to Miami twice to visit our friends and look for space for a shop, and he went with us to Paris for Fashion Week a year ago."

"Okay, thanks, Mr. Corona." I sat down.

Michael Santini walked to the lectern. "Do you have any proof of this purchase of a shop here?"

"I saw the owner in the hall. I assume she's going to be a witness."

"Where did the cash you gave Luis come from?"

"From my corporate bank account."

"Now you love your son. I can see that. You don't want anything to happen to him, isn't that right?"

"Of course that's right. I am in pain looking at what you people have already done to him."

"I don't have any other questions of this witness." Santini sat down.

"Your Honor, my next witness is Paulina Morrero."

Catherine escorted Ms. Morrero down the aisle. She was using a cane and looked like each step was an effort. She looked shocked when she saw Luis. She asked the judge if she could be seated while she took the oath. "Sorry, Judge, I am awaiting surgery on my hip. I thought I'd have concluded the turnover of my shop to the Coronas by now. I've rescheduled my surgery twice," Paulina said.

"Are you the owner of a boutique that carries your name, ma'am?" I began my questioning.

"Yes, I own Paulina's in the Gables.

"Are you in the process of selling this shop?"

"Yes, to the Coronas. They are lovely people, and I especially liked young Mr. Corona. He has a certain *joie de vivre* that I thought would be enjoyed by the clients of the shop."

"Do you see the young Mr. Corona in the courtroom?"

"Yes, he's sitting over at that table next to the interpreter who's speaking into his ear, but I must say, he looks nothing like he did when he came to the shop to negotiate the contract. He looks as if he's been ill."

"What were the terms of the sale?"

"Luis was to bring me the cash down payment at the beginning of June. We worked out a payment schedule for the next few years. I was anxious to retire. As you can see, I have some health problems."

"Okay, thank you for coming to court today."

Santini stood next to his table. He didn't even bother to go to the lectern.

"Ms. Morrero, isn't it unusual to request so much money in cash?"

"Not in my country. In the Dominican, American cash is the most reliable currency."

"Do you have any proof that you own this boutique that you speak of ?"

"Obviously, you aren't from Miami. Everyone knows Paulina's. But Ms. Katz said you might ask that, so I brought my business license and my certificate of occupancy." She pulled the papers out of her oversized designer handbag and held them out.

Santini approached and studied the papers. "Do you wish to see these, Judge?"

"That won't be necessary. I do live in Miami, and, fortunately or unfortunately, my wife has bought an occasional gown from Paulina," Judge Hammel said. The spectators laughed appreciatively and Paulina rewarded the judge with a huge grin.

"What else do you want to know, young man?" Paulina tapped her cane impatiently.

"That's all, ma'am." Santini sunk into his seat.

Catherine helped Paulina down the two steps from the witness chair and took her arm as they proceeded slowly up the aisle.

"Your Honor, my next witness will be my client, Luis Corona."

"Maybe this is a good time to take a break," the Judge said. "It sounds like he may be a long witness. We are in recess for ten minutes."

CHAPTER SIXTY-TWO

I moved up the aisle to talk to Luis's band of supporters. Miguel had rejoined Maria in the courtroom now that he was finished testifying. Mr. Marquez stopped me.

"I thought I'd be called as a witness," he said.

I'm leaving you in case I need to call a witness after the government has put on their case. You can discredit many things they may imply."

I moved on to talk to Carlos. Angie was out of her seat as I approached.

"Mary, darling, I am so shocked at what the government has done to Luis. Is he as sick as he looks? And you are just amazing. I told Carlos he could have his hands full with you, you clever girl," she said.

"Thanks, I think." I was never sure with Angie whether she was giving me a compliment or a veiled insult.

Carlos interrupted Angie before she could level more backhanded remarks. "I apologize again for getting you into this," he said. "I never imagined that Luis's arrest would become an international cause."

Before I could say a word to Carlos, Harlan McFarland was standing in front of me. "Have you been able to assess your client's physical condition? If he is freed, will you be suing the government?"

"Harlan, I can't really answer any of those questions now. Let's talk later." I pushed past him and headed for the restroom before anyone else had anything else to say.

A few minutes later I tried to calm Luis. He was very weak and very scared to answer questions in court. In these few weeks, it seemed to me that he had been brainwashed into believing that whatever he said would cause authority figures to inflict more physical and emotional punishment.

"Just remember, I'm here with you to protect you and so is Judge Hammel," I said as the judge resumed his seat and called us to order.

"Ms. Katz, your client will have to testify from his seat at your table due to the government's insistence on his being restrained. Can you manage this?"

"Certainly, Judge." I moved to the aisle separating my table from the Washington lawyers and positioned myself so the judge and Luis could see me. The Washington boys would be looking at my rear, which seemed fitting to me.

"Luis, can you raise your right hand a little, so you can take the witness oath?"

Luis complied. We were off and running.

"Luis, tell the judge your full name and age."

"Luis Miguel Corona. I am twenty-two."

"Luis, I see that you are answering my questions in English. If at any time you don't understand a question or you feel more comfortable using the services of the interpreter, please consult her. Tell the court where you live and where you went to school, a little about your background."

"Well, I was born and raised in Buenos Aires in my country, Argentina. I have always lived in the same house with my parents and I still do. I attended the Academia de Santa

Maria near La Plaza Mayor. I graduated there with high marks in everything except science. Then I finished at the Pontificia Universidad Católica Argentina. We call it UCA for shorthand. There I learned much about design and business to assist me in my duties in my family's business."

"Have you ever lived in any other countries?"

"No. I have visited in this country, and in France. I vacationed in the island of Barbados two years ago."

"Now you boarded a plane a few weeks ago to come here to Miami. Why were you coming here?"

"To open a shop for my family."

"Was this plane an Argentine plane or an American plane?"

"It was American. It offered the best fare."

"Did you go through a security check when you boarded the plane?"

"Yes, of course."

"Tell us about that."

"Well, I put my carry-on bag on the carousel with my shoes and my belt, like they said to do. I showed the lady my passport and ticket and my work papers that I had received a few days before. I filled out a paper showing the money I was bringing and that I was traveling for business. A man looked at my bag in the x-ray and I showed him my little bottles of cologne and deodorant. I put the things from my pockets into a little bowl and the man looked at all of it."

"Did anyone take anything away from you and tell you that you couldn't bring it on the plane?"

"No, no one. Could I have some water, *por favor*, I mean please?"

I quickly poured a glass from the carafe on the table. "Are you okay, Luis?"

"Just a little weak."

"Once you got on the plane and got in the air, what, if anything happened next?"

"I had taken out my magazines to read, and the man next to me said they looked interesting. We started to talk. We had some drinks. Well, I guess I had some drinks. I felt very festive, coming to Miami, being trusted to start a business.

"He asked if he could look at my magazines and I said okay. We started talking about our governments. He was American. I think he asked me what I thought of the war in Iraq. Pretty soon we were quarreling. It got a little heated. Finally, I told him the rest of the world was laughing at his country for getting into such a war. The flight lady came and told us to stop shouting. The man told her that I had hit him and she should go tell the pilot. I said to him, 'I didn't hit you. I just poked you in the chest to make my point.'"

"What happened next?"

"I was embarrassed so I shut up and I guess I fell asleep for a while. Then the flight lady brought out our dinners. I tried to buy the man a glass of wine, but he refused."

"You were trying to apologize?"

Santini was on his feet. "Judge, she's asking leading questions. I object."

"That last one was leading, but I haven't heard any others. Ask direct questions, Ms. Katz. And Mr. Santini, I haven't forgotten that you're there. You'll get your opportunity in a few minutes to refute any testimony."

"Luis, did anything else happen on the plane?"

"Many things. After dinner and café were served, I got up and went to the bathroom. What I did was wrong, I know. I lit up a cigarette. It's a long flight, but I knew better. I just couldn't resist. The smoke alarm went off. Then people pounded on the door and a man shouted to come out of there with my hands up."

"How were you able to light your cigarette?"

"I had a little lighter in the shape of a pen. It was in my pocket."

Did you put the lighter through the x-ray machine at the airport?"

"Sure. It was with all my stuff that I put in the little bowl."

"What happened next?"

"When I came out of the bathroom, two men threw me on the floor. I saw one of them was the man from my seat. I didn't know he was a policeman."

"What did the men do next?"

"They pulled me down the aisle in front of all the passengers and put me in the back of the plane where they pour the drinks. They handcuffed me to a cart. They asked me many questions all at once like where was I going? Why did I try to light a fire? I tried to answer everything, but they were screaming at me. They searched my pockets and took everything away."

"Did you ask them what you had done or why they were searching you?"

"No, I was so scared."

"What happened next?"

"I think the next thing that happened was they got my suitcase and they started taking everything out of it and asking me more questions."

"Did they ask your permission to search your things?"

"No, never."

"Did they explain to you that you didn't have to talk to them or that you could have a lawyer?"

"No, they just kept taking things out of the suitcase and

holding them up. The man from the seat said, 'Look at all this money.' I told him that it was for my shop. I tried to tell him to call Paulina, but he wouldn't listen. They opened my shaving kit and took out my mustache scissors, and they all nodded their heads. By then the flight lady was there too."

"No one removed the scissors at the airport?"

"No one. Then they pulled out the white powder wrapped in the prayer paper."

"What powder was that?"

"Our housekeeper is from Cuba. She practices Santeria. It's a kind of religion. She buys the powder at the bodega and she always puts it in our bags when we travel. She says it's to bring us home safely."

"Do you know what's in the powder?"

"I don't know. They got real excited about it. They put on gloves and took it somewhere. Then the man from the seat started asking me about my magazines. But whenever I tried to answer, they all just laughed at me."

"What are those magazines, Luis?"

"They are what is called—" Luis leaned over to the interpreter and whispered some words. "They're called in English graphic comics. They are imported from Japan. They're very popular with many people my age."

"What are they about?"

"They're like Superman, only the strong guys invade the earth and have battles with humans. It's not real, it's—"

"Science fiction?" I asked.

"Yes, that's it."

Once again Santini pulled his heavy frame out of his seat. "She's doing it again, Judge. I object to her leading her witness."

"I apologize, Judge. I was just trying to move things along, but while we are stopped, I need to know if the government has brought these items confiscated from my client to court this afternoon. I'd like to introduce them so you can see how innocuous these possessions are."

"Well, Judge, we don't have them. We tried to get them here, but we aren't sure who has custody of them." Santini looked at his shoes, and not at the judge.

"You see, Your Honor, these lawyers in no way thought you would hold this hearing today. They made no preparations."

"Yes, I do see that, Counsel." Judge Hammel frowned. "Please, continue with your questions." He nodded in my direction.

"Luis, what else happened on the plane?"

"They took out my passport and all my papers, and started asking me what my real name was and where I was from. They looked at my reservation at the Floridian Inn and they were nodding to each other. They took turns watching me until we got to Miami. I figured everything would get cleared up once we were in Miami, but they took me off the plane in handcuffs and to the jail. I begged to call my parents or Paulina or our friends, the Martins. They said no phone calls for the enemy."

"How have you been treated during these weeks?"

"I have been alone in a cell in different jails. They shaved off all my hair. Every few hours someone asks me the same questions over and over. Why am I here? Who sent me? What is my real name? I answer the truth and they hit me. They play loud music and have bright lights so I can't sleep. I just don't understand how this could happen to me, who never wants to hurt anyone." Luis began to sob.

I was fighting tears too. "Okay Luis. The government lawyers want to ask you questions now." I sat down.

Santini walked over and stood in front of Luis, but Judge

Hammel told him to stay next to his own table. Luis was shaking.

"Isn't it a fact that you came to Miami with a plan to meet a known terrorist at the Floridian Inn?"

"No, I don't know any terrorists."

"Why did you try to start a fire on the airplane? Weren't you just trying to terrorize the crew? Weren't you trying to take over the plane?"

"I have answered these same questions for days. All I wanted to do was smoke a cigarette after dinner. Now I am cured of smoking, I will never look at another cigarette."

"*Gracias al los dios*," came a voice from the audience. I realized it was Maria. She had broken the tension in the courtroom. I saw that Judge Hammel was suppressing a laugh.

"Now tell us the name of the people you were going to meet at the Floridian Inn," Santini continued.

"I expected to see the Martins, J.C. and his wife and their son, Carlos. They're sitting right there." Luis pointed to them. "My parents told me to be sure to invite them to dinner, and, of course, I was going to meet Paulina at her shop."

"I'm asking you about someone who was at the inn. Judge, please instruct the witness to answer my question."

Hammel frowned at Santini. "Mr. Corona, were you going to meet anybody at the Floridian Inn?"

"No, Judge, I've answered this same question for weeks." Luis put his head down on the table.

"Let's go back to the publications you were bringing into the country. You have called them graphic comics. Do you deny that they show a group of men with explosives? Do you deny that the pictures show the steps they took to make some kind of explosives?"

"They show men using all kinds of weapons. That's true. They are supposed to be from another planet."

"Isn't it a fact that these pamphlets are instructions about making bombs and attacking Americans?"

"Actually, they are attacking Japan. Japanese artists draw these comics."

"Isn't it a fact that you concealed a sharp scissors and a lighter onto the plane in hopes of terrorizing the flight crew?"

"No, it's not true. I've told all of your officers over and over." Luis began to sob and beat his one free fist on the table.

"I'm done with this witness," Santini said, and took his seat.

I patted Luis's shoulder. "Calm down, and try to hang in there just a little longer," I whispered.

"Is your client able to go on with this hearing?" Judge Hammel asked.

"I believe he can, Judge. I have two other witnesses to call."

"You're kidding," the judge said. "I thought your client was your last witness."

"I want the court to hear more. May I continue?"

"Yes, go ahead."

"We call Natalie Byron."

Catherine was on her way up the aisle as I spoke. She returned with an elegant black woman, carrying some papers. She nodded at the judge, took her place in the witness chair, and raised her right hand before being asked to do so.

"Please state your name and profession."

"I am Natalie Byron. I am a senior crime lab technician at the Miami-Dade Crime Lab."

"How long have you been in your current position?"

"Twelve years. Before that I was a training officer in the crime lab of the FBI in Quantico, Virginia."

"What are your duties in the crime lab?"

"I oversee the testing of suspect substances. It is my job to check the work of a group of technicians whenever they have been unable to identify a substance, or when there is some special question about a substance."

"Now, were you asked to look at a white powder submitted by federal officers in which the substance had been removed from someone named Luis Corona?"

"Yes, I was. If I may look at my report, I will tell you on what date that occurred."

"Judge, I want to look at that report first," Santini said.

"That's fine with me, Judge, but he has the report in his file. I got Ms. Byron's name from him just this morning."

"Go ahead, look at the report, but let's move this hearing along."

Santini studied the report for a few minutes and handed it back to the witness.

"I was asked specifically by Homeland Security to test this substance myself and to send through a report as soon as possible. That was on June sixth. I was further asked to keep all information from the tests as highly confidential, not to be shared with others in the lab."

"Is it unusual for you to test substances for federal agencies?"

"We do the testing of almost all evidence seized in this county. Since I was an FBI employee and an instructor, I am often asked to handle federal cases rather than having them transport evidence to their own lab."

"Was there anything at all unusual about this evidence?"

"Yes and no. What was unusual was that there was no case number assigned to any of the paperwork. Also the name of the arresting officer was missing. Instead there was a badge number to be used to transmit the report to Homeland Security, and the name of a deputy in the Justice Department named Golightly. I assigned a lab case number prior to examining the substance. I unsealed the evidence envelope and saw what was not at all unusual. There was a white powder wrapped in a piece of colorful wrapping paper. The paper contained a prayer written in Spanish. I recognized this as a Santeria prayer."

"By your answer do I understand that you've seen this kind of paper and powder on other occasions?"

"Many times. Santeria is a popular religion with many Hispanic people. The prayer and the powder are like a St. Christopher medal, to protect the person who carries them."

"Did you test the substance?"

"Yes. First I carefully opened the paper. I wore a mask and gloves in case the paper was a ruse. As soon as I looked at the powder, I knew it wasn't going to contain any illegal substances. It certainly wasn't anthrax or its progeny or the people who viewed it at the arrest would already have been ill. Next I placed the powder on a glass slide and added some drops of chemical to it. There was no reaction. I completed the more complicated tests for heroin and cocaine. I already knew that it wasn't either of them, but it's my job to complete all of the tests that would identify even a drop of an illegal substance. Finally, I identified that the powder was a combination of talcum powder and sugar. This is most often what is sold in the bodegas. Sometimes flour is used."

"After making these determinations, what did you do next?"

"I resealed the evidence in a lab evidence envelope, placed my initials on the envelope, and resealed it in the original envelope in which it was submitted. I tried to call the gentleman at the Justice Department, but he never returned my call. I placed the evidence in the evidence locker in the secure room in the lab. Then I sent copies of my report to the badge number at Homeland Security and to the Justice Department."

"Have you had any further communication with any other agency in this case regarding your tests or this substance?"

"Not until today. I received your telephone call asking me to appear here voluntarily today and to bring the evidence in this case. I also received a call from my office when I was on my way here, regarding a call from someone at Justice. I was told it was about this case. I told the office to tell the caller I was on my way to testify here and they could speak with me here. Mr. Santini did speak with me outside the courtroom and I shared with him the results of my tests."

"Okay, thank you Ms. Byron and thanks for appearing at the last minute without a subpoena."

Santini began his questions before he was out of his chair. "Ms. Byron, you don't know the defendant in this case, do you?"

"No, I never know anything about any of the accused. I just know about the substances that are seized."

"So just because the powder in this case was not a narcotic or any other harmful substance, you don't know whether there was any other criminal evidence in Luis Corona's case?"

"No, of course not. I don't even know what he is charged with."

"That's funny, neither does he." The words popped out of my mouth before I knew it.

"Ms. Katz, please, you know better," Judge Hammel said before Santini could make his objection.

"I'm sorry, Your Honor," I said.

"I don't have any other questions for Ms. Byron," Santini said.

"Judge, my last witness will be Consul General Philipe Marquez. He is seated here as a spectator, but the government never invoked The Rule, so they can hardly complain that the witness has been tainted by hearing the other testimony here today. I actually had planned to call him as a rebuttal witness to the government's case, but I believe it makes more sense to call him now. It may save some time."

"I'm all for that," Judge Hammel said.

I looked up at the judge and thought how tired he looked.

Señor Marquez came up the aisle as Ms. Byron left. He was quickly sworn in and I jumped right into my questions.

"State your name and position, sir."

"I am Philipe Marquez. I am the officer in charge of the Argentine consul in Miami. This has been my position over the last four years during the current administration in my country."

"Are you acquainted with the Corona family from Buenos Aires?"

"I knew of them by reputation. They have put Argentine fashion designers on the map. I do not know their son, Luis, but since Luis's arrest I have come to know Miguel and Maria Corona quite well. I have also looked into the background of Luis."

"Please, tell the court what you have learned about Luis Corona"

"I felt it important to investigate what kind of person Luis is. His parents contacted our embassy in the U.S. I was then contacted to assist our citizens who were unable to find out why their son was being held prisoner. I found nothing in Luis's background such as arrests or any criminal activity. He graduated from university cum laude and has worked for his parents. I couldn't even find a traffic infraction. My office in Buenos Aires interviewed his professors and some of his friends and neighbors. Nothing points to any reason he should be in any trouble in a foreign country."

"Tell the court what actions you took to try to find Luis or to gain any information regarding any charges pending against him in the United States."

"I spoke immediately with the U.S. embassy in my country and asked them to assist me in finding Luis. They have only said that they were trying to find him but were unable to. I spoke with the office of the U.S. Attorney in Miami. I was told that they were unable to help me, because Luis's charges were being handled by Homeland Security. I was rebuffed when I called that office, given what I believe you call 'the runaround.'"

"How did you locate Luis?"

"In desperation, I called a press conference. We received several anonymous tips and one of them led to Luis at the federal detention center in this county. We further found that no charges had been filed against him in the weeks following his arrest."

"Now, one of the questions which Luis was repeatedly asked was who he was sent to meet at the Floridian Inn. Do you have any idea why Luis was under suspicion because he was holding a reservation at that hotel?"

"A few days before Luis traveled to Miami, a man was found murdered at that hotel. The murdered man registered using an Argentine passport. My consulate here was asked to check into his identity. I learned that the passport belonged to an Argentine gentleman who had died a year ago."

"Did you ever learn who the murder victim actually was?"

"He was a Colombian who was involved with a drug organization and a rebel group in his country. In fact, this information surfaced as part of a case centered in the state

criminal courthouse here. This morning's news media confirmed this in their lead stories. There was no connection to
Luis Corona in any way."

"How many rooms does the Floridian Inn have, if you
know?"

"I do know, because I have booked rooms there for many
business travelers from my country. There are over two hundred rooms."

"Thank you, Señor Marquez. I have nothing further."

Santini got to his feet slowly. He moved to the lectern
and read the notes on his pad. The courtroom was quiet. The
pause was long. The judge's stare was piercing.

"Mr. Santini, are you going to ask any questions, or are
you just stretching your legs?" Judge Hammel asked.

"Sorry, Judge. Mr. Marquez, you have told us you don't
know Luis Corona. Correct?"

"That is correct."

"So would it be fair to say that you don't know whether
or not Luis had any other reasons to come to Miami?"

"Yes, that's correct. It's just that everything is clear that he
was here to open a shop for his family."

"Your job is to represent the Argentine government and
citizens here in Miami, isn't it?"

"Of course."

"And it would be best if no one from your country got
into trouble in this country?"

"Of course, but even if an Argentine was charged with a
crime, I would still provide the services available to our citizens. It's just that in Luis's case, there are no charges."

"You've answered my question, sir. I didn't ask about this
case."

"Mr. Santini, you must realize that my government is

aware that Luis has been held without charges and without a hearing to set bail. This is very upsetting. Our Department of State is considering some formal action to resolve this."

"Judge, please instruct the witness that he is to answer my questions and not to make a speech." Santini's frustration was obvious.

"Mr. Marquez, sir, please, try to answer without going into other areas. I understand your feelings, but we must adhere to the rules of evidence and procedure," Judge Hammel said.

"This is my last question, Mr. Marquez. Isn't it a fact that the person who told you about the identity of the murder victim at the inn was Luis Corona's attorney, Ms. Katz?"

"Yes, that's correct, but it was splashed all across the *Herald* and CNN this morning."

Santini took his seat, and I stood to announce that we rested our case.

"Your Honor, I think the court can see that Luis Corona is being held without charges, without bail, without access to his attorney, all in violation of our constitution, that he was about to be spirited out of this country on the flimsiest evidence I've ever encountered. I ask this court to release him forthwith and with the apology of our government." I sat down and as I did, I couldn't believe that applause thundered out of the spectators' seats.

"Please, Ladies and Gentlemen, there must be no further emotional outbursts or I'll be forced to clear the courtroom. Everyone please stay in your seats." Judge Hammel's voice shook with exhaustion.

The federal watchdogs behind me were on their feet towering over Luis and me. The applause ceased and the watchdogs sat down.

"Mr. Santini, are you ready to call your witnesses?" the judge asked.

"Shouldn't we take a break first, Judge?" Santini looked hopeful.

"No, let's just soldier on, please."

"We call Marta Alonso." Santini sent the bailiff to call the witness.

A fortyish woman in a stylish suit and spike heels was escorted to the witness chair by the bailiff.

"Do you know who this woman is?" I whispered to Luis.

"I think it's the flight lady from the airplane," he whispered back.

Santini began his questions as soon as the witness was sworn and seated. "Tell the court your name and your occupation."

"I'm Marta Alonso. I'm employed by Overseas Airways as a flight attendant."

"How long have you been a flight attendant, Ms. Alonso?"

"I began at Eastern Airlines when I finished college and worked there until they went out of business. Then I joined Overseas Air, so I guess altogether twenty-eight years."

"Were you working on flight nine-eight-nine from Buenos Aires to Miami on June fifth of this year?"

"Yes, I work that route on a regular basis as the senior flight attendant."

"Did you come in contact with a passenger named Luis Corona on that flight?"

"Yes, I did."

"Do you see him in court today?"

"I guess he's the one at the table there."

"Ms. Alonso, please don't guess," the judge said. "Can you be sure?"

"I'm sorry, Judge. It looks a little like him. I see a lot of passengers, you know. It sorta looks like him, but he doesn't look the way he did on that flight."

"Ms. Alonso, tell us when you first became aware of Luis Corona."

"A little while into the flight, I saw that he was seated next to the sky marshal, the security officer who rides most of our flights dressed as a passenger. I always take note of who is seated around the officer. Then later, I heard him arguing with the officer. The conversation became louder. Mr. Corona had ordered a few drinks before that. He seemed to be in a happy celebratory mood when I served him the drinks. You know, kidding around with me and some of the other passengers, so I was surprised when I heard the argument."

"Did you do anything at that point?"

"I saw that other passengers were turning around and staring, so I went over to Mr. Corona and told him he'd have to quiet down. The marshal said that Corona had hit him and that I should tell our captain. When the marshal says to alert the captain, I do that immediately. It means he suspects a problem."

"Did anything else happen?"

"Not for a while. I think Mr. Corona was sleeping or resting. Things quieted down. A few hours later, I served dinner and wine, and everything seemed fine. Sometime after dinner, I heard the smoke alarm start wailing. By the time I got to the area of the restrooms, the marshal and the copilot had Mr. Corona on the ground. He was struggling. They put him in the back of the plane and handcuffed him."

"Were you present when the marshal searched his bag or questioned him?"

"Part of the time, but I had to take care of all the other passengers. Many of them were frightened. Rumors were traveling throughout the plane. Some people thought we had been highjacked. I served free drinks to many of the passengers and tried to reassure them."

"Do you remember any item examined during the search or anything that Mr. Corona said?"

"I saw some things from his shaving kit. There was a tiny scissors the marshal was looking at. There were several packs of cigarettes. The only thing I remember about Mr. Corona was that he was crying and begging them to let him get off the floor."

"Is there anything else that you remember about this incident?"

"Not really. No."

Santini sat down, and I moved to the lectern.

"Ms. Alonso, in your many years as a flight attendant, have you seen more unruly passengers than Mr. Corona?"

"My goodness, yes, I've seen fist fights in the aisle. I once saw a husband actually beat up his wife. Once I caught two people having sex right at their seats. You see everything on these long flights."

"Were you suspicious that Mr. Corona was some kind of troublemaker from his demeanor?"

"Not until the sky marshal told me to alert the captain."

"Now you said that Mr. Corona ordered several drinks early in the flight."

"That's correct."

"Was he drunk?"

"Maybe a little. It seemed like he was in a happy mood until the argument."

"You served him wine with his dinner even though he seemed a little drunk and the marshal had you alert the pilot?"

"Sure. He wasn't falling down drunk or anything."

"What did the pilot tell you to do when you alerted him?"

"Just to keep an eye on things and let him know if anything else happened."

"You mentioned seeing packs of cigarettes. Did Mr.

Corona have a cigarette in his hand when he was pulled out of the bathroom?"

"I saw one on the floor in the bathroom. It was still lighted. I was the one who put it out so we could reset the smoke alarms. That was after they took the passenger to the back of the plane. Then I went into the restroom to see if everything was okay so other passengers could use it. It's awful on a full, long flight when one restroom goes out of use."

"Okay, thank you, Ms. Alonso."

I took my seat. For the first time, Luis smiled at me. Santini stood and renewed his request to take a short break.

"All right, we'll be in recess for ten minutes," Judge Hammel said.

Santini had a further request. "Your Honor, may I ask if all counsel could meet with you in chambers for a few minutes."

The judge nodded, and we all stood as he left the bench.

"What does this mean?" Luis asked.

"Darned if I know, but don't be scared. I think we're doing fine. I'll be back soon."

Marcia Lu was standing in front of us. "I'll take you and Mr. Santini back to chambers," she said.

I grabbed my pad and pen and followed her out of the courtroom. The two feds behind us hovered over Luis like buzzards over roadkill.

CHAPTER SIXTY-THREE

We waited in the outer office while Marcia went to see if the judge was ready for us. I paced the area, looking at the books lining the walls of the office, feigning interest in the federal statutes, cases, and rules in their enormous volumes in historical order. My nerves were screaming with impatience. Why were we here? What did Santini have in store?

"You're a real scrapper," Santini said. He was standing right behind me. I moved away as if I'd been slapped. "I heard you liked to play hardball in court."

"I'd hardly call this brief hearing an example of playing hardball," I said.

"I meant it as a compliment," he said. I realized he was smiling at me.

Marcia appeared in the doorway and ushered us into Hammel's inner sanctum. It was a large office with a desk at one end and a conference table at the other. There were photographs of Miami's skyline over the years, going from flat white buildings, to glass skyscrapers. One wall was filled with all kinds of awards. It was a comfortable space that exuded a friendly calm.

Marcia motioned us over to the table and we sat on either side. The judge took his seat at the head of the table. Marcia sat at his left, with her laptop computer open and ready in front of her.

"All right, Mr. Santini, why are we here?"

"Thank you, Judge Hammel, for seeing us in chambers and for your patience this morning. I don't want to take up more of your time without good cause. I hope you can understand that I couldn't have this discussion in the courtroom. Judge, my only other witness would be the sky marshal. He is here and reluctantly ready to testify. However, once he takes the stand in open court, his cover is blown. He cannot travel anonymously to perform his duties. His face will be known. Even though we have no cameras allowed in federal courtrooms, we do have artists who draw the faces, and we do have TV crews outside as well as print media who will be all over him."

"Does he have other evidence concerning Mr. Corona other than what I've heard today already?" Judge Hammel asked.

"Judge, I'm just trying to do my job. I can only work with what I'm handed. I believe there was, how can I put this, an overreaction on the part of the government in this case."

"So what you're saying is that if I free Mr. Corona based on what I've heard here today, the government will not be taking an appeal or even objecting."

"That's about it, Your Honor."

"Well, I have to say I've heard a lot of gobble-de-gook from the government over the years, but this really tops it all. Does the Justice Department or whoever pursued this case realize that they may be opening themselves to a civil case for big damages? That young man out there looks traumatized, and physically ill. The representative of the Argentine government looks very upset. I had a call from Ambassador Francis Miller early this morning. He's been told that Argentina considers this an international slap in the face. Can you tell me why this incident has dragged on this long without more evidence? Is it now our government's policy to arrest first, and then hope to find some evidence?" Judge Hammel's anger showed more with each word he spoke.

I jumped into the fray. The important thing was to get Luis out of here. "Judge Hammel, given what I've just heard, I ask you to find that there is not and never was a reason to detain my client. I ask for an order granting my habeas corpus petition with an immediate release of my client. Although no charges have ever been filed against him, I'm asking for an expungment of any record of his arrest. I would also like Mr. Santini to clear Mr. Corona's name from any enemy lists. The last thing Luis needs is to go to an airport somewhere and find he's on a no-fly list."

"That seems a reasonable request," the judge said, nodding his agreement.

"The government disobeyed your last order and tried to spirit my client out of the country, so I'm afraid your order alone won't insure that he isn't hassled further."

"I will grant your order in full, but I want your assurance on the record, Mr. Santini, that there will be no further inclusion of Luis Corona on any enemy list. To that end, I will speak to Ambassador Miller to expedite the removal of Mr. Corona from any such lists," Judge Hammel said. "I have to say that I have never felt so sad seeing the paranoia that has permeated the top ranks of our government. I assume Ms. Katz may walk her client out of here this afternoon."

"I'm not sure about that, Judge. He has to be returned to his last detention center and cleared from there."

"Oh, no, Judge," I said. "This is just a trick for the feds to get their hands on Luis again. They were about to send him to Guantanamo. Please, don't let them take him away from here."

Judge Hammel stood up. "If you want to further detain this young man, file charges against him now. Then I will set a bond, and he'll walk out of here anyway. You have thirty minutes to file something."

"Well, Judge, I can't do that. My agency can't proceed in that fashion."

I stood up and looked at Santini. "Judge, the way to resolve this is for us to return to the courtroom and allow the sky marshal to testify. Then it will be up to Your Honor to render a final order of release for Luis. I think the real embarrassment to the government will be the marshal's inability to add one new piece of evidence. That's the real reason for his reluctance to testify. I won't accept a suspension of the hearing unless I can take my client out of here completely cleared this afternoon."

"I am in agreement, Ms. Katz. What's it going to be, Mr. Santini? And if the officers who brought Mr. Corona in here have some disagreement with this, I will handle them. Just let them know if they ignore my order, they may be the ones sitting in a holding cell."

Marcia Lu began typing on her laptop. "I'll have a draft order ready in a few minutes for you, Judge. I think I have your exact wording. I've been taking notes."

"Judge, my hands are tied. There's nothing else I can do except to accept this result. The only thing I simply can't agree to is to waive our right to appeal. My superiors must make that decision," Santini said.

"Fine. I wish they would appeal. I'd like to see the faces on the appellate judges when they read the transcript of this hearing. Right now I'm going to return to the courtroom to read my order into the record." Judge Hammel began to review Ms. Lu's work.

I returned to the courtroom and put my arm around Luis. " It's over," I said.

CHAPTER SIXTY-FOUR

Thirty minutes later, Catherine and I escorted Luis out of the courtroom. He was so weak that we actually were holding him up. His parents hugged him, Carlos hugged me. J.C. and Angelina hugged all of us. Señor Marquez bowed and kissed my hand and then kissed my cheek. Ambassador Miller went to the judge's chambers. Ms. Lu had summoned him as soon as the order was read.

"Come, we will have a great party, a fiesta at our hotel," Miguel said.

"Miguel and Maria, Luis is ill. I want to get him to a hospital right away and document his injuries and any other physical problems. Maybe J.C. can call Dr. Andreas for us," I said.

I was worried about Luis, who looked as if he couldn't apprehend anything being said. I also knew we would need proof of his treatment while jailed and its aftermath if the Coronas decided to sue the government. The foundation had been laid in the transcript of today's hearing for false arrest and defamation.

We delivered Luis to the hospital and left him in the hands of Luis's parents and Doctor Andreas. I asked for a full report as soon as possible.

Catherine and I headed back to the office. Carlos drove his parents home. Señor Marquez went with them. I was glad to see everyone leave. For once, I wanted peace and quiet and no one within a mile who had a problem.

We arrived at the office to find a stack of messages on voice mail and e-mail. Most were comments of congratulations on the courthouse drug case from friends and colleagues. There were requests for appointments from potential new clients. One was from a city commissioner who claimed he was about to be indicted. "Nothing new there," I said to Catherine.

The message that puzzled me was from Liz. She asked if she could come to see me in the morning. *Now what?*

Catherine returned several calls for me, and I went home to feed Sam and crawl into bed. I unplugged my landline and turned off my cell and BlackBerry. I slept straight through until five the next morning when I made a huge sandwich and drank a pot of coffee before heading back to the salt mine.

CHAPTER SIXTY-FIVE

I picked up a newspaper on the way to the office and settled back to read it and watch the TV news. Both were filled with Luis's hearing. TV carried a shot of Catherine and me leading a disheveled Luis down the courthouse steps. For once someone looked more disheveled than I did.

This must be a record. Front page news two days in a row. Harlan McFarland wrote a great story. It was another banner headline day for him. Something told me he would be going from intern to full-time reporter before the end of June.

At eight o'clock, Liz knocked at the still-locked front door of the office. She looked more like her professional self. I liked her better in jeans and ponytail.

"What's up?" I asked as we settled in our usual seats on either end of the sofa.

"I wanted to catch you up on what happened yesterday, and then I need to ask your advice," she said.

"It's not a legal problem, is it?" I asked.

CHAPTER SIXTY-SIX

The Last of Liz's Story

The morning after the arrest of Gladys and Anne, Liz was awakened by the phone. As soon as she finished speaking to Mary, she was startled by pounding on her condo door. She peeped through the safety hole and saw Joe. She opened the door, still rubbing sleep out of her eyes.

Joe held out the morning paper. Headlines broke through the fog in her brain.

"Why didn't you call me last night? You've been through so much. Why didn't you reach out to me for help?" Joe looked like a wounded child.

"I really couldn't tell you much, except that I was part of an investigation. Mary told me not to divulge anything to anyone. Last night I was just wrung out. I didn't learn about Anne until this morning, and I was too upset to call you. Come on in. I'll make coffee."

"I didn't think I was just 'anyone,'" Joe said. Now he was pouting.

"Look, Joe, I didn't know who to trust. Anne used me. Gladys used me. I need to be sure about the decisions I make from now on."

"What does this mean for us? I thought we were planning

a wedding. I've even started making honeymoon plans."

"Don't you think I should be involved in plans for a trip? I don't recall any discussions about places we both might like to go. I need a little time and space to sort out everything. My life has been turned inside out. Please try to understand and give me a little time," Liz said. "Right now I need to get to the courthouse. The first thing I need to get straight is where I will be working."

"I'll give you plenty of time. I won't bother you again. When and if you want to be with me, you can call me." Joe dropped the newspaper on the floor and slammed the door as he left

Liz had no more tears left. She sat dry-eyed and read the stories in the *Herald*, the headline of Anne's arrest, and the sidebar about Mary and Mark and her and how they had uncovered the drug cartel's use of the criminal court system. She looked like a real hero in the story. She felt like an idiot, trusting people who used her. She was nobody's lapdog. It was time to take control of her life, starting with her job as a judge.

Liz arrived at the criminal courthouse before nine a.m. She had phoned Patricia from her car. Patricia was at her post as usual. She cried when they had talked about Gladys, but she promised to hold down the fort until Liz could get there.

Liz went directly to Chief Judge Paul Marconi's chambers.

"Is he in?" Liz asked the secretary in the outer office.

"He is, but he's on the phone. If you'll have a seat, I'll see if he can see you as soon as he's off his private line," she said.

"Never mind," Liz said, as she strode to the mahogany door of Marconi's private lair and threw it open. The secretary tried to follow her, screaming about how she couldn't just go in unannounced. Liz slammed the heavy door in her face.

Marconi was not on the phone. His back was turned. He

was staring out the window and sipping a cup of coffee. He whirled around as the door slammed, spilling the coffee down the front of his white shirt.

"Good morning, Paul. I trust you've seen the morning paper and I know you spoke to Detective Morris last night. I thought that you'd call me immediately," Liz said. She seated herself without being invited.

"I didn't want to disturb you last night, but I intended to call you this morning," Judge Marconi said as he dabbed at the ugly brown stain on his shirt.

"Yes, well the road to hell is paved with good intentions. I'm here to tell you that I will be returning tomorrow morning to my criminal division. I don't know of anything I can do about the orders Gladys forged in my name. That will be for the state and the appellate court to sort out."

"Maybe you should let things settle down a bit before you go back," Paul said.

"No way. The best way for me to revive my reputation is to resume my normal duties, which I intend to do. It's hard for me to believe that you had no idea that Judge Ackerman was dirty. You must be a terrible judge of people to have appointed her to be the head of the criminal court. You knew that she was notorious for having concealed firearms on the bench and in her chambers, among other rumors about her."

"You trusted her, too, Liz," Paul said.

"But I have come off as the hero who set her up and cleared the courthouse of criminal activity. I may have posed as her friend just to catch her, while you put her in a position to further her illegal activity. That can't look good for your future."

"That sounds like a threat. I'm sure you didn't mean it that way."

"You can call it whatever you like. I'm surprised that you were happy to help Jason investigate me when all along you could have pointed out Anne's unusual behavior, but that's in the past. I'm ready to move forward in my new appointment next week as chief judge of the criminal division."

"I beg your pardon. I haven't made that decision yet."

"Sure you have. I'll expect the announcement any time now. You know where to find me; back in my chambers in the criminal division. Better get coverage for that family division I've been holding down." Liz swept out of Marconi's office. As she left, she glanced around his suite. She planned to run against Marconi for chief of all courts next fall.

I applauded when Liz finished her description of her meeting with Marconi.

"So what's the problem you wanted to discuss, Liz?" I asked. "It sounds like you've got things under control."

"In my professional life, but my personal life is a mess. It's about Joe. I can't trust my own judgment. I'm not Cinderella looking for the prince to save me. That's how I felt when Joe said he was planning a honeymoon without even consulting me. Maybe I would be jumping into this marriage. You're so objective. I thought maybe you could give me some advice."

I couldn't help myself. I began to laugh hysterically. I couldn't stop. Liz stared at me. I still couldn't control the laughs that poured out of me like a waterfall. I laughed until tears rolled down my cheeks.

"What is the matter with you? Is my problem that hysterical?" Liz stood up and looked ready to bolt from my office.

"No, Liz, you're not funny. It's just that you are asking a woman who can't stay engaged to anyone. I've had two broken engagements, and now I've got Carlos, who I'm wild about, pressuring me for a commitment, and I can't make up my mind what to do. You really came to the wrong place for advice."

Then Liz began to giggle. "I get it. We're a great pair."

When we finally finished acting like two junior high kids, I thought for a minute.

"Liz, how about this solution? Why don't you suggest that Joe move in with you for a while and you try out how you get along. If things are smooth and you feel comfortable, there's always time for a wedding. If not, you'll both know it."

"Do you think I can make a better judgment after a few months?"

"Sure. You can look for little signs, like if he leaves the toilet seat up more than twice after you yell at him to quit it, or if he always drinks the milk straight out of the carton."

That picture sent us both into more uncontrolled laughter. When we settled down again, Liz reached over and squeezed my hand.

"See, Mary, I knew you'd help me find an answer. Maybe I can help you. We could talk about Carlos and how you feel."

"Thanks, but I think I'm beyond help. Anyway, I'm glad you like my suggestion, and there's no charge for this consultation."

CHAPTER SIXTY-SEVEN

Later that morning, Catherine came in to say that Miguel and Maria Corona were in the waiting room.

I went out and brought them into the office. They both tried to hug me at the same time. I was lucky they didn't break my ribs.

"You will never know how grateful we are," Miguel said. "Carlos told us how brave you were to stand up to public opinion in representing our son when people believed he was a terrorist. He told us you lost other clients too."

"Please, it's been a real pleasure to see you united with Luis. How is he, and will you be taking him home to Argentina soon?"

"Dr. Andreas is keeping him in the hospital for another day. He has developed a strep infection from the jails and he has some very bad bruises that need attention, but nothing is life threatening, thank God."

"So you'll be leaving soon?"

"Oh, no, we started this whole project to establish a business for Luis in this country and we intend to complete this purchase. Ambassador Miller is assisting us in getting our funds returned that the federal officers seized. Paulina is ready to turn over the shop to us. We would like you to look at our agreement and to attend the closing with us."

"I'd be happy to do that. I'm just surprised that you would

want to have anything else to do with this country after Luis's ordeal here," I said.

"We know that the things that happened to Luis are not the fault of you and all the fine citizens like you. In our own country, we have had governments that don't reflect the people they govern. We understand. Now we are here to bring you a check for your legal work for Luis. You haven't even sent us a bill." Miguel slid an envelope across the desk.

I opened it and removed a certified bank check for $200,000. My hand shook and I dropped the check on the floor. As I pawed under my desk to pick it up before they took it back, I said, "This is really too much."

"Not at all," Maria said. "As soon as the shop is open, you and Catherine are to come and pick out any designer outfits that you like. We'll never forget what you did for our family."

As soon as the Coronas left, I raced out to Catherine. "Turn on the voice mail. Turn off the computer. We're going out for the most expensive lunch we've ever had. Anywhere you want to go." I waved the check in front of her.

"Wow, with that check we could have lunch in the Bahamas, but I have to be home when the boys get home, so let's go to Joe's Stone Crab on South Beach. I've always wanted to go."

"Well, you can get stone crabs at every fish market and eat them at home, but if that's what you want, let's do it." We locked the office and roared out of the parking lot. Free at last.

CHAPTER SIXTY-EIGHT

We spent the afternoon gorging on stone crabs and downing a bottle of sparkling wine. We even took a walk on Ocean Drive and ogled all the tourists who were ogling us. I dropped Catherine at her house. The humidity was intense. Mixed with the sun and the wine, I was drenched in sweat as I swung back into the office parking lot. Carlos was parked there in the Escalade. I actually saw the car a block before I turned into the lot. It's hard to miss.

"Where have you been? Are you okay? Where's Catherine?" he asked in rapid sequence.

"We went to lunch, and aside from being a bit drunk, I've never been better," I said.

"Lunch? It's four thirty. You're turning into a regular Latin *muchaca*. I must be rubbing off on you. Listen, I want to talk to you about something. I've been thinking. We never go out on a date. We haven't been to a movie or dancing."

"Well, that's because every time we have the time to be together, we end up in bed. That's not a complaint," I said.

"Saturday night, I want to go somewhere exotic for dinner. What do you say?"

"I say great. I'm in the mood to celebrate. It's a date."

I waved to Carlos as he drove off. He said he had some business to attend to. I decided to check the messages before heading home. I was just finishing reading the e-mails when the phone rang. It was Harlan McFarland.

"Harlan, great story in today's paper. You must be the newest ace reporter down there," I said.

"Thanks, Mary. I have been offered a full-time job starting right after the Fourth of July, but that's not what I'm calling about. I wanted to get a statement from you about Judge Hammel."

"Judge Hammel? What do you mean?"

"Oh, I guess you haven't heard. It's been all over the radio and TV. Judge Hammel died this morning. He had a massive heart attack. Died in the ambulance on the way to the hospital. Yours was the last case he ever heard."

"Oh my God. I can't believe it. Do you think Luis's case did him in? Wait, that's not my statement for your paper," I said.

"I know. I wasn't writing it down. No, I think he was very sick during the hearing. We all commented about how exhausted he looked. He looked bad during the first hearing you had too."

"How old was he?" I asked.

"Seventy-eight. You were lucky that he was the judge who heard Luis's case. He had no fear about standing up to the boys from Washington."

"Just say that I was very proud to be in his court and that he set the example of the importance of an independent judiciary in protecting our constitution."

"I've got it, Mary. I spoke to his son a few minutes ago. He told me that his dad loved hearing Luis's case, and he thought you were a great young attorney. His son spoke to the judge last evening. He said the judge had chest pains when he got up this morning. His wife called 911 and the judge died on the way to the hospital, even with the paramedics working on him."

"Thanks for calling me, Harlan." I hung up and had a good cry.

Friday began with a tropical downpour; thunder, lightening, and street flooding. By ten o'clock it was over and there was a freshness in the air. July was almost here and the change from hot and wet was ending up just plain hot. It's almost always in the nineties for the Fourth.

Catherine and I spent the day going over files and catching up on the small cases that had been languishing. Of course, no one's case is small to them, so there was plenty of work ahead of us. Catherine hit on her familiar melody. It's time to add another attorney or at least an intern. I promised to think about it.

I was just putting out the lights and getting ready to head home when the phone rang. I was tempted to let it ring. The long daylight of June beckoned me to get Sam out for a good run. I glanced at the caller ID and saw the printout "Angelina Martin." I tried to think of some reason for Carlos's mother to be calling. Nothing came to mind, so curiosity got the better of me. Sam got put on hold and Angelina got answered.

"Mary, darling, where is your secretary? You spoil your help."

"How are you, Angie? Everything okay?"

"Yes, of course. Don't say I only call you when something's wrong."

"No, I wasn't saying that."

"Well, the reason I am calling is I have the best news, and it's all because of you. Chicky is coming home."

"Chicky? Who is Chicky, another cousin?"

"No, Chicky is Celia's nickname. You know, Carlos's sister, my little girl."

"She's leaving Argentina?"

"Yes. It's so wonderful. Miguel and Maria decided that Luis would need help organizing the shop and running it. She's agreed to accept their offer of a position as manager of the boutique. She'll be perfect for the position. She's so into high fashion. You'll love her, darling. And this would never have happened if you hadn't taken Luis's case and freed him from those locos."

"That's great news, Angie. I'm so pleased for you and J.C. How did Celia get the name Chicky?"

"I think Carlos and his brother used to tease her that she talked all the time, like a chicken squawking, but it's really an endearing quality. I'm dashing around finding her a condo or a townhouse or something. She simply refuses to move in with us. So when I see you, I will give you a giant hug and kiss. I'm on my way out, so ciao."

I took a deep breath as Angie clicked off. A high-fashion, constantly talking replica of Angie who is fondly called Chicky. Just my type of girlfriend.

CHAPTER SIXTY-NINE

Saturday was a sunny, very hot day, a perfect time to give Sam a bath. I hosed him down, soaped him up, and received several showers myself as he continued to shake himself off. We both sat on the grass in the sun, drying off and snoozing.

My second job of the morning was phoning both brothers and my parents. The whole family, amazingly, had left me alone while I was up to my eyeballs in the two big cases. No one answered at either brothers, but Mother picked up immediately.

"I can't believe you're actually calling me without my leaving you six messages," she said.

"Enough with the sarcasm. How is everybody?"

"I know how you are," she answered. "I read about you every day in the papers. You even made the *Palm Beach Post*, right next to the banner headline about a new hospital opening. And I saw you and Catherine on CNN coming out of court with that poor boy."

"So you know I've been busy. What about Dad and the doctor's appointment."

"I'm so grateful to J.C. for getting him to that nice Dr. Andreas, who persuaded him to go to the cardiologist. He's on some cholesterol-lowering pills. I always warned him about eating all that chopped liver and the other stuff his mother made."

"How about your southern fried chicken? I don't think it's fat free."

"He's also on some other heart pills, but he passed his stress test,"

"Sure he did. He puts the rest of us into stress," I said.

"Now who's being sarcastic? Anything else new there?"

"Well, Carlos is taking me out for some fancy, shmancy dinner tonight."

"Yes, I know. At least Carlos calls me when you're too busy, so I know you're still breathing. Are you getting your hair done for the evening?"

"No, Mother. Carlos likes my hair. Gotta go."

I had completed all my duties and it was only noon. For the first time, I relaxed and watched baseball on TV with popcorn and beer for lunch.

I decided to wear my one good slinky black dress. I bought it a year ago while I was still engaged to Franklin to wear to a client's anniversary party held at the Miami Club. It used to be off-limits to Jews, blacks, and Hispanics, but having fallen on hard times, it now was only too happy to admit anyone with the $50,000 initiation fee.

The dress still fit, even after the beer and popcorn. I poured two glasses of merlot from the case Lillian Yarmouth sent me. She continued to supply me with more wine than a nonalcoholic could consume.

Carlos arrived promptly at seven looking like a page from GQ again, navy blazer, heavenly blue shirt, Gucci loafers. Heads turned when we were shown to our table at the Forge Restaurant. The problem was that all the heads were women admiring Carlos.

The Forge is not far from the street where I grew up in Miami Beach and even closer to Katz's Kosher Market. But it's a world away from the places my family frequented.

My menu had the prices deleted so I snatched Carlos's and after a quick glance, I returned it to him before it spoiled my appetite. A bottle of champagne arrived while we ate our appetizers of escargot, which are really snails, but bigger than the ones I clean out of my garden.

"You said you had some worries about your next project. We never had a chance to talk about what's happening after the oceanfront condos," I said.

"I was worried. I smell a slowdown coming. Look around, and you see Miami-Dade is overbuilt. Downtown Miami has thousands of condos being completed. That's why I built in Fort Lauderdale. I have a lot of land that I've bought, but I was reluctant to start a building that might not have buyers. I was almost tempted to take a trip to Abu Dhabi or some other Arab place where they're building on every inch of land, but that wouldn't solve keeping my crews working."

"You said you were worried. What changed?"

"For one thing, I'll be remodeling Luis's boutique. Miguel decided it needs a complete update, so that'll keep one crew busy. And then I got the contract to build some affordable townhouses at the university for grad students. I had some land in Little Havana, not so far from the Gables. The university bought the land, and I'll start the project as soon as the last crew finishes in Fort Lauderdale. So, just like that, everything is moving again."

By the time we got to coffee and brandy, we were feeling pretty mellow. Carlos took my hand and I felt that electric feeling when we are together.

"You know you never ask me for anything. I didn't even know the date of your birthday 'til I asked your mother, and it's not until November. Isn't there anything that you want?" Carlos asked.

"Yes, there is," I said. "The only thing I miss about my old job is that the firm had season hockey tickets. Hardly anyone ever used them, so I got to go to a lot of the games."

"You mean the Florida Panthers ice hockey at that arena way up there in west Broward County? You really drove all that way?"

"It's not that far and, yes, I love hockey. Have you ever gone to a game?"

"Just once. I was invited to sit in a suite, but I was busy making friends with the elected officials there, so I didn't see much of the game. If that's what you want, consider it done for your birthday, but meanwhile I have another present for you."

Carlos reached in his pocket and produced a small box wrapped in elegant silver paper. "Open it," he said. He smiled that disastrous smile that always makes me forget everything, including a warning signal flashing in my mind.

I carefully and slowly removed the paper. The little box felt like it was burning a hole in my hand. Carlos was still smiling expectantly. I opened the box and saw the biggest diamond ring I had every seen, even on TV. It was surrounded by emeralds. The light from the candles on the table made the ring look like sparks were bouncing off of it.

"What is this for? I mean what does this mean?" I stuttered.

"It's to replace the rock that you seem to miss that you returned to Frank, and it can mean whatever you want it to mean. I want it to mean that we are together forever, but I know how you feel. If you want to wear it, it will mean a lot to me, or you can keep it until you're ready to wear it. It's your call."

I stared at the ring, and then I looked at Carlos. His expression reminded me of a kid who just got his first car.

"I think I'd like to wear it sometimes, as long as you can live with my not being ready to get married," I said.

"It's a start," Carlos said. He leaned across the table and gave me the kind of kiss that made me tell him to hurry up and get the check so we can go home.

So as I told you at the beginning, I answered two phone calls that changed my life. Liz and Luis brought me all kinds of new clients, but best of all they became my friends for life. Elected officials from all over the state are calling to hire me after they are indicted. After all, this is Florida. I've even had a call from the American Bar Association looking for defense attorneys to represent Guantanamo detainees, but that would mean leaving my practice and Carlos and Sam. I may need to listen to Catherine and hire another attorney just to screen the cases.

Right now, I'm sitting in my living room looking at the diamond ring and wondering where it is leading me.

The phone is ringing. "Hello?"

"Mary, it's Franco. Thank God you're home. I'm at the Dade County jail. Can you come down here?"

"Of course, what happened?"

"I got in a little altercation with my wife and she called the cops. When they got there they said they had a warrant for my arrest for bribing a cop."

"When was that?"

"When I paid that guy to get your car out of the impound lot."

"I'll be right there, Franco. Don't talk to anyone. Tell them your lawyer, Mary Magruder Katz, is on her way."